Dearest Enemy

Nan Ryan

THORNDIKE
CHIVERS

This Large Print edition is published by Thorndike Press, Waterville, Maine, USA and by BBC Audiobooks Ltd, Bath, England.
Thorndike Press is an imprint of The Gale Group.
Thorndike is a trademark and used herein under license.

All characters in this book have no existence outside the imagination of the author and have no relation whatsoever to anyone bearing the same name or names. They are not even distantly inspired by any individual known or unknown to the author, and all the incidents are pure invention.
The text of this Large Print edition is unabridged.
Other aspects of the book may vary from the original edition.
Set in 16 pt. Plantin.

LIBRARY OF CONGRESS CATALOGING-IN-PUBLICATION DATA

Ryan, Nan.
Dearest enemy / by Nan Ryan.
p. cm. — (Thorndike Press large print romance)
ISBN-13: 978-0-7862-9892-1 (alk. paper)
ISBN-10: 0-7862-9892-8 (alk. paper)
1. Large type books. I. Title.
PS3568.Y392D43 2007
813'.54—dc22 2007026239

BRITISH LIBRARY CATALOGUING-IN-PUBLICATION DATA AVAILABLE

Published in 2007 in the U.S. by arrangement with Harlequin Books S.A.
Published in 2007 in the U.K. by arrangement with Harlequin Enterprises II B.V.

U.K. Hardcover: 978 1 405 64268 2 (Chivers Large Print)
U.K. Softcover: 978 1 405 64269 9 (Camden Large Print)

Printed in the United States of America on permanent paper
10 9 8 7 6 5 4 3 2 1

For
My dearest friend, Heather . . .
Now, like me, an only child.

Dearest Enemy

Washington, D.C.
November 1864

Wintertime in Washington.

A heavy snow was falling on that frigid November afternoon when the tall, lean, thirty-six-year-old Union naval officer hurried in out of the cold. Once inside the remote cottage long owned by his wealthy family, the handsome officer hung his musette bag on the coat tree in the small foyer. Then he stamped his booted feet and shrugged out of his heavy greatcoat.

Shivering and rubbing his hands together, he turned and went into the parlor, crossing directly to the cold fireplace. He began tossing logs into the grate to build a much needed fire. Within minutes flames shot up the chimney and a healthy blaze began to warm the chilled room. The officer smiled, pleased with his handiwork.

He turned and crossed to the mahogany

bar that stretched along one side of the large room's back wall. He took down a couple of gleaming crystal brandy snifters from a shelf behind the bar. He snagged the glasses in one hand and grabbed a carved decanter of cognac with the other, carrying both to the fire. He placed them at the edge of an enormous fur rug that lay spread out on the floor directly before the blaze.

He rose to his feet and waited.

Rear Admiral Mitchell B. Longley had slipped away from his fleet command to rendezvous for a brief hour or two with the luscious red-haired, blue-eyed enchantress with whom he was falling in love. It wasn't wise, he realized, to be away from his weary sailors even for a short time. But in this case, it was necessary. He hadn't seen his beautiful sweetheart in weeks and the long separation was making it increasingly hard for him to concentrate. To be as sharp and cunning as a naval commander needed to be in a time of war.

This tryst, he reasoned, was essential. To him and to the Union Navy. After a sweet hour in his angel's arms he would leave this place calm and keen-minded, ready to go back into battle against the hated Rebs. Who would begrudge him a few stolen moments of bliss that might well save his sanity?

Mitch heard her coming up the front walk. He rushed to the door and eagerly yanked it open. And felt his heart hammer against his ribs when he saw her. Native Virginian and irresistible charmer, Suzanna LeGrande stood on the stoop smiling up at him. The hood of her long cape covered her glorious hair, but her brilliant blue eyes were sparkling with life and her berry-red lips were turned up in a dazzling smile.

"Am I late?" she teased, and tossed her hood off to reveal the fiery red hair that framed her fair face.

"Right on time, darling," Mitch said, drawing her inside and shoving the door closed as he bent and kissed her.

Suzanna sighed and placed her hands on his trim waist. She loved the way Mitch kissed her after they'd been apart. His first kiss was always so powerful, so potent, as if he was starved for the taste of her. Now, just like those other times they had met after being apart for days or weeks, this thrilling kiss went on and on and made her knees weak and her stomach contract.

When at last he took his lips from hers, Mitch said against her perfumed hair, "We haven't much time, my love."

"Then let's don't waste a minute of it," she breathlessly replied.

"My thoughts exactly," Mitch said as he unfastened the hook beneath her chin and shoved her heavy cape off her slender shoulders.

He hung the velvet wrap on the coat tree beside his still-damp greatcoat and bulging black musette bag. And then smiled with pleasure as he watched Suzanna hurry toward the fire, struggling with the buttons going down the back of her blue woolen gown.

The pair laughed and teased each other as they hurried to undress.

"I'll bet I beat you," taunted Mitch, his dark navy blouse already stripped off and tossed aside.

"Not on your life," Suzanna retorted, stepping out of her lace-trimmed petticoats.

Articles of clothing flew across the room as the laughing competitors raced to be first to get naked.

"Looks like I'm going to win, Miss LeGrande," Mitch proclaimed, as he stuck his thumbs into the waistband of his white linen underwear, the only article of clothing remaining on his tall, lean body.

"I don't think so, Admiral Longley," Suzanna squealed as she kicked off her white ruffled pantalets.

Naked, they stopped laughing. Wordlessly

they stepped into each other's arms atop the soft fur rug. Both shuddered at the initial touch of bare flesh on flesh. They kissed passionately and sank to their knees.

Too long denied the kind of ecstasy that was impossible to ever forget, they couldn't wait. In seconds Mitch was making eager, anxious love to Suzanna on the lush dark fur, while the flickering flames tinted their enjoined bodies a pale orange hue. Their shared orgasm occurred almost the minute he was inside her. That's how hot they were for each other. Neither minded that it was over so soon.

In fact, both were again laughing as the spent Mitch fell over onto his back beside Suzanna. Struggling for breath, they kidded each other about their lack of control. But when finally the laughter subsided and the gasping for breath ceased, Mitch turned onto his side by Suzanna, raised up on an elbow and laid a hand lightly on her stomach.

The tip of his forefinger circling the small indentation of her navel, he said with a sheepish grin, "I don't want you calling me the 'five-minute man.' "

Suzanna smiled. "Then you'll have to convince me that you aren't."

Mitch did just that.

He made love to Suzanna again, this time taking it slow and easy, stretching out the pleasure for the better part of an hour, each savoring every sweet moment of the incredible bliss.

"I've just enough time for a bath," Mitch finally said with a yawn. "Care to join me?"

"Mmm, too lazy," Suzanna replied, not stirring. "I might just take a catnap right here."

"Good idea, sweetheart." Mitch kissed her turned-up nose and agilely rose to his feet.

Once he was out of the room and safely in his tub, Suzanna quickly rose. She rushed out into the foyer and took down Mitch's black naval musette bag, which she carried into the parlor and placed atop the mahogany bar. She opened it and anxiously went through the papers, searching for pertinent dispatches.

Her eyes widened in horror as she read a document setting forth the timeline and exact location where the Union Navy planned to launch a major attack on the unsuspecting Confederate Rapidan River stronghold. Suzanna was trembling with emotion as she carefully placed all the documents back inside the musette bag and returned it to the foyer.

When Mitch walked into the room with a towel around his waist, Suzanna was just as he had left her — stretched out naked before the fire, seemingly dozing.

Mitch looked down at her and weakened. "Perhaps I could stay awhile longer."

"Could you, darling?" she trilled, rolling up into a sitting position and tugging playfully at his covering towel.

Mitch exhaled heavily. "No. No, I really can't. I must get back to the fleet."

Reluctantly, he got dressed. When he was once again in full dress blues, he came to her, cupped the back of her head, bent from the waist and kissed her goodbye.

When he straightened, he said, "I'm not sure when I'll be able to get away again."

Suzanna smiled in understanding, laid her cheek against his trousered leg and said, "Kiss me as if this were the last time."

He crouched down on his heels, kissed her passionately and said, "I love you, darling."

"Please be careful," she murmured in reply.

Rear Admiral Mitchell B. Longley had barely exited the cottage before Suzanna jumped up, took a sheet of vellum paper from the desk in the corner and wrote down everything she had read in the damning dispatch.

She then dressed and trudged two miles through the deepening snow to reach the landmark — a carefully chosen leaning rock near her home — beneath which she consistently hid messages laying out information she had gleaned from the unsuspecting enemy.

A fearless spy for her beloved Confederacy, Suzanna LeGrande hesitated a moment before placing this particular missive under the rock.

If she passed on this vital information, she could be endangering Mitch's life. She could be responsible for her Yankee lover's death. Her heart squeezed painfully in her chest. She felt suddenly dizzy and her cheeks were hot despite the cold of the afternoon.

Suzanna closed her eyes and strongly considered tearing up the note. But only for an instant. She drew a labored breath, hardened her heart and dutifully placed the message beneath the cold stone.

One

On a chilly autumn morning in 1859, the lively mistress of a magnificent mansion came flying down the curving staircase, her lilting laughter echoing throughout the grand residence. Eighteen-year-old Suzanna LeGrande was a happy, carefree young aristocrat who had lived all her life in this stately two-story Virginia manse on the rolling banks of the Potomac River.

The laughing young belle lived with her widowed mother, forty-nine-year-old Emile, and her older brother, twenty-two-year-old Matthew. The frail, quiet Emile LeGrande loved her daughter dearly, but the mercurial Suzanna's rambunctious behavior was prone to give her mother headaches.

The LeGrande siblings were close, and Matthew, being the man of the house, was very protective of his beautiful younger sister. Since the high-spirited Suzanna had turned sixteen, hopeful young suitors had been drawn to the vivacious miss. She was, and had always been, stunningly beautiful, with her flaming red hair, large, wide-set blue eyes and milky-white skin. But Suzanna was not vain about her looks. She had turned heads her entire life and thought nothing of it.

Besides, it was a great deal more than her startling beauty that attracted a growing army of male admirers. She possessed a great zest for life and threw herself into everything she did with such blazing intensity it charmed the young bucks and frightened her sedate mother. Suzanna had a compulsion to dramatize, which made her tremendously fascinating to all her friends.

She was high-strung, sensitive, warm-hearted and endlessly entertaining. There was never a dull minute around Suzanna. At an early age she had learned — from her gregarious, red-haired father — to spin yarns that left her listeners wide-eyed and hanging on to every word. It was not only boys who found the outspoken Suzanna intriguing, but girls as well.

She was impetuous and impatient, but so filled with the joy of living that she lifted spirits with her mere presence. Added to her talent for storytelling was her unique ability to read palms and predict futures, an art she had learned from her beloved old nursemaid, now deceased. Naturally, all the young belles wanted to know what romantic adventures lay in store for them. The boys were unconcerned about the future, but looked on the palm reading as an opportunity to hold Suzanna's hand.

Suzanna was totally feminine, yet she had a masculine directness that was captivating. She spoke her mind, was never coy or ambiguous, nor was she particularly diplomatic. While Suzanna took after her deceased father, the lovable, outgoing Lawrence LeGrande, Matthew was more like their mother. He enjoyed a good time as much as the next fellow, but he had no compulsion to race through life as if the world might stop turning should he miss a picnic or party or ball.

An honor graduate of West Point, Matthew took duty, honor and country seriously. And he felt that his most important duty was to see to it no unprincipled male took advantage of his sister. While he was away at the institute, Matthew had worried about what calamity might befall the trusting Suzanna. A scholar who easily excelled in his studies, Matthew had completed his education at the ripe old age of twenty, and had immediately returned home to take up his post as head of the LeGrande household.

"For heaven sake, Suzanna," Matthew said now, looking up as a laughing streak of flaming hair and lilac ruffles dashed past the open library doors. "Isn't it time you displayed a bit more decorum?"

Suzanna skidded to a stop at the umbrella stand in the foyer. As she reached for a woolen cape and matching bonnet, she said over her shoulder, "Do forgive me, Matt. You see, I'm in an awful hurry and really must fly." She turned and flashed a smile at her tall, sandy-haired brother, who had stepped out into the foyer.

"At breakfast you failed to mention you were going out this morning," Matthew casually commented.

"Did I? Well, I have a great deal on my mind, what with next week's reception at Stratford House. That's why I'm in such a hurry. I'm on my way now and —"

"You're planning to be the first guest to arrive?"

"Don't be silly!" Suzanna said as she tied her bonnet's long grosgrain streamers beneath her chin. "I promised I'd help Mrs. Grayson and Cynthia Ann decide on the decorations and finalize the extensive menu." She added excitedly, "It's a stellar guest list to be sure. More or less the beginning of our upcoming Washington social season. Why, even Colonel Robert E. Lee and his wife, Mary, are expected at the festivities, did you know that?"

Matthew nodded. Colonel Lee, a West Point graduate and superintendent at the Point, was home on leave from his regimental duties on the Texas frontier.

"I'll be very surprised if the colonel attends, Suzanna. You know very well that his dear wife is in poor health and rarely leaves Arlington House and therefore . . ."

"Colonel Lee with be at the reception, Matthew," Suzanna stated emphatically. "He's far too polite and too political to disappoint a hostess as powerful as Jennie Grayson." She crossed to her brother, stood on tiptoe and kissed his cheek. "After all, the colonel likely plans to —"

"You have no idea what Lee's plans are," Matthew interrupted, quickly changing the subject. "Let's discuss *our* plans. Have you given any thought to what you'll wear this evening?"

Suzanna stepped back. Her well-arched eyebrows shot up and she looked genuinely puzzled. "This evening? Is there something special about this evening?"

"Suzanna, you do try my patience. I told you several days ago we have an important dinner guest joining us this evening. I expect you to be here."

"Why, I wouldn't miss it for the world," she said with a shrug of her slender shoulders. "Another unsuspecting candidate for my hand in marriage?"

Matthew frowned. "Just promise me you'll be home in plenty of time to get properly dressed to receive our guest. And that you'll be on your best behavior. Ty Bellinggrath is a fine man, Suzanna, and —"

"You can count on me, brother, dear," Suzanna said with a teasing smirk. "I'll scrub my face and cinch my waist and be on display when he arrives. Then you may point out all my finer qualities as I slowly pirouette for the prospective bridegroom."

"Now, Suzanna."

"Do me one small favor, Matt. Promise that if I'm not married by the time I reach twenty-five, you will give up and stop bringing young gentlemen here in hopes of marrying me off!"

For the first time Matthew smiled as he said, "Bellinggrath will be here at seven o'clock, my dear. And so will you."

"I shall look forward to a most enjoyable evening," Suzanna said sarcastically. "Now I really must be going. Poor old Durwood's waiting out in the cold with the carriage."

Two

Suzanna sighed with pleasure as she settled herself comfortably inside the roomy brougham. Old Durwood, in full livery, sat proudly up on the box, handling the pair of matched bays with ease despite his worsening arthritis. The horses were fine specimens, curried to a high gloss, and the gleaming black, silver trimmed carriage had seats of soft burgundy leather.

With her bonnet off and slapped down on the seat beside her, Suzanna gazed out the window at the natural beauty of her native Virginia. How she loved the broad avenues and the glittering streams. The familiar sights never failed to take her breath away.

Suzanna was eternally grateful that this was her home, the place where she had been born, the place where she would live all her days. She considered herself fortunate to have had a father who had been so forward thinking and such a brilliant businessman.

It was true that the late Lawrence LeGrande had inherited a tidy sum from his British ancestors, but he hadn't been content to simply let the cash lie in the safety of a bank vault. Instead he had invested wisely in land and had, over time, accumulated a vast fortune from varied endeavors.

There were the tobacco fields in northern Virginia, a coastal cotton plantation in South Carolina, indigo crops in northern Georgia and a host of other well-chosen investments in rail and shipping. The holdings were diverse and profitable and afforded the LeGrande family a life of splendid ease in the stately riverside mansion known as Whitehall.

Suzanna loved her life and her home and prayed that nothing would ever change. She wanted everything to remain just as it was on this crisp autumn morning in October of 1859.

Suzanna was halfway out of the brougham before it came to a full stop in the pebbled drive of Stratford House in the heart of Georgetown. Nonplussed at his young mistress's less than ladylike behavior, old Durwood laid the long leather reins aside and gingerly swung down to the ground.

"Why you want to act like a boy, Miss Suzanna?" he scolded, taking firm hold of her arm as she jumped from the carriage. "Folk'll be gossipin' 'bout us if you don't behave and . . ."

But Suzanna, skirts lifted, bonnet left behind, was already dashing up the front walk, calling Cynthia Ann's name. The dark-haired girl stepped out onto the shaded veranda, spotted Suzanna and came dashing forward to greet her best friend and trusted confidante. The young women threw their arms around each other and embraced as though it had been weeks — not hours — since last they'd seen each other.

"You'll have lunch with us," Cynthia Ann stated as they walked into the house, arm in arm. "Then spend all afternoon?"

"So long as I'm home by seven," Suzanna replied. "Matthew is up to his old tricks. He has invited a poor naive fellow to dinner." She made a face. "Be grateful you don't have a big brother!"

Both laughed, then Cynthia Ann asked, "How does Matthew keep coming up with new prospective beaux? Surely you've met all his friends by now. At least all the ones he'd hope you might marry."

Suzanna sighed and shook her head wearily. "Hopefully this is the very last one! His name is Ty Bellinggrath. He and Matt were classmates at West Point, but Bellinggrath left home right after graduation. As I understand it, he's been in Europe for the past couple of years. He only returned a week ago and Matthew immediately pounced on him." She quoted her brother, " 'I'll have you know, Suzanna LeGrande, that my good friend Ty Bellinggrath is the respected scion of an old Virginia family. He excelled in his studies at the institute and is considered quite a catch.' " Suzanna laughed and added, "I can just imagine what he looks like. Matt is so anxious to marry me off he's scraping the bottom of the barrel now."

Inside the wide foyer of Stratford House, the slender, still handsome Jennie Grayson waited to welcome her. "We're awfully glad you could come this morning, Suzanna," she exclaimed with a warm smile. To her daughter, she said, "Cynthia, dear, why don't you take Suzanna upstairs, where the two of you can relax for an hour before lunch?" Her attention shifted back to Suzanna. "After we've had a leisurely noontime meal, we'll go over the party menu and give you our ideas regarding the decorations. You're always so innovative, the final decision will be yours."

■ ■ ■ ■

In Cynthia Ann's bedchamber, a spacious room at the front of the mansion, the two friends gossiped and laughed and shared secrets. With their slippers and crinoline petticoats kicked off, stays loosened, they lay on their backs atop the canopied feather bed.

"Read my palm, Suzanna," Cynthia Ann said suddenly, turning onto her stomach and holding out her hand.

"Again? I just read it last week."

"I know, but perhaps something has changed since then. Maybe Davy is going to propose after the party." Her brown eyes danced at the thought of marrying her gallant sweetheart.

"I don't understand you, Cynthia Ann Grayson," Suzanna said, toying with the lace jabot at her throat. "Why would you want to get married and ruin your life? Married women don't have any fun, nor thrilling adventures. Worse, no one pays any attention to what they have to say. They're expected to keep silent on any controversial issue as though they don't have a brain in their head. Such a life couldn't possibly be fulfilling."

"It would be if . . ."

"I shall never marry. Why should I? I have no need of a husband to take care of me. I can and will take care of myself. And I'll be free to speak as I please and do as I please without having to seek permission from some domineering male."

Cynthia Ann just shook her head and laughed. She'd heard it all before. She felt certain that Suzanna would change her mind about marriage when the right man came along.

"You have exactly twenty-five minutes to make yourself presentable," said an annoyed Matthew when Suzanna raced up the front steps of Whitehall at 6:35 that evening.

Laughing, she patted her brother's stern cheek and said, "I need only twenty, so I'll have five to spare."

He exhaled heavily and followed her inside the well-lit mansion. While he turned toward the paneled library to join their mother, Suzanna climbed the stairs, struggling to unhook her dress. In her rose-and-cream suite at the head of the staircase, Suzanna's ever-patient personal maid, Buelah, waited to help her young charge get dressed.

Impressive in her black-and-white uniform, the stout, six-foot-tall Buelah didn't scold the girl she often called "my baby." She admired Suzanna's free spirit and always laughed at her antics. Besides, she knew that with her help, Suzanna would be dressed and ready within fifteen minutes.

"Your tub is drawn and waitin'," said Buelah. She took Suzanna's arm, turned her about and made quick work of unhooking her dress.

"Ahh!" Suzanna sighed when, three minutes after walking into the suite, she sank down into the heated water.

Buelah, on her knees beside the tub, scrubbed Suzanna's glistening back with a long-handled brush while Suzanna drew a soapy washcloth down each slim arm.

"I laid out the pale blue velvet dress, the one you've never worn. It'll bring out your eyes. I'll brush your hair up atop your head and hold it in place with that oyster-shell comb." Buelah chattered on as she drew Suzanna to her feet and began briskly rubbing her dry with a fluffy white towel. Then she followed her young mistress back into the bedroom and helped her don the silky stockings and lacy underthings laid out there. Nineteen minutes after arriving home, Suzanna came down the grand staircase fully clothed and breathtakingly beautiful.

She heard masculine voices and then her mother saying, "So glad you could come this evening, Mr. Bellinggrath."

Suzanna frowned. She wasn't glad. She fully intended, immediately after dinner, to plead a headache and retire to her suite.

She took a deep breath, stepped down off the bottom stair, crossed the marble-floored foyer and walked into the high-ceilinged drawing room.

The two men came to their feet.

"Ah, there she is," said her brother. "Ty, may I present my sister, Suzanna. Suzanna, this is my good friend Ty Bellinggrath."

"Miss LeGrande," said Ty, taking her offered hand in his. "A genuine pleasure to meet you." He raised it to his lips and brushed a quick kiss to its soft back.

Young Bellinggrath did not immediately release her hand. Instead, his much larger one closed possessively around her fragile fingers. They stood there staring at each other while her mother and brother looked on.

For the first time in her life, Suzanna was speechless. She didn't say she was pleased to meet him. She didn't say anything. Not one word. She gazed up at the tall, slim, handsome blond man and felt her breath catch in her throat. His pale golden hair gleamed in the light of the chandelier and his luminous blue eyes sparkled with unmasked interest.

After several silent seconds, Matthew cleared his throat and said, “I believe Cook is signaling that dinner is ready.”

Suzanna and Ty had momentarily forgotten they were not alone. Both broke into nervous laughter.

But he didn’t let go of her hand.

THREE

"Shall we go in to dinner?" Matthew said, helping their mother to her feet. "Suzanna, why don't you show our guest into the dining room."

Suzanna freed her hand, but immediately slipped possessive fingers around Ty's arm. "If you'll kindly come with me, Mr. Bellinggrath," she said, and flashed him her most dazzling smile.

"Indeed, I'd be honored, Miss LeGrande," said the shy, well-mannered Bellinggrath.

He graciously allowed himself to be propelled into the candlelit dining room by the determined Suzanna. Behind them, Matthew and Emile exchanged looks of surprise. Never had they seen Suzanna exhibit such unveiled interest in a would-be suitor.

Ty pulled out the chair Suzanna indicated, and she slipped into it. But when Matthew drew out the chair directly beside it, Suzanna said, sweetly but firmly, "Mother, why don't you sit across from us? Mr. Bellinggrath will sit here by me."

Again Matthew and Emile exchanged glances, and Matthew couldn't hide a hint of a smile as he ushered his mother to the other side of the table. When Emile was seated, Ty sat down in the chair beside Suzanna, while Matthew took his own at the head of the table.

After shaking out a white damask napkin and draping it over his right knee, Matthew lifted the small silver bell beside his plate. He gave it a forceful shake. A pair of male servants in spotless black uniforms and snowy white gloves instantly appeared. One poured iced water into crystal goblets and port wine into tall stemmed glasses. The other placed bowls of chilled vichyssoise before each diner.

The meal began.

For the first time in her life, Suzanna found that she was not hungry. Not at all. Neither was Ty Bellinggrath. Hot yeast rolls and creamery butter did not tempt either of them. They hardly touched the rare roast beef and carefully steamed vegetables. Even the baked Alaska, Suzanna's favorite, sat melting on their plates.

Suzanna had no appetite, no interest in

food. She was interested only in Ty Bellinggrath. His blond, blue-eyed good looks and quiet, gentlemanly manner made him tremendously appealing. She liked hearing him speak, his voice pleasingly low and well-modulated. She liked the way he shyly smiled, the corners of his full lips lifting ever so slightly. A bashful little-boy smile, touchingly adorable. At the same time there was about him a calm demeanor and dignified bearing that denoted strength and dependability.

Added to his physical attributes was his sharp intellect. He was wise and well-versed on a wide range of subjects, yet modest, clearly averse to flaunting his knowledge. He challenged her own keen mind, and she could tell by the look in his eyes that he was heartened to find her so smart. But he was not astonished as most gentlemen were.

The dinner conversation was lively and diverse, and Suzanna listened as, prompted by Matthew, Ty spoke about his recent travels through Europe. He painted vivid word pictures of Paris, that fabled City of Light. He told of the cafés lined with tables facing the street, where he had sat in the warm sun and sipped vermouth while watching the passersby. He described the flower sellers with their fresh blossoms. The boulevardiers in long-tailed coats and goatees. The open-air carriages rolling by conveying happy, handsome couples. The shop windows on the Rue de la Paix. The tree-bordered Champs-Élysées.

Concluding, he pointed out that he had returned to America only last week and that he was very glad to be home. He glanced at Suzanna when he said it, and she nodded, smiling. She was very glad as well.

The meal ended and the foursome went back into the drawing room. Inclining his head, Matthew suggested Suzanna play the piano for their enjoyment. Generally, such a suggestion drew quick protests and mean faces from his sister. She was no circus performer! She would not would jump through hoops to prove she had laudable feminine talents that might make her more attractive to the opposite sex!

But Ty gently coaxed, "Yes, Miss Suzanna, won't you, please . . . ?"

"Only if you'll agree to sit beside me while I play," she said sweetly.

"It would be my pleasure," he replied in that low, soft drawl that so suited him.

Matthew and Emile sipped their coffee, unable to believe what they were seeing — Suzanna seated at the square pianoforte, playing Chopin beautifully and smiling warmly at the blushing blond man who sat beside her.

The impromptu recital ended.

Ty rose and drew her to her feet. "That was lovely, Miss Suzanna. I truly enjoyed it." Suzanna beamed with pride. Ty then turned and said, "Mrs. LeGrande, Matthew, thank you so much for inviting me to dinner. It was a most pleasant evening and I appreciate your hospitality. Now I really must be going."

"So soon?" Suzanna said, visibly disappointed. "Why, it's early yet, not even nine. Don't go."

"You're kind, Miss Suzanna, but . . ."

"What would it take to make you stay?" she asked anxiously, her heart overruling her head. "I can do more than just play the piano, you know. I read palms! I can predict the future. I do some great tricks with a deck of playing cards. I can tilt my head back, balance a full wineglass on my forehead and, without using my hands, sink all the way down to the floor and stretch out on my back without spilling a single drop! I can —"

"Mind your manners, Suzanna!" Matthew scolded. Emile frowned disapprovingly at her daughter.

Ty Bellinggrath was laughing, charmed by

this outspoken young beauty. With her at his side, he crossed to the sofa, smiled at her mother and said, "Good night, Mrs. LeGrande. Again, thank you so much."

"Do come back again, young man," said Emile.

Matthew was on his feet now, ready to see his guest to the door. But the shy, retiring Ty said, "Please, stay where you are, Matt. Miss Suzanna will see me out." He shifted his focus to her. "Won't you?"

"I will!" she eagerly exclaimed, lifting her bell-like skirts and preceding him out of the room and into the foyer. When he would have paused there to bid her good-night, she drew him out the front door and onto the chilly, moon-splashed veranda. There she turned to face him and eagerly asked, "Are you going to the Graysons' reception next Saturday evening at Stratford House?"

"If you are, I am."

She liked his answer and told him, "I'll be there."

"Then so will I."

Suzanna started to speak, but Ty lifted a hand and touched her cheek lightly. His eyes flashed in the moonlight when he whispered, "Till then, Suzanna."

Four

The pressure of Ty's hand at her waist was intensely exciting to Suzanna. That and the warm look in his eyes as he gazed down at her.

The two of them spun about the ballroom's crowded floor at Stratford House, oblivious to the other dancers. Lost in the first thrilling blush of budding romance, they were only vaguely aware of the seductive milieu surrounding them, engulfing them. Bouquets of freshly cut hothouse flowers. Candlelight falling on the polished parquet floor. The subtle scents of expensive perfumes. The swish of silks and satins and the flash of diamonds. Soft laughter and haunting violins and chilled champagne.

The romantic evening was to become even more so when, midway through the glittering reception, the clearly smitten Ty said against Suzanna's ear, "It's grown quite warm in here, hasn't it?"

To which she laughed and promptly replied, "Mother said never say 'hot.' Why don't we go outdoors and get a breath of the fresh night air?"

Ty paused midstep. "I was hoping you'd say that."

"And I have, so let's go."

"I wouldn't want to compromise you, Miss Suzanna. Matthew would have my hide if I —"

"Matthew need never know. And will you kindly stop calling me *Miss* Suzanna?" She glanced warily around, then whispered, "I'll pretend I need to freshen up. Once upstairs, I'll slip down the back way and meet you in the rear gardens. No one will be there."

"An ingenious plan," he said admiringly, and eagerly ushered her off the floor and through the crowd. Suzanna stopped just before they exited the ballroom, reached out and plucked an ivory gardenia from a huge bouquet in a tall porcelain vase beside the arched doorway. Then she preceded Ty into the foyer.

But before they could cross the crowded vestibule, they encountered Matthew.

"Have you heard the news?" he asked, taking no notice of the fact that they had left the ballroom. "Colonel Robert E. Lee has sent his apology. He will not be attending this evening."

"Is Mrs. Lee feeling worse?" asked Suzanna, hoping she didn't look guilty.

"No, it's not that. Lee's leave has been abruptly canceled. He has been called back to duty immediately."

Ty Bellinggrath frowned. "The John Brown raid at Harper's Ferry?"

"Yes. Our host, Ronald Grayson, just told me that Colonel Lee's been dispatched to Harper's Ferry in command of the United States troops. He received orders from the secretary of war to take the evening train there."

"The affair must be more serious than we'd presumed," said Ty thoughtfully.

Matthew nodded, sharing Ty's concern. "They're holding a number of citizens hostage and threatening their lives. It's a dangerous situation that could erupt —"

"I'm sure Colonel Lee will soon have everything under control," Suzanna interrupted, anxious to get away from her brother, refusing to allow anything to spoil this perfect evening. "You'll excuse me, Matt," she said. "I was just going to freshen up."

"Yes, of course. Go ahead." Matthew made a move toward the ballroom. "You coming, Ty?"

"Ah . . . no . . . I . . . You go on," Ty said, feeling heat rising to his face. "Think I'll step out onto the veranda for a minute. It's growing quite stuffy inside."

"Good enough. See you both later," said Matthew, and left them.

"That was close," Ty commented.

"He doesn't suspect a thing," Suzanna assured him.

At the base of the grand staircase, Ty winked at Suzanna and whispered, "Five minutes."

"Make it four." She lifted her bronze taffeta skirts and dashed up the stairs.

On the landing, Suzanna encountered Cynthia Ann coming out of her bedroom. Suzanna immediately put her finger to her lips, then she drew her best friend close and whispered in her ear, "I'm meeting Ty Bellinggrath in the terraced back gardens!"

"Suzanna LeGrande!"

"Shh! Don't tell a soul. We bumped into Matt downstairs and I told him I was going to your room. Should he mention my absence, assure him I am upstairs."

Nodding, happy to share her friend's secret, Cynthia Ann asked, "Are you going to let him . . . kiss you?"

"Bite your tongue, Cynthia Ann Grayson! Of course not," Suzanna stated emphatically. Then she grinned and whispered, "But I will make him wish he could kiss me." Both girls giggled. "I must go," said Suzanna, hugging her friend. Then she was gone, with Cynthia Ann looking after her.

Unhurriedly, Ty crossed the wide foyer, nodding to acquaintances, exchanging respectful pleasantries with his elders. Once out the front door, he anxiously crossed the veranda and skipped down the wide stone steps. His heart beginning to beat rapidly, he sprinted around the mansion.

He found Suzanna waiting beneath a decorative marble statue, the moonlight striking her full in the face, the night breeze swirling locks of her hair around her head. In her hand she held the fragrant gardenia she had plucked from the bouquet inside the ballroom.

Ty approached.

When he reached her, neither said anything. They stood for a long moment, gazing at each other. Finally, Suzanna lifted the gardenia, carefully tucked it into Ty's lapel, and said, "Next time I do this — put a blossom in your lapel — it will be our secret signal that you will be allowed to kiss me before the evening is over."

Ty trembled at the prospect. He reached

for her hand and took it in both of his. "Will it be long before you . . . ?"

"We'll see," she teased, and knew she'd done just what she had set out to do. Ty Bellinggrath was dying to kiss her and wouldn't rest until she let him.

"Are you cold? I could lend you my . . ."

"No," she said with a provocative smile, "I'm almost as warm as you."

Ty laughed, bewitched. Hand in hand they strolled down a pebbled path that criss-crossed the manicured gardens of the vast estate. At a white settee at the far edge of the property, they paused. Ty took a linen handkerchief from his inside breast pocket and carefully spread it on the bench. Once Suzanna was settled, he took a seat beside her.

He draped an arm along the settee's high back behind her. Unconcerned with the chill of the autumn night, they sat in the moonlight and talked and laughed and became better acquainted. Suzanna made Ty promise that he would come to Whitehall again for dinner one evening.

"I will," he replied.

"And not some distant date in the future," she said. "Join us tomorrow night."

Again he laughed. "I'll be there," he said. "And speaking of the future, is it true you can read palms?"

"It certainly is," Suzanna proudly assured him. "I've a real talent for it. Shall I read yours?"

"Have we enough light?" He glanced up at the full white moon.

"I'm sure we do. Give me your hand and I'll tell you what you can expect in the years ahead," she said with authority.

Ty was smiling as he held it out, palm up. Suzanna was smiling, too. She took hold of his large hand, raised it a little closer to her face and studied the open palm for several long seconds. Her eyes widened, then narrowed. Her smile fled. Watching her intently, Ty caught the change of expression and wondered what had caused it. Suzanna lowered his hand, wrapped both of her own around it and pressed it to her waist.

"Well? What did you see?" Ty was still grinning.

"Nothing," she said in clipped tones. "I saw nothing." She smiled once more and told him, "You were right, there's not enough light."

"I'm disappointed," he said, studying her face. "I was hoping you would tell me . . ."

"Ty, I can't actually predict the future. I was teasing you. It's just something I do for fun." Quickly changing the subject, she said,

"We had better get back inside before we're missed and my overprotective brother has you horsewhipped."

FIVE

The courtship had begun.

Utterly enchanted with Suzanna, Ty Bellinggrath was ever the gentleman. He treated his beautiful sweetheart with the utmost respect at all times. He waited patiently, hopefully, for the magical moment when Suzanna would step up to him and place a blossom in his lapel.

Nights passed.

Then weeks.

Yearning to taste her soft, full lips, Ty had begun to wonder if he would *ever* be allowed to kiss the woman with whom he was falling deeply in love.

And then, when he least expected it, when it was the dead of winter and the trees were bare and a blanket of snow covered the ground and Christmas and New Year's had come and gone, the unpredictable Suzanna surprised him.

On a bitterly cold February evening, as he

waited with Matthew and Mrs. LeGrande in the library before a blazing fire, Suzanna, looking especially lovely in a high-necked, long-sleeved dress of rich brown velveteen, suddenly appeared. Ty and Matthew came to their feet and while Matthew mildly scolded his sister for making their dinner guest wait, Ty felt his chest tighten.

On this freezing winter's night, Suzanna wore a fragile ivory gardenia in her blazing red hair. Would she place it in his lapel? If so, he knew what that meant. He would, at long last — if he could figure out how to get her alone for a few precious moments — be allowed to finally kiss his adored sweetheart.

Suzanna caught the look in Ty's eyes and knew what was running through her beau's mind. She would, she decided, let the expectation build awhile longer. She didn't immediately place the blossom in his lapel. She made him wait. Made him wait all through a leisurely five-course dinner. Made him wait while she and her mother sipped their coffee in the library and Ty and Matthew shared a brandy. Made him wait until the tall cased clock in the foyer struck the hour of ten and Ty said he should be going. Made him wait until she saw him to the front door and he had taken his heavy caped cloak down from the coat tree, but had not yet swirled it around his shoulders.

"Good night, Ty," Suzanna said sweetly as they stood facing each other in the foyer.

"Suzanna, I . . ."

She smiled as she took the gardenia from her hair and carefully tucked it into the lapel of his dark frock coat. And before he knew what was happening, Suzanna put her arms around his neck and lifted her lips for his kiss. Nervous, afraid Matthew or Mrs. LeGrande might decide to come out of the library, he nonetheless couldn't resist. He bent his head and kissed Suzanna squarely on the lips.

It was the sweetest of kisses, a kiss he would never forget. When their lips separated, Suzanna rested her forehead against his chin for an instant.

"Promise you'll never again kiss anyone but me," she said.

"I promise."

Ty waited a full year.

He formally proposed to Suzanna on October 12, 1860, the anniversary of the night they had first met. Suzanna eagerly accepted.

"You'll take me to Paris for our honeymoon?"

"I will, darling girl," he promised.

Suzanna immediately expressed the strong desire to be a June bride. Ty hated to wait, especially since he was all too aware of the troubling unrest sweeping the country. But he could deny her nothing, so he agreed.

The date was set. Elaborate wedding plans were put in motion. Engraved invitations were ordered. Suzanna settled on a wedding dress of snow-white satin trimmed with thousands of tiny, hand-sewn crystal beads. Months in advance, wedding gifts began pouring into Whitehall.

Happy as only the very young can be, Suzanna looked eagerly forward to becoming the bride of Ty Bellinggrath, and Ty was anxiously counting the days.

But on April 12, 1861, two months before the big day was to take place, Fort Sumter in the Charleston harbor was fired on from a Confederate artillery battery. The next day the fort surrendered to Southern forces. War Between the States was unavoidable.

When Suzanna heard the disturbing news, she knew that her wedding plans might be postponed indefinitely. She suggested to Ty that they elope, marry quickly before the coming conflict got under way.

Ty talked her out of it, reasoning that it wouldn't be fair to her. She wanted a big church wedding and she deserved to have one. He assured her that even with the worst happening — the Confederacy going to war against the Union — the hostility wouldn't last. It would be over in a few short weeks and they could get married just as planned.

On the 15th of April, President Lincoln issued a proclamation calling for seventy-five thousand militia to serve for ninety days to put down "combinations too powerful to be suppressed by the ordinary mechanism of the government." The proclamation infuriated the South and spurred the uncommitted states into action.

On April 17, Virginia seceded from the Union, along with North Carolina, Arkansas and Tennessee. On the twentieth, Robert E. Lee resigned his command as colonel of the First Regiment of Cavalry in the United States Army. Word spread that the decision broke Lee's heart and that he had stated, in a missive to General Winfield Scott, "Save in defense of my native state, I never desire to again draw my sword."

The news all over Washington was of Colonel Lee's resignation. When Ty came to Whitehall that evening, Suzanna met him at the door and threw her arms around his neck. "Don't go, Ty. Please don't go."

"He has to go, Suzanna," Matthew said, stepping into the foyer with their mother at his side. "Just as I must go."

On April 25 Virginia joined the Confederate States, and both Ty and Matthew warned Suzanna and Mrs. LeGrande that the two of them should quickly move to a place of safety. War was now inevitable and could explode around them at any minute.

"No! This is our home. We are not leaving Whitehall," stated the usually gentle Emile LeGrande, demonstrating a surprising flash of mettle.

"Mrs. LeGrande," Ty said, with respect. "Won't you please consider closing up the house and going to New Orleans until this is over? I've cousins there who will be more than happy to —"

Interrupting, Suzanna said, "Mother is right, Ty. We are going nowhere."

No amount of reasoning could change the women's minds. Ty and Matthew prepared to ride to Richmond to join Colonel Lee's Virginia Provisional Army.

Two short weeks after the capture of Fort Sumter, the dashing young men stood on the broad veranda of Whitehall saying goodbye. Mrs. LeGrande cupped her son's dear face in her hands and fought back tears. Suzanna stood in Ty's embrace and admonished him to write every day. He promised he would.

"It's time," said Matthew, and Ty nodded without looking up.

Disengaging himself, he held Suzanna at arm's length and told her, "We'll be back before you know it, sweetheart."

She nodded, smiled, took an early blooming rose from her hair and tucked it into his lapel. "Kiss me," she challenged.

Ty's handsome face flushed. He had never dared kiss her in front of her family. He glanced over her head at Mrs. LeGrande and Matthew. Then, realizing it might be weeks before he could kiss her again, he tossed caution to the wind. Ty lowered his head and soundly kissed Suzanna.

Then he stepped back from her and was gone.

Suzanna stayed on the veranda long after Ty and Matthew had disappeared. Chilly despite the warmth of the sunny spring day, she fought one of those "disturbing feelings" that sometimes came over her, a strong premonition of danger.

She had never discussed those inexplicable sensations with anyone other than the understanding Cynthia Ann. Sharing such unexplainable anguish with her levelheaded brother would have brought only mild scorn and a swift reassurance that such feelings meant nothing. Had she confided in her mother, it would have further upset the older woman. And Suzanna tried never to needlessly worry the fragile Emile.

Lost in troubled thought, Suzanna blinked and came back to the present when she heard Cynthia Ann calling her name. The Grayson brougham had rolled to a stop in the driveway and Cynthia Ann was rushing up the walk. Heartened, Suzanna hurried to meet her.

As the two young women embraced, Suzanna said, "Oh, Cyn, I'm so glad you came because —"

"I know," Cynthia Ann interrupted. "We passed Ty and Matthew riding away at a gallop. I knew you'd be upset, but they'll soon be back and . . ."

"It's more than their leaving, Cyn. It's . . . I'm experiencing one of those eerie, awful feelings. Like something really terrible is going to happen."

Cynthia Ann squeezed Suzanna's narrow waist. "Suz, I'm so sorry. Let me stay here with you until it passes."

"Would you? I'm frightened and I can't worry Mother." She pulled back, looked at the shorter girl, and was startled to see bright tears shining in Cynthia Ann's eyes. "What is it? Has something dreadful already happened? Is that what I sense?"

"We're going away, Suz."

"Going away? But . . . why? Where?"

"Boston. Father is sending Mother and me to stay with my maiden aunt in Boston until this is over."

"Oh, Cyn, must you?"

"Father says there's sure to be bloody battles right here in and around Washington." She swallowed hard and added, "Dearest friend, you and I are to be on opposite sides in this war. Father's pledged allegiance to the Union Army and so has my darling Davy."

"Dear Lord, I hadn't thought of that," Suzanna said, realizing with horror that scenes such as this were taking place all over the city. The war was tearing apart lifelong friends, even families.

"It isn't my fault, Suz," said the now weeping Cynthia Ann. "Please don't hold it against me."

Tears spilling down her own cheeks, Suzanna said, "Darling Cyn, nothing could ever change the way I feel about you. You're the sister I never had, and I shall love you always. None of this is your fault, nor mine. It changes nothing between us."

"I knew you'd understand."

"When are you leaving?"

"Mother and the servants are busy packing now and . . . Tomorrow. Early tomorrow morning."

"So soon? It's like a knife through my breast," Suzanna said honestly. "This — your leaving me — must be responsible for the terrible feeling I have." She looked hopefully at Cynthia Ann. "That's it, isn't it, Cyn? That's the bad thing I perceived was going to happen."

"I'm sure it is, dear. And I'm so sorry to be deserting you when you need me most."

"I'll be all right, truly I will. And you will write me often and I will answer. And when this conflict ends, you will come home and we will be just as we always were."

"Yes. Yes, we will. Nothing can ever damage our friendship."

"Absolutely not. Now come on inside and let's enjoy our last afternoon together."

Six

July 1861

Creamy white flowers covered the rose-bushes that grew just outside the open floor-to-ceiling windows. The fragile blossoms undulated in a gentle breeze blowing out of the south. The rhythmic shimmering stirred the flowers' seductive fragrance, sending the subtle scent wafting through the windows and into the spacious ground floor bed-chamber.

"Umm, smell that," purred a voluptuous naked woman lying stretched out on the silk-sheeted bed, arms flung above her head, midnight hair spilling across the lace-trimmed pillows. "Like the sweetest of honey."

"I smell you," said the man who, shedding the last of his clothes, came down onto the bed beside the woman.

"And how do I smell?" she asked, turning on her side and raking long fingernails through the coal-black hair covering his broad, muscled chest.

"Hot. Pungent. Like a highly aroused female in need of immediate sex," he said, unworried that she might take offense.

No chance of that. Mitch Longley knew her too well. Mrs. Dawn Bell Thompson Bond Merriweather, a wealthy and beautiful twice-widowed, once-divorced brunette who was accepted in Washington society mainly because she was extremely wealthy, had let him know the night they met exactly what she wanted from him.

As they had danced in the ballroom of this very mansion — one of three grand residences she owned — she'd wasted no time in explaining why Mitch had been invited to the evening's glittering soiree.

"Admiral Longley," she had said, "since the afternoon when I was walking past the War Department with a good friend and you and I very nearly collided, I have thought of little else but you."

"Madam," Mitch had reminded her, "the incident happened only yesterday afternoon."

She'd laughed gaily and said, "Well, you can't very well expect a lady to live in torture forever, now can you, Admiral?"

"I'm afraid I don't quite follow."

"Don't you?" she said, and none-too-subtly insinuated her chiffon-gowned knee between his. Her gloved hand firmly urging his head down, she'd put her lips against his ear and whispered, "I want you to make love to me. Tonight. Here in my home. In my bed. After my guests leave. Or before. It's up to you. We can go to my suite right now if you like. It's just down the hall." She pulled back to judge his reaction.

Mitch Longley was unfazed. Hers was not the first, nor would it be the last, decidedly unladylike proposition he had received from a spoiled, desirable woman. He made no misstep. His handsome face did not change. She might have been commenting on the weather for all that registered in his continuing calm demeanor.

Taken aback, Dawn said, "Perhaps you still don't fully understand me, Admiral. I am suggesting that —"

"I'm not titillated by the prospect of making love to a woman while she's entertaining a houseful of people." He smoothly danced his brash hostess to the edge of the floor and deposited her there. Speaking loudly enough for others to hear, he thanked her for the dance and for the evening. Dawn Merriweather's face fell with disappointment.

Then Mitch leaned close and whispered in her ear, "Get rid of them. I'll be back at midnight. If you're not alone, don't expect me to stay."

Without another word, Mitchell B. Longley, wealthy Maryland native, Union naval officer, graduate of the Naval Academy at Annapolis, class of '48, turned and left, with Dawn Merriweather staring after him.

When Mitch returned to the mansion at the stroke of midnight, a uniformed butler admitted him into the silent house and directed him to a set of closed double doors at the end of the wide downstairs corridor.

Pausing before those doors, Mitch raised his hand, then lowered it without knocking. He walked into the white-and-blue-decorated suite and closed the door behind him. She was not in the spacious sitting room, where huge white sofas and overstuffed blue easy chairs rested before a white marble fireplace. Mitch crossed the room. He went directly to the open connecting doors, stepped inside the candlelit bedroom and saw her.

The beautiful Dawn Merriweather, in a virginal white dressing gown, with her lustrous black hair falling loose around her shoulders, stood beside the big feather bed.

"I thought perhaps you weren't coming,"

she said, seductively running a thumb and forefinger down the lapel of her shimmering robe to call his attention to the rigid nipples pressing proudly against the shiny fabric.

"You knew very well I would come," he said. "Take that thing off." He gestured to her garment.

"No," she said, letting her arms fall to her sides. "You take it off, Admiral."

Mitch shook his head and turned to leave.

"Wait! Come back. It's off! The robe's off!" she said, frantically yanking at the sash and sending the slippery covering to the carpeted floor.

Mitch stopped, turned and smiled. She was naked, her voluptuous body as beautiful as her face. She was Venus di Milo in the flesh, yet this goddess of love and beauty had arms with which to hold him.

In seconds Mitch was as naked as she. In minutes they were atop her feather bed going at each other in a no-holds-barred frenzy of raw sexual hunger. Mitch learned on that very first night that Mrs. Merriweather was insatiable. And that, not surprisingly, she was a highly experienced lover who was able to teach him a trick or two.

Now on this hot July afternoon a month after they'd met, the delectable Dawn sat astride the prostrate Mitch and aggressively rode him, determined to keep him hard and hot and here inside her. Her heavy breasts swaying with her slow undulating movements, midnight hair whipping around her face, she gazed steadily into his hooded green eyes and praised his prowess as a lover.

Mitch knew all her games. He knew exactly what she was up to on this particular afternoon. He had informed her the minute he arrived that he could stay for only an hour. He'd gotten his orders. He was to report to the Washington navy yard to board the USS *Pawnee* at 4:00 p.m. By dusk the Union warship would sail with the tide to Alexandria, Virginia.

Prolonged lovemaking was enjoyable. Still, Mitch had no choice but to take matters into his own hands and bring them both to a hasty release. He rolled up into a sitting position, slipped his hands beneath Dawn's bent knees, pressed them to his sides and firmly clasped the twin cheeks of her buttocks. While she anxiously hugged his head to her breasts, Mitch pumped into her with a fury.

"Nooo!" she protested when her climax began. "Not yet, Mitch, I . . . I . . . ooh, yes, yes!"

Seven

Despite the war, Suzanna had lost none of her youthful optimism. She constantly reminded her worried mother that the conflict would soon be over and the South would be victorious. Then Matthew and Ty would come riding home, heroes on horseback.

Suzanna looked eagerly forward to the few short letters she received from Ty. She read them over and over again. Then she carefully placed those precious missives in an empty, ruffle-trimmed bonbon box to keep forever. Her last letter from Ty had come from Manassas, reaching her on July 19.

Dearest Suzanna,
I miss you so much it is a physical pain. But I do have something of you — the rose you placed in my lapel on the morning we parted. I keep it with me at

all times, inside my tunic, next to my heart.

Matthew and I have not suffered so much as a scratch. We're fortunate to be together and even more fortunate to serve in the Confederate Army of the Potomac under the flamboyant Brigadier General Pierre G. T. Beauregard.

Dearest, we are bivouacked outside Manassas, near the railroad junction where the massing of Confederate troops continues. We are hoping to engage and vanquish the enemy very soon. Ours is a mighty force, sweetheart. Do not worry.

All my love,
Ty

Even prior to receiving Ty's letter, Suzanna had heard that a buildup of both Union and Confederate troops was taking place in Manassas. She realized a battle was inevitable.

She did not allow herself to worry. She continued to plan for the lavish wedding and for the romantic honeymoon in Paris that Ty had promised her. She happily envisioned the day when she would walk down the aisle on Matthew's arm to become Mrs. Ty Bellinggrath.

Until that much-anticipated hour, she

would keep busy and quietly do whatever she could to aid the Confederacy.

Suzanna tirelessly rolled bandages and collected spare medications for the troops from those families she knew to be sympathetic to the Cause.

Since her Virginia home was just across the river from the bustling Union capital and its hordes of uniformed Yankee soldiers, she had to be extremely cautious about declaring her loyalty to the South. Hardly anyone supportive of the Confederacy had remained in the Washington, D.C. area. Most had fled shortly after war broke out.

Suzanna missed her friends, especially Cynthia Ann Grayson, with whom she had always shared her secrets. Now she had no one to confide in. She was lonely for those absent companions, but didn't allow herself a great deal of time to dwell on her isolation.

Since Matthew was away, the responsibility for looking after their mother and overseeing the family businesses had fallen on Suzanna's shoulders. She never bothered her mother with complicated affairs of enterprise. Emile LeGrande, married as a young girl, pampered by her husband and then her son, had never paid any attention to complicated concerns of commerce.

Emile had always taken their wealth for granted and had never been curious about any of her husband's business ventures. Indeed, she had no idea what they owned or how much they were worth. After Lawrence LeGrande's passing, Matthew had rightfully stepped into the role of manager of the estate.

Suzanna was acutely aware that she could not enjoy the luxury of disinterest where their holdings were concerned. In the days prior to his leaving, Matthew had patiently schooled his sister on the diverse LeGrande interests.

Now, in his absence, Suzanna spent a great deal of time poring over various ledgers, attempting to make sense of the neat columns of numbers. Deposits from profits, deductions of payouts for labor rendered. She made every attempt to keep informed on where they stood financially.

Suzanna didn't mind the responsibility. She prided herself on being as intelligent as any man, and assumed that she could easily shoulder the task until Matthew's return. She loved her mother dearly and was resolved never to burden her with worries regarding their livelihood.

Keeping the family ledgers balanced was not Suzanna's only duty. When the war began, a number of the servants had deserted Whitehall. Of the few who remained, none wanted to journey too far from home. Understanding their confusion and fear, Suzanna assured them that they need not leave the safety of the mansion. If they would see to the household chores, she would do the necessary marketing.

In truth, she rather enjoyed venturing forth to choose fresh fruits and vegetables from the sidewalk stalls just across the river. And it afforded the opportunity to eavesdrop and learn about the war's progress, to hear news of troop movements. Her mere presence in the staunchly Union city was an unspoken assurance that her alliance lay with the North. In the interest of self-preservation, she allowed that assumption to go unchallenged. Indeed, she enhanced it by pretending delight on hearing people proclaim that the mighty Union would make short work of putting down the rebellion.

At market on the blistering hot afternoon of July 22, 1861, Suzanna observed great numbers of the shattered Union Army marching wearily into Washington. When she inquired about the meaning, an old gentleman who was clearly disappointed informed her that "the upstart Confederates have been victorious at Manassas."

"Ah, that's too bad," Suzanna commented, hoping her face did not betray her true feelings.

She went on carefully choosing ripened peaches and placing them in the basket over her arm, suppressing the smile that was playing at her lips.

Then, all at once, from out of the blue, one of those dreaded "feelings" came over her. The blood drained from her face. Her basket of fruit fell to the ground. She didn't bend and pick it up. She immediately left the outdoor market. She hurried back across the bridge, anxious to get home, plagued with an icy fear that something had happened to Ty or to Matthew.

Her heart drumming in her ears, she fought the panic that was threatening to choke her. By the time she reached the circular drive of Whitehall, she was out of breath and had a painful stitch in her side.

She stopped at the front gate, pressed a hand to her aching side and blinked away the sunspots dancing before her eyes. Her anxiety escalated when she looked up and saw her frail mother standing on the veranda. Old Durwood, the only male servant still at Whitehall, was at her side, supporting her.

"No," Suzanna murmured soundlessly, "please, God, no. No, no, no." She lifted her skirts and raced up the front walk.

She reached her mother, looked at Emile with questioning eyes. The older woman said nothing, but her wet cheeks and ashen face spoke volumes. Suzanna looked from her mother to Durwood and back again.

"Matthew? Is it Matthew?" Suzanna asked, studying her mother's face. No reply. "Ty?" Suzanna could hardly get his name out. "Dear Lord, it's Ty, isn't it? Ty has been . . ."

"B . . . both," Emile LeGrande barely managed to whisper. "Both of them," she murmured, and then began to sob so violently she could say no more.

"Both? No! No, that's impossible. It can't be, it cannot be true." Suzanna, refusing to believe, looked at the stooped servant. "Durwood, tell me this is all a terrible misunderstanding! It has to be a mistake. Why, I just heard at the Blakely Street market that the Rebs have had a stunning victory at Manassas, so you see . . . it . . . they . . . Matt and Ty . . ."

"Miz Suzanna," said the kindly Durwood. "Miz Emile was not feeling well, so she send me round to Doc Ledet's for some —"

"Ah, there, that's it!" Suzanna seized on

the possible misunderstanding. "Mother's feeling ill and she had a bad dream while napping. The same thing has happened to me many times." Nervously, she smiled and stated, "Mother hasn't been out of the house, so she couldn't possibly have heard that . . ."

"Miz Suzanna, I tol' you I was at Doc Ledet's. The doctor, he had been out and he checked the weekly casualty list." Durwood swallowed hard. "He assumed we knew. He thought that's why I come for him, 'cause Miz Emile she be so distraught over . . ." His words trailed away.

Suzanna was shaking her head, refusing to accept it. "If it were true, Dr. Ledet would have come right over. . . ."

"He did, Miz Suzanna. The doctor come home with me to be with Miz Emile."

Suzanna felt her world swiftly spinning out of control. "He came? Then where is he? Surely he wouldn't be so callous as to leave Mother alone when . . . when . . ."

"He had to go, Miz Suzanna. He's needed at the hospital to tend Union wounded coming in from Manassas."

For a long moment, Suzanna said nothing more. She just stood there staring at her grieving mother and the teary-eyed servant. When she did speak, it was in level, well-modulated tones. "Durwood, are you absolutely certain that Dr. Ledet said . . ." She drew a shallow breath. "Both of them? Matt and Ty both . . . killed in battle? They're gone? They are never coming home?"

"Yes'em, he was sure," the old man said. "If it be any help, the doctor said this first land battle of the war was a clear victory for the Confederacy."

Suzanna nodded feebly. She closed her eyes, opened them. She dutifully stepped forward and put an arm around her mother's trembling shoulders.

Suzanna drew a spine-stiffening breath and said softly, "Yes, Durwood, it does help. It helps a great deal. I am certain that Ty and Matt were heroic and that we can all be very proud of them both. Thank you so much. You may go."

"Anything I can do, I will, Miz Suzanna."

"I'll call if we need you."

The old man nodded and, blinking back tears, crossed the veranda and moved gingerly down the steps. He slowly circled the mansion and went to his quarters in the carriage house.

Suzanna heard a roaring in her ears. She felt faint and sick. She longed to scream in pain, but she didn't. She had to be strong for her helpless mother. She held the weeping Emile in her arms and comforted her, soothing her as if she were a fretful child.

When, finally, Emile was so exhausted she stopped sobbing and had calmed a little, Suzanna took her inside. She put her mother to bed and gave her a small amount of the laudanum that Dr. Ledet had supplied. She sat with her mother until Emile fell into a welcome slumber.

It was nearing sunset when Suzanna tiptoed out of the room and quietly closed the door. She walked down the grand staircase as if in a trance. In the foyer she paused and wondered, *Should I turn and go into the library? Or should I make my way to the kitchen and see about the evening meal? Or perhaps go up to my room and write a note of sympathy to Ty's parents?*

What exactly did a person do when she'd just received word that the two men she loved most in all the world were dead? When she'd been told that she no longer has the protective big brother who had been with her all of her life. That she would *never* be the bride of the handsome young man who'd promised to take her to Paris and to cherish her forever?

For a long, tortured moment, Suzanna stood there unmoving in the silent foyer, wondering how she could possibly endure this double tragedy. How she could go on when all was forever lost.

She couldn't.

It was too much.

She couldn't stand it.

At last, that much-needed release swamped her.

Suzanna put her hand over her mouth to stifle the wrenching sobs that were tearing at her tight throat. She flew out of the house, across the veranda and down the front steps. She raced around the mansion and out into the back gardens. She ran until her legs finally grew too weak to carry her, and her heart was burning in her chest, her hot face wet with rapidly flowing tears.

She had reached the riverbank when her knees buckled. She fell forward, sprawling on her belly, her hooped skirts belling up behind her. She didn't rise. She screamed and cried and beat on the ground with her fists, overcome with grief and pain. She cried until there were no tears left and her eyes were swollen half-shut. Until her head throbbed painfully and her fists were bloody from striking the ground.

Then she fell silent.

And still.

Completely still.

She stayed there until the summer sun had

completely gone down and a pale silver moon had lifted above the treetops and was inching up into the night sky.

With great effort, Suzanna turned over onto her back. She lay there for some time, then finally sat up. She wearily rose to her feet and walked toward the house.

And as she climbed the back steps, she squared her tired shoulders, lifted her chin and silently promised her sweetheart and her brother that she would avenge their deaths.

She would not rest until she had caused Yankee blood to spill. Somehow, some way, she would make the hated Union pay for what they had done. She didn't care who she had to hurt. She didn't care what she would be required to do to exact reprisal. Nothing could be too dishonorable or too distasteful if it meant the certain defeat and death of at least one hated Yankee bastard!

EIGHT

Suzanna understood her mother's suffering. She shared that pain, but dealt with her own loss in a very different way. While Emile languished in her room, often too distraught to even come downstairs, Suzanna paced the drawing room restlessly, scheming, plotting, considering how she could best help the Confederacy.

Impatient to begin an endeavor wherein she could be of genuine value to the Cause, Suzanna realized she had to bide her time until her mother grew a bit stronger. But she despaired of her mother *ever* growing stronger.

Suzanna was determined to help the war effort and, more importantly, to avenge the deaths of her beau and her brother. While she waited for her mother's health to improve, she considered and discarded idea after idea.

Then, one cold February morning in

1862, Dr. Milton Ledet, the family physician who had delivered both Matthew and her, unwittingly came up with the perfect strategy for Suzanna. One she hadn't seriously considered, but which was ingenious.

The caring physician had stopped by to check on Emile, as he did regularly. After spending a few minutes with his frail patient, listening to Emile's heart, checking her pulse and assuring her that by spring she'd be fit as a fiddle, he came back downstairs.

Suzanna was waiting in the foyer to question him about the progress of the war. At her insistence, he shared the latest news. News that was not favorable. He had, he told her, heard that the Federals had attacked the Confederate positions on Roanoke Island, off the coast of North Carolina.

"The Union Navy sent in such a large fleet they easily overwhelmed the Confederates. The ships unmercifully bombarded the Rebels dug in along the shore." He shook his head sadly. "The Rebs couldn't hold their position against such a mighty force. Those that weren't killed had no choice but to surrender."

Suzanna gritted her teeth and silently cursed the Union's powerful navy. In frustration she said, "When the war began, everyone — you included — said it would be over within weeks. It's coming up on a year and . . ." Her words trailed away. Then she asked point-blank, "Are they going to beat us, Doctor Ledet?"

"Us? My dear, I've warned you time and again about referring to the Confederacy as 'us.' I'm constantly careful, and you must be as well. If you and Emile refuse to flee, then you must pretend alliance with the Union."

"I know, I know," she said, waving a hand dismissively. "Don't worry, I only confide in you." She sighed wearily. "Everyone else on our side is gone."

"Not quite everyone," he said with a sly smile. "Last evening I was at the home of one of Washington's most noted hostesses, an old friend I've known for years." He looked around as if someone might be listening, then lowered his voice to just above a whisper and confided, "Mattie Kirkendal frequently entertains Yankee officers in her palatial mansion." He paused for effect. "I'll betray a confidence here, because you and your family go back a long way. Mattie Kirkendal strongly sympathizes with the Confederacy." His light eyes twinkled.

Suzanna's eyes twinkled as well. "And hosting these parties for Yankee officers allows her to learn the enemy's pernicious secrets. Mattie Kirkendal is a spy for the Confederacy!"

"Shh. Now, Suzanna, don't you dare breathe a word of this to anyone." He took hold of her elbow and guided her into the drawing room. Continuing to speak in low tones, he asked, "Have you ever heard of a lady named Rose O'Neal Greenhow?"

Suzanna shook her head.

"Mrs. Greenhow was also a prominent Washington hostess who sympathized with the South. It is said she was responsible for the Confederate victory at Manassas last summer. She managed to get an important ten-word message to General Beauregard that helped win the battle!"

Her blue eyes dancing with excitement, Suzanna said, "That's it!"

"That's what?" The doctor's brows knitted.

"Get me an invitation to one of Mattie Kirkendal's social gatherings. Can you do that?"

"I suppose I could, but . . ."

"How old is this Mattie Kirkendal?"

The doctor shrugged. "Mmm, mid to late fifties. Why?"

Suzanna's smile was cold, calculating. "If a middle-aged woman can pry secrets out of the enemy, think what I might be able to glean."

The doctor was already shaking his head worriedly. "No! Absolutely not! I have made a dire mistake in discussing this with you. I shouldn't have told you about Mrs. Kirkendal or Rose Greenhow. Did I fail to mention that Mrs. Greenhow is now in prison? You don't understand, child. Spying against the Union is punishable by death!"

"Only if you're caught," she stated coolly. "I won't be."

Stern and fatherly now, Dr. Ledet said, "You just put such wild notions right out of your head and forget all about this. As I said, I should never have mentioned —"

"I will not forget about it! I know now exactly how I can be of use, and I am going to do it. You refuse to help? You won't get me an invitation to one of Mrs. Kirkendal's affairs?"

The doctor wore a pained expression. "Please, Suzanna, you mustn't even consider such a dangerous endeavor. Why, it would kill poor Emile if —"

"Doctor," Suzanna interrupted. "What's killing my poor mother is the loss of her only son. And although she is unaware of it, we are losing most of the family fortune as well. If this war drags on much longer, we will be left with nothing."

"Surely it won't come to that, my dear."

As if he hadn't spoken, Suzanna said firmly, "I am going to spy for the Confederacy with or without your help. My mind is made up."

"You don't know what you're saying. You have no idea what you'd be letting yourself in for." His face flushed when he added, "You are much too young and innocent to realize what unpleasant . . . ah . . . chores might be required of you."

"Tell me," she said. "What exactly would I have to do?"

The physician exhaled heavily. "Suzanna, you're a very beautiful young woman and . . . these Union officers that Mattie entertains would undoubtedly be physically attracted to you."

"Well, I should hope so," she stated emphatically. "Else how would I ever get any pertinent information out of them?"

His brow was furrowed. "Must I spell it out for you, child? Do you actually suppose that all you'd need do was smile at these seasoned officers to make them confide in you?"

"I am willing to do whatever it takes to

bring down the Yankees," she said defiantly, chin raised.

Nine

Suzanna wasted no more valuable time.

That very afternoon, after Dr. Ledet had gone and her mother was napping, she had Durwood bring the carriage around to drive her across the river. When she reached the baronial, two-story mansion of the wealthy widow, Mattie Kirkendal, a distinguished-looking butler answered the bell. Suzanna handed him a note of introduction from one Dr. Milton Ledet.

"If you'll kindly wait in the drawing room," the butler instructed, taking Suzanna's fur-lined cape.

He directed her into a spacious parlor where expensive oil paintings hung on silk-covered walls, and overstuffed chairs and sofas of shimmering brocade faced a blazing fire in the huge, marble-manteled fireplace. Suzanna moved toward the blaze, stretching her cold hands to its warmth.

"Miss LeGrande?" A throaty female voice

soon came from behind her, and Suzanna turned to see a short, stout, handsomely dressed, gray-haired woman whose round face immediately broke into a wide smile. Hands extended in greeting, the woman eagerly bore down on Suzanna, saying, "My dear, welcome to my home. I'm Mattie Kirkendal."

"Suzanna LeGrande, Mrs. Kirkendal," she answered, taking the soft, plump hands.

"My, my, aren't you a lovely little thing! Absolutely exquisite!"

"Thank you, Mrs. Kirkendal," Suzanna said, embarrassed by the flattery.

"Call me Mattie. Now come, Suzanna, let's you and I sit and get acquainted. Dr. Ledet's note gave me very little information other than the fact that he has been your family physician and friend for many years. He gave no hint as to why you would want to meet me. So tell me about yourself. To what do I owe this unexpected pleasure on such a cold afternoon?"

As the two women settled themselves on one of the brocade sofas, a servant appeared bearing a silver tray with a china plate of golden-brown croissants and two steaming cups of a dark, thick beverage.

"Half coffee, half cocoa," Mattie Kirkendal pointed out. "You'll find it quite delicious, I believe." She reached for a cup. "I've served this particular blend of hot chocolate since the days I first tasted it as a young, carefree girl on holiday in Paris. It brings back so many fond memories and . . . and . . ."

Mattie Kirkendal caught the wistful expression that crossed Suzanna's face at the mention of Paris, and was puzzled. "My dear, what is it? Have I said something to upset you? Did you have an unpleasant experience in Paris?"

"I've never been to Paris, Mrs. Kirkendal." Before the older woman could respond, Suzanna said, with a decisive shake of her head, "It's nothing. Nothing is wrong. Really."

But while Mattie Kirkendal gingerly sipped the rich chocolate, Suzanna never touched hers.

Without preamble, she declared with fervor, "Mrs. Kirkendal, I *desperately* want to do something — anything — to aid in the war effort and to help the South defeat the Yankees. I will not be content until every last one of the blue-coated devils has gotten what he justly deserves! Therefore I am here to offer my services if you have any need of me."

Mattie was surprised and delighted that

such a young, beautiful belle would be willing to aid in the Cause. At the same time she was skeptical.

"And why, pray tell, are you sharing this dangerous desire with me?"

"I know, Mrs. Kirkendal. I know all about you. Dr. Ledet told me, but please don't get angry with him. Your secret is safe with me and I admire you for what you're doing to help the South. I want to be a part of it."

"I see. And just what has happened in your young life to cause such fierce passion where the Yankees are concerned?"

Her blue eyes narrowing, Suzanna said, "They have taken everything from me. Everything. My sweetheart. My brother. My livelihood."

The thoughts and words coming in a rush, Suzanna talked of her handsome blond fiancé and her strong, dependable brother. She revealed how her storybook world had been forever altered. She confided that she had been left alone to care for a sickly mother and that the once great LeGrande fortune, which had been carefully amassed by her deceased father, was rapidly dwindling away due to the destructive war. Dry-eyed, she made her case, demonstrating her resolve.

When at last she fell silent, Mattie Kirkendal said softly, "You've suffered far too much for one so young. I can understand your fierce need to make the Yankees pay for your misfortunes. But I am not convinced that you are up to the task of spying for the Confederacy."

"Yes, I am," Suzanna stated with calm authority.

"You can't possibly comprehend what you'd be getting yourself into. I can't allow —"

"Allow? Allow! Mrs. Kirkendal, with all due respect, it is not up to you to allow me to do anything I've set my mind to. If you refuse my services, that's fine with me. I will find someone else who is eager for my help."

Mattie Kirkendal exhaled heavily and set her china cup aside. Frowning, she said, "If you are bound and determined, then . . ." She shrugged chubby shoulders. "But I must warn you, Suzanna, what you're volunteering to do will be neither easy nor pleasant."

"I never supposed that it would be."

Mattie spent the next half hour explaining to Suzanna exactly what would be expected of her. "You realize that you will be called on to dance with, flirt with and butter up the very men you so despise."

Undeterred, Suzanna assured Mattie that she was up to the challenge. "I can and will be of invaluable assistance, Mrs. Kirkendal. I have spent many years socializing with friends and acquaintances who have chosen to remain with the Union. I can easily convince them that I have as well. I will spy for the Cause and no one will suspect me."

"Bless you, my child," exclaimed Mattie at last, keenly aware that a beautiful young lady like Suzanna would be an invaluable asset to the Confederacy. "How soon may I expect you to begin to help us?"

"Today. Now. This afternoon."

Mattie laughed heartily and patted Suzanna's knee. Then she sobered and said, "Are you aware of the punishment for spying on the Union?"

"Death," Suzanna stated without emotion. "By hanging."

"You are willing to take such a risk?"

"Yes, I am."

Suzanna could not be talked out of the perilous scheme. She regretted that she couldn't share her thrilling secret with her mother, but she didn't dare confide in the frail Emile, who, if she knew of her daughter's intention, would surely weep and worry and beg her to reconsider.

So Suzanna kept the truth a secret. She

mentioned casually that she had been invited to a social gathering at a Mrs. Mattie Kirkendal's and that she wanted to attend.

Emile agreed that it was a good idea. "Darling, you deserve an evening out occasionally. I hope you enjoy yourself."

"I will, Mother," Suzanna lied. "And you're not to worry."

But when, just forty-eight hours later, Suzanna came into her mother's bedroom to say good-night before going out, Emile gazed at her strikingly beautiful daughter and became uneasy.

Buelah, Suzanna's stalwart maid and the only female servant still at Whitehall, was trailing after her charge, grumbling, "You got no business going out dressed like that, Miz Suzanna. This is not decadent Europe. It's Washington City and folk'll think you are a loose woman."

Emile, in bed despite the early hour, tossed back the covers and rose to her feet with effort.

"Suzanna, perhaps Buelah is right, dear. Don't you have something else you could wear, something more appropriate?"

"I tried to talk her out of it, Miz Emile," Buelah said, hands on her hips. "I did my best."

"You may go now, Buelah," said Suzanna. The servant turned and left, still muttering under her breath.

On this cold winter night, Suzanna was going to a glittering reception at Mattie Kirkendal's. It was the first of many such social gatherings she would be expected to attend, a gala where there would be a host of prominent guests and a number of Union officers. Officers who were sure to notice her. Suzanna had made certain of that.

She was dressed for the occasion in a gorgeous gown of shimmering yellow faille. One of the many ball gowns purchased before the war, it had a very tight bodice that accentuated Suzanna's small waist, and a décolletage cut so low it not only revealed her bare throat and shoulders, it exposed a generous expanse of her pale soft bosom.

Emile recognized the stunning ball gown as part of the expensive trousseau purchased for her daughter to wear on her Paris honeymoon. Neither it, nor any of the many traveling suits, ball gowns, bonnets and shoes and gloves, lacy lingerie or gossamer negligees had ever been worn. All had been stored away shortly after Ty and Matthew were killed.

"Suzanna, you're not really going to wear that to the reception, are you?"

"Yes, Mother, I am. Since I will never have a honeymoon, never go to Paris, I see no need to save it."

Emile stepped close, brushed a flaming lock of hair off her daughter's bare shoulder, and said, "I know you feel that way now, dear, but in time you'll find someone else who —"

"I'm late, Mother. I really must go now."

Ten

Suzanna had inherited uncommon strength, inflexible will and great charm from her father. She would need all three in the endeavor in which she was about to engage. She had volunteered for a thankless ongoing task that would be both distasteful and dangerous. But she never for a moment considered changing her mind and backing out.

This was war and she had enlisted.

Now, as the carriage rolled down Connecticut Avenue, then past the White House, Suzanna gazed out at the stately residence and thought of the sallow-faced president who lived there. Was Lincoln half as sorry as she that the nation was bitterly divided? Could he hear, from inside the White House, the low pounding of distant artillery and an occasional crackle of musket fire?

When the war broke out, Washington, D.C. had immediately turned into a training ground, arsenal and supply depot. In the well-fortified city, streets constantly reverberated under the wheels of heavy cannons. Sacks of flour, stacked against a siege, surrounded the U.S. Treasury, and the Union Army had built a ring of earthen fortifications around the city.

Sadness swamped Suzanna as she stared at the unfinished dome of the Capitol. She had passed this place so many times in all the different seasons. Now it was the center of the Northern Union! This was no longer her country, but the enemy's. Suzanna looked away, more resolved than ever to make the Yankees pay.

Soon the carriage turned into the circular drive of Mattie Kirkendal's palatial, well-lit residence. Suzanna had arrived fashionably late for Mattie's glittering reception. She had planned it that way. She wanted to attract as much attention as possible when she made her entrance.

She succeeded.

Once a servant had taken her wrap and directed her down the wide central corridor to the ballroom, Suzanna paused just outside the open double doors. Male voices, music, laughter and the clink of champagne glasses reached her. She swallowed anxiously, then nervously smoothed her yellow skirts and swept her loose red hair back off her shoulders. She took a deep breath that made her full breasts swell above the top of her low-cut bodice.

She almost weakened. She wanted to turn and run.

She closed her eyes and thought of Ty.

She opened her eyes and confidently stepped forward.

Utilizing the strongest ammunition in her arsenal — her youthful beauty and charm — Suzanna plunged headlong into battle, taking the ramparts, coolly sizing up the enemy. For a moment that seemed like an hour, she stood framed in the arched doorway, calmly awaiting her hostess.

Guests quickly caught sight of the flame-haired young woman in the shimmering yellow dress. Laughter lulled. Conversations stopped. Heads snapped around. Men stared. Women frowned.

Suzanna didn't flinch under the scrutiny. Beautifully gowned and groomed, she exhibited a cool facade of self-assurance, although inwardly she churned with anxiety and doubt. Could she really go through with this? Could she convince these Union officers that she found them charming and fun and romantic, when actually she despised them all?

"Ah, there you are now," trilled Mattie Kirkendal, finally coming forward to greet Suzanna. Leaning close, the older woman said, "I did it on purpose, you know. Left you standing here alone. I wanted to give all the gentlemen ample opportunity to notice you."

"And have they?" Suzanna asked.

Mattie's reply was the pursing of her lips and the twinkling of her eyes. "Now, come, I'll introduce you around."

"I can hardly wait," Suzanna said.

At once she was the center of attention. As she entered the brilliantly lit ballroom there were audible gasps at her youth and proud bearing, her shimmering yellow gown with its off-the-shoulder sleeves and low-cut bodice, her lustrous mass of flaming hair framing her fair, flawless face.

With the beaming Mattie at her side, Suzanna moved among the guests, nodding, smiling and offering her hand.

"And I've been waiting all evening for the opportunity to dance with you, Miss LeGrande," said a pudgy, ruddy-cheeked, heavily bearded Union officer who was a good six inches shorter than the tall, willowy Suzanna.

The gala was finally beginning to wind

down as the hour of midnight fast approached. Throughout the trying evening Suzanna had talked and laughed and danced with at least a dozen officers. She was tired and sleepy and could hardly wait to get home.

But no one would have guessed as much by watching her.

"Why, Captain Rood, I'm flattered," she said now, and favored the short, rotund captain with a dazzling smile. "I kept hoping that you would ask me." She lowered her lashes seductively.

"You did?" he said, his small, dark eyes widening with disbelief, his mouth stretching into a foolish grin.

"Why yes," she lied. "Shall we?"

Captain Rood swallowed convulsively, took her hand and led her onto the floor. In his arms, Suzanna fought the revulsion she felt at having his bristly beard tickle her bare throat as he turned his face toward hers. That and the way he breathed, like a steam engine puffing to pull uphill. His hands were clammy and the brass buttons on his uniform blouse were pressing against her stomach. And, not surprisingly, he was a terrible dancer, totally without grace. He stepped on her toes at every turn.

But Suzanna endured the ordeal with

aplomb and listened attentively as the Yankee captain, in an attempt to impress her, spoke freely of the Union's latest deployment of troops.

"Why, Captain, I'm afraid I've been a bit too sheltered. What exactly does 'deployment' mean? And when and where will it happen?"

His wet, fleshy lips now grazing her throat, the captain cheerfully did his part to educate her. And to set her mind at ease. "You have no need to worry, my dear, we greatly outnumber the Rebs."

"I'm relieved to hear that, Captain," Suzanna said. "So, if there should ever be a battle in or around Washington proper, we townspeople wouldn't be in danger?"

Captain Rood laughed merrily. "Ah, how charmingly innocent you are, Miss LeGrande. The truth is, you couldn't be in a safer place than right here in this heavily fortified Union city."

Suzanna nodded and bit the inside of her bottom lip. She could well remember the first days of the war, when Ty and Matthew had optimistically predicted that "we'll make Washington the new capital of the Confederacy."

When at last the music mercifully ended, Suzanna gave no indication of her troubled thoughts. She was glowing, as she had been all evening, her enormous blue eyes flashing with gaiety and good health. The talkative captain was left with the impression that this beautiful young woman found him quite interesting.

That idea was solidified when a young major stepped forward to claim Suzanna for the next dance. Suzanna playfully winked at Captain Rood over her partner's shoulder. Then she quickly turned her full attention to the man in whose arms she now found herself.

Suzanna charmed everyone.

The enchanted officers laughed at her bold comments and saucy frankness. She could be wickedly funny and highly entertaining. She found it incredibly easy to dominate these would-be warriors and convince them to confide in her.

But it was tiring, and she was glad when the evening was finally over.

"What a fantastic performance!" praised Mattie Kirkendal when the last of the guests had gone and only she and Suzanna remained. "You were absolutely superb, my dear. Thank heavens you're on the right side of this!"

"But I learned nothing of value," Suzanna said with a weary yawn.

"Don't be so impatient, Suzanna," Mattie gently scolded. "Go on along home now and get some well-deserved rest. I'm planning a wine supper for Tuesday next. May I count on you to attend?"

"I'll be here."

Eleven

Suzanna had declared a strong alliance with the Union, and no one doubted her sincerity. A small number of friends and acquaintances she'd known prior to the war had stayed on in Washington because their loyalties lay solidly with the North. They took it for granted that the same was true of her. There was no reason for them to suspect otherwise.

Suzanna easily insinuated herself into the social crowd of Washington. After attending only a couple of Mattie Kirkendal's soirees, she was added to the guest lists of other noted Washington hostesses. They jealously vied for her, insisting that she attend their gatherings. All agreed that Suzanna LeGrande was an asset with her beauty, charm and wit. Her mere presence ensured a lively party, with the gentlemen officers being entertained and thoroughly enjoying themselves.

Suzanna played her part well. But it was not easy. Many times it was extremely difficult to act as though she were delighted with news of the war's progress. Such as on the hot, hot summer evening of July 4, 1862.

Suzanna was at a crowded soiree when a beaming Union officer strode into the great hall, leaped up onto the orchestra platform and raised his hands for silence.

Then he eagerly shared this message. "Good news, my friends! The Confederate general Robert E. Lee has suffered a terrible defeat at Malvern Hill!"

Suzanna was heartsick on hearing of Colonel Lee's defeat at the hands of the Union's Major General George McClellan. But she concealed her anguish. All around her whistles and shouts rang out from the joyous crowd, and many of the guests happily embraced. When the orchestra again struck a chord, the smiling Yankee captain who'd delivered the message stepped down off the platform and came straight toward Suzanna.

She found herself swept up into his arms as he stated with a pleased grin, "McClellan's a military genius, no doubt about it."

"Indeed," she managed to reply, smiling up at him. "Did General McClellan thoroughly trounce Lee then?"

"Handed traitor Lee a crushing defeat! The Johnny Rebs suffered more than five thousand casualties without gaining a single inch of ground!"

"Ah, that is wonderful! A stunning victory for us," she stated, hoping she sounded genuinely joyful.

"Yes, yes it was, miss."

"After the victory, did . . . ?"

"McClellan wisely retreated to the James River. He's encamped at Harrison's Landing."

"Oh? Is it safe for his men there?"

"Couldn't be safer. They're under the protection of the big guns on all those navy warships anchored there."

"Thank goodness."

Throughout the summer and fall of 1862 and on into the New Year, Suzanna attended a neverending round of receptions and parties and balls, where she met and charmed her share of Union officers and sympathizers. She flirted and teased and promised more than she ever aimed to deliver. And she gleaned as much information as possible from the captivated officers.

Suzanna pretended nonchalance and lack of interest when the conversation was of the war. But she hung on every word spoken regarding the conflict's progress, troop movements and coming battles. She memorized each place name, each mention of a direction or objective. She carefully committed to memory the names of men she'd not yet met, but whose daring deeds peppered the conversations of the officers with whom she danced. Such names as the well-regarded Captain Dan Stuart. Brigadier General Samson Weeks. Major General Skillman Bond.

And Rear Admiral Mitchell B. Longley.

The admiral's name kept coming up in conversation, the officers eagerly exchanging stories of Longley's heroic exploits. Suzanna learned that Rear Admiral Mitchell Longley was highly respected for his brilliance and his bravery. It was said that he was fearless and cunning and as cold as ice. Confident to the point of arrogance, having no need of acclaim or accolades. A laconic loner who disdained social gatherings.

Suzanna was just as glad the lauded admiral didn't bother coming to the galas when he was in the Washington area. Such a man couldn't be counted on to share tidbits of valuable information; therefore, she had no desire to meet him. She was interested only in those officers who became amazingly loose-lipped after a few glasses of champagne.

Suzanna invariably sipped her own wine very slowly, but she often laughed and behaved as if she were tipsy. Those gentlemen she charmed would never have believed that, unfailingly, Suzanna was as sober as a judge. Or that on those occasions when she excused herself to freshen up, she immediately went in search of a private spot to write down anything of interest that had been carelessly disclosed. She was extremely careful and if she could find no privacy, she silently repeated the tidbit to herself, over and over, memorizing what she had heard.

When she did reduce an item to writing, she used a code concocted by one of the trusted couriers she and Mattie used to slip through enemy lines to deliver messages to the Southern commanders.

Suzanna had quickly learned what she was to be on the alert for. Always get the name of the military unit and commander. Find out, if possible, where the officer and men expected to be sent. The place from which they had arrived. Which scouts they had and the scouts' whereabouts. And to *never* be caught with a message that would give her away and endanger the troops.

She'd had a couple of close calls. Once, she was holding a hastily scribbled note in her hand when an officer came up from behind, surprising her. She had managed to shove the damning scrap of paper into her bodice before turning to smile at the man. On another occasion, when she'd volunteered to carry a missive through the Union lines herself, since a courier was unavailable, she had carefully concealed the paper in her hair, intricately dressed atop her head, with large curls circling her crown. Stopped by an armed picket on the outskirts of the city, she was forced to hand over her cape and reticule and bonnet, all of which were thoroughly searched, then handed back.

The missive had remained safely hidden in her hair.

Suzanna was proud of her modest accomplishments. She felt she was doing something constructive, contributing in some small way. She had received the gratitude of more than one Southern commander who had acted on gathered intelligence to save precious lives. Success spurred her on. She had become adept at drawing out the Union officers. More than one was guilty of disclosing information that should never have been shared with her. And she had managed to give nothing in return other than a few harmless kisses, which had been decidedly distasteful, but had had no lingering adverse effects.

Anyone who saw her at one of the glittering gatherings would have sworn Suzanna had not a care in the world.

Nothing could have been further from the truth.

Twelve

Suzanna spent most evenings in a seemingly carefree pursuit of pleasure, but her days were spent worrying and wondering how much longer she could maintain Whitehall. In the early weeks of the war, Colonel Robert E. Lee's Arlington plantation, just down the river from Whitehall, had fallen into Union hands. Occupying forces now lived in his stately home, Arlington House. Suzanna went to bed each night fearing that blue-coated devils would come swarming into Whitehall.

Her own apparent alliance with the Union had thus far saved Whitehall. Still, there was the ever-present danger that she would be unmasked for the Confederate sympathizer she was. Should that occur, she had no doubt the Yankees would immediately seize the estate.

Even if that never happened, she worried that she would soon lose the mansion. The lengthy war had been financially devastating. The sizable LeGrande fortune had been lost. The tobacco fields of northern Virginia had long since been trampled down by thousands of marching feet. Months ago a letter had come bringing the distressing news that the once-profitable coastal cotton plantation in South Carolina had been taken over and occupied by the Yankees. There were no longer any indigo crops in Georgia. No huge amounts of capital rested safely in banks generating interest. No cash poured into the coffers to offset expenses for necessities. There was, although Suzanna never hinted as much to her ailing mother, next to nothing left.

Nothing, save her beloved Whitehall.

Suzanna prayed that the war would soon end. She prayed that the Yankees wouldn't learn the truth and occupy the mansion. She prayed as well that she could somehow, some way, manage to hold on to the big white house on the river, the only home she had ever known. She lost sleep worrying how she could pay the exorbitant taxes owed on the estate, an astronomical sum that was mounting daily.

The imposing mansion where the LeGrande family had once hosted barbecues and balls now had most of its rooms closed off because she couldn't afford to heat them. Suzanna unfailingly kept the fire in her sickly mother's bedroom burning brightly, but the rest of the house was often chilled and drafty. There were times when the shivering Suzanna wondered if she'd ever be really warm again.

A terrible year in every way, both for her and for the Confederacy, 1863 finally drew to a close. But 1864 proved to be just as cold — and in more ways than one. Days into the New Year, Suzanna was forced to do something that was far more difficult than simpering and flirting with the hated Yankee soldiers.

She had no choice.

Snow flurries swirling about her head, Suzanna stood on the wide veranda of Whitehall on a frigid January morning, saying goodbye to the stooped, white-haired old butler-driver, Durwood, and the proud, statuesque maid, Buelah. The only servants left at Whitehall were being sent away.

Tears swimming in his dark eyes, Durwood said, "How will you and Miz Emile get along without us to take care of you?"

Suzanna smiled at him and pulled the lapels of his too-large greatcoat together over the old man's narrow chest. The finely tailored coat had belonged to her brother. Durwood hadn't wanted to take it, but she had insisted that "Matt would have wanted you to have it."

"It won't be easy for us without you," Suzanna said now, "but we will manage, and you two will be better off."

"But this is our home, Miz Suzanna," he argued. "We belong here, takin' care of you and Miz Emile."

As if he hadn't spoken, Suzanna repeated what she had explained to them a dozen times in the past week. "Now our second cousins, the Thetfords, have a fine home in Baltimore and they've assured me that you'll both be warmly welcomed into their household." She smiled and added, "I'm certain their house is warm and that the food is always plentiful."

"Don't eat much," the old servant muttered, pleading his case.

Suzanna choked back tears. "It's only a visit, I promise."

Her bearing as proud as ever, handsome face sullen, Buelah said, "I never liked Maryland!"

Suzanna laughed despite the gravity of the situation. "Why, Buelah, you've never even been there, so how do you know?"

"I know all right! Besides, our place is

right here, with you and your momma. She in bad health, she need us."

"She'll feel better once spring comes," Suzanna said, not actually believing it. "Now, you're going to miss your train if you don't hurry. It's a long walk to the depot." Suzanna hated the fact that the pair had to walk to the station in the cold, but there was no choice. The fine carriage and matching bays had been sold months ago, and there was no money to hire a hansom cab. She barely had enough to pay for their train tickets.

"You two take care of yourselves," Suzanna said.

"Sure gonna miss you and Miz Emile," said Durwood.

Shaking a finger in Suzanna's face, Buelah warned, "I've said it before and I'll say it again, I know what you're up to. You don't fool me. No sir. And you are gonna get yourself in serious trouble trifling with those Yankee soldiers you dance with at all those parties you been goin' to." She reached out, put her hands over Durwood's ears and told Suzanna, "You're gonna meet one of those Yankee officers who 'spects a bit more than a few flirtatious smiles. Mark my words!"

Suzanna felt a chill of apprehension skip up her spine at Buelah's prediction, but she smiled confidently and said, "I can take care of myself."

Buelah huffed and shook her head.

"Please don't worry," Suzanna said, then affectionately hugged both loyal servants and sent them on their way.

Buelah, still scowling, took Durwood's elbow and propelled him down the steps. Suzanna stayed on the veranda and watched as the tall, imposing Buelah, firmly gripping Durwood's thin arm, gingerly guided the slow-moving old man along the front walk. She watched as the pair made their way onto the circular driveway and finally out to the tree-lined boulevard beyond.

There they paused for a moment, and Suzanna felt her heart squeeze in her chest. But they never looked back. They turned and headed down the street.

Soon they disappeared in the worsening snowstorm, and Suzanna went back inside.

THIRTEEN

Spring finally came in that harshly cold year of 1864, but it was too late for Suzanna's ailing mother. Still grieving over the death of her adored son, Emile now had to be informed of yet another terrible truth.

As gently as possible, Suzanna explained to her sheltered mother that they had lost the LeGrande fortune, including the family mansion. Come the end of May, they would be forced to move out of Whitehall.

It was too much for Emile LeGrande.

She couldn't bear the thought of leaving her home. Tearfully, but resolutely, she told her daughter that she would not go. Never! They couldn't make her! This was her home and she would not vacate the premises.

As it turned out, Emile LeGrande never had to leave her beloved Whitehall. The sickly woman contracted pneumonia and, despite all the best efforts of her caring daughter and the family physician, Dr. Ledet, she died in the big four-poster where she had slept every night since arriving there forty years earlier as a blushing bride.

The same bed where both of her children had been conceived and born.

With her mother's death, Suzanna's hatred of the Union grew and became white-hot. The Yankees, damn them all to Hades, had taken everything from her. She had nothing left to lose.

Suzanna took what little money was left and moved into a set of rented rooms in the heart of Georgetown. On the first night she spent there, she awakened sometime after midnight and for a long moment didn't know where she was. Frantic, she looked around and saw none of the familiar furniture of her spacious bedroom at Whitehall, where she'd slept every night of her life.

Then the truth dawned.

Suzanna sighed wearily, lay back down on the strange, narrow bed and turned onto her side. She curled up into a fetal position and fought back the tears that were stinging her eyes. Never in her life had she felt so alone, so afraid, so desperate.

Or so determined.

"Leave it. Leave the bottle."

"As you wish, sir."

"I wish," said the tall, fatigued officer as he flipped open the buttons running down the center of his blue uniform blouse.

By the time the bellhop closed the door of the Washington, D.C. hotel suite, Rear Admiral Mitchell B. Longley was bare chested. The weary naval officer sank down onto an easy chair and took off his tall black leather boots. He reached for the filled glass, downed the dark liquid in one long swallow and made a face.

He set the empty glass aside, stood up and started to unbutton his trousers. Before he could succeed, a loud knock sounded. Annoyed, Mitch Longley crossed to the door and yanked it open.

"I asked that I not be disturbed," he said, frowning when he saw a sheep-faced lieutenant looking up at him.

"I know, sir, and I'm very sorry. But it's important."

"It had better be."

"Sir, it's Senator Davis Baxter. The senator, like everyone else in D.C., has heard about your impressive victories and . . . ah . . . how you torpedoed the *Albermarle* in a daring night raid on the Roanoke River down in North Carolina, so . . ." Aware of Mitch's deepening scowl, he hurried on. "The senator wants the opportunity to congratulate you in person."

Mitch was instantly exasperated. He'd bet everything he owned that he knew where Senator Baxter had heard he was back in Washington. Edna Earl Longley. Mitch's paternal aunt and closest living relative had likely tipped off her powerful friend, the senator. Mitch had written to his aunt, telling her that he would arrive in Washington sometime near the end of the week. Today was Wednesday. The formidable woman had a sixth sense about such things. He had been in the city for less than an hour and she already knew he was here. Damnation! Now she'd feign great hurt because he hadn't come directly to her house.

"Kindly tell Senator Baxter that you have passed along his congratulations," Mitch said, and started to close the door.

The lieutenant put out his hand to stop him. "You don't understand, sir. The senator has strongly requested your presence at a gala this evening. He believes, and rightly so, that you being there with some of your fellow officers would be good for morale." Again the lieutenant looked sheepish. "I'd say it's more like an order than a request, sir."

"Lieutenant, senators do not issue orders to naval officers. Now if you'll kindly excuse me . . .”

“Please, Admiral Longley,” said the lieutenant, thrusting a small velum envelope at Mitch. “As I understand it, the soiree should be most relaxing and enjoyable. It’s at the Washington mansion of a Mrs. Mattie Kirkendal, and the officers who have attended her gatherings in the past have raved about the flowing champagne and exquisite food and beautiful women.”

Mitch nodded. Now he knew this was his aunt’s doing. She and Mattie Kirkendal were old acquaintances. “I’ll think about it.”

“The party is tonight, sir.”

“Out of the question. I’m dead tired and all I want is to get into bed and sleep for the next twenty-four hours.” This time Mitch did close the door.

He turned and went back into the sitting room. He glanced at a decorative clock resting on the mantel. Ten minutes past two in the afternoon. Hands at his waist, Mitch moved to the tall front windows of the Hotel Washington, which looked out on the street below. Carriages rolled by with laughing people inside. Mitch scowled. It was as if they didn’t realize there was a war going on. That men were being killed daily.

Mitch drew the heavy drapes against the

strong May sunlight and turned away. At the drum table where he'd left the bottle of bourbon, he paused, finished unbuttoning his blue trousers, then shoved them down his slim hips to the carpeted floor. He stepped out of the trousers, kicked them aside and reached for the bourbon bottle and glass.

He took both with him as he crossed the sitting room and stepped into the shadowy bedchamber. The heavy curtains were all tightly drawn. Mitch went directly to the huge four-poster, where snowy-white sheets were turned back invitingly. He sat down on the edge of the mattress and poured himself another stiff drink.

This one he slowly savored. It had been weeks since he'd tasted liquor. He smiled. He could, he reasoned, drink all afternoon and into the night if he so desired. And he definitely so desired. He was presently on a much needed furlough from his fleet command and would not, therefore, be putting anyone's life in jeopardy should he get pleasantly drunk.

If he drank enough, perhaps he would forget, at least for a while, the faces of all those young, innocent boys he had seen die in battle. Faces that haunted him.

Mitch emptied the shot glass and poured

himself another. Leaving the full glass where it sat beside the bottle on the night table, he yawned, rubbed a hand across his naked torso and stretched out on his back in the soft bed. Sighing with pleasure at the touch of the silky sheets against his bare flesh, Mitch Longley slowly reached a long, leanly muscled arm out toward the full glass of bourbon.

But he never picked it up.

His empty hand fell to the side of the mattress.

Rear Admiral Mitchell B. Longley, the hero of Roanoke River, was sound asleep.

Fourteen

". . . And if all goes as planned, we will have caught the biggest fish in the pond!"

That was Mattie Kirkendal's prediction when she told Suzanna that she was expecting a very important guest for this evening's reception. Summoned to the Kirkendal mansion in the early afternoon, Suzanna had barely walked through the door before an excited Mattie rushed forward to meet her.

"Thank you so much for coming on such short notice," she had said, taking Suzanna's arm.

"My pleasure, but what — ?"

Interrupting, Mattie eagerly confided that the conquering naval hero, Rear Admiral Mitchell B. Longley, had just arrived in Washington for a week-long leave and consultation, and would be at tonight's gala come twilight.

"It's up to you, child," she had told Suzanna. "You must work your magic on Admiral Longley. I've no doubt that he knows pertinent facts regarding Union plans and decisive military actions that are in the offing. Oh, Suzanna, the intelligence he might share with you could be invaluable to the Confederacy!"

"What if the admiral shows no interest in me?" Suzanna had ventured.

Mattie laughed gaily. "My dear, Admiral Longley is a virile, handsome thirty-six-year-old male who has been on fleet command for months without leave. One look at you and he will be instantly captivated. The only danger you'll face is keeping him in line and —" Mattie's face flushed when she added softly "— protecting your virtue."

"That will pose no problem," Suzanna stated confidently. "You've seen me easily handle any number of amorous officers over these past few years."

Mattie smiled benevolently and shook her head. "Admiral Longley is not like the rest, Suzanna."

"He's a Yankee, isn't he? Then he's just like all the rest to me. Now, how will I know him? You must introduce me the minute he arrives."

"That won't be necessary," said Mattie. "He's sure to spot you the instant he steps into the ballroom." Her eyes twinkled when she added, "And I've an idea you'll notice him as well."

As sunset approached, Suzanna was at home in her rented rooms, dressing for Mattie's gala. While she moved about the bedroom, she idly wondered if this Admiral Longley was "like all the rest." Mattie had told her Longley was a handsome, charming gentleman all the ladies found exceedingly attractive.

Suzanna hoped he actually was relatively attractive. She was sick to death of having to flirt, tease and dance with officers who were physically unappealing, intellectually boring and tiresomely predictable in their declarations of admiration for her.

Ofttimes, at the end of yet another trying evening, she felt guilty and dishonest and repulsed when she allowed one of the smitten Yankee fools to kiss her on the lips. While they swooned and sighed and attempted to press her closer, she fought the impulse to grit her teeth and forcefully shove them away. She had never allowed an eager suitor more than one good-night kiss and even then she had never permitted a single officer to see her home. She had a signal worked out with Mattie's butler.

When she motioned to the aristocratic servant that she was ready to leave, he nodded, and within five minutes one of Mattie's carriages was brought around to drive her home.

Alone.

Suzanna unhurriedly stripped down to the skin and stepped into a steaming tub of hot water. She soaped her slender arms and considered what she should wear for this momentous occasion. She supposed she should choose one of her more daring ball gowns in an attempt to catch the admiral's discerning eye.

Swirling the soapy washcloth over her gleaming throat, Suzanna considered how she could best stand out from the crowd. She would not be the only young lady present, and if this naval admiral was actually handsome and charming, she would surely have competition for his attention.

Suzanna found that her interest was mildly piqued. It was like a game she wanted to win. She had always been competitive, enjoyed setting goals and attaining them. She was, she realized with surprise, determined to catch the admiral's eye.

Her bath finished, Suzanna rose from the tub and toweled her slender body dry. She glanced at the room's locked door, then shyly stepped in front of the freestanding mirror. Critically examining her pale, naked body, Suzanna touched her full breasts and flat belly. She turned away from the mirror and glanced over her shoulder. She slowly pivoted until she was again facing the mirror. She studied her reflection, and her breath caught in her throat when she imagined a man's burning eyes observing her, touching her, caressing her.

Feeling strangely sensual, Suzanna strolled naked to the huge armoire. She took out a pair of silky stockings, saucy satin garters, a lace-up corset and covering camisole, and a pair of naughty, lace-trimmed French pantalets that had never been worn.

Before donning the underthings, she took a seat at her vanity and dressed her lustrous red hair. She chose the elaborate style of the day, long ringlets dripping from a high oyster-shell comb. She turned her head this way, then that, and was pleased to see the flaming curls dance with her movements.

She rose. She struggled to lace the corset as tightly as possible, holding her breath, wishing Buelah was there to help her. Finally Suzanna managed to get the corset completely laced up. The boned undergarment accentuated her small waist, so she didn't mind that it was hard to breathe. The corset firmly in place, she donned the rest of her underwear and drew on her stockings.

When she lowered the frothy, blue chiffon ball gown over her head and let it fall into place, she smiled, pleased. The ruffled bodice dipped low; the corset pushed her bared bosom up. Catching her bottom lip in her teeth, Suzanna put her hands beneath her breasts and lifted them higher still, then urged the gown's bodice lower.

She picked up a small bottle of lavender water and dabbed a drop in her cleavage and behind her ears. She took one last look in the mirror.

"Will the admiral approve?" she asked her reflection, and experienced a sudden tingling sensation, part fear, part excitement.

"I can't imagine what has happened! Why isn't he here?" said an upset Mattie Kirkendal that evening as the hour of ten o'clock fast approached.

Strangely disappointed that the Union admiral had not shown up for the gala, Suzanna laughed off the woman's concern. "For heaven sake, Mattie, it's not the end of the world. You said yourself that Longley arrived in Washington only today. The poor man's probably tired and has chosen to rest this evening."

The two friends were in Mattie's spacious boudoir, Mattie searching for the smelling salts, Suzanna applying Mattie's heated curling iron to the ringlets gone limp from too many dance partners pressing their cheeks to hers.

Downstairs, the party was loud and lively, the absent admiral being the only invited guest who had not shown up.

Her red curls bouncy again, Suzanna said, "Let's go back down, Mattie. Forget about Admiral Longley."

The woman's stout shoulders lifted in a heave of dejection. "I had so wanted him to meet you."

"There'll be other opportunities. Surely he'll be in the city for a few days. Now come, we owe it to your guests to return to them."

"I suppose," said Mattie.

Fifteen

The heat was so intense he could feel it blistering his face and singeing his eyebrows. He couldn't see through the thick black smoke, but he could hear the reports of guns from both sides and the cries of men as they were struck by incoming fire. Amidst the melee he stood resolutely on the hurricane deck of the steel ram, shouting orders to those crew members who were still on their feet. The fierce firing continued as the heavy guns boomed and the dying screamed out in agony.

In midcommand, he felt the hot lead pierce his flesh, felt the wet blood coursing down his chest, soaking his uniform blouse, draining his energy.

"Keep firing!" he shouted, feeling his legs buckle beneath him. "Don't let up! Keep firing! Keep firing!"

"Keep firing!" Mitch was shouting as he lunged up from the bed, sweating profusely, awakening abruptly from the recurring nightmare. His breath coming fast, heart hammering, he checked his bare chest with searching hands, half expecting to find a mortal wound.

Mitch exhaled raggedly and raked his hands through his disheveled hair. He tossed back the sheet and swung his legs over the edge of the mattress. He dropped his head into his hands and sat there in the darkness for a long minute, collecting himself, fighting a bout of panic, the kind that seemed to seize him more and more regularly of late. A deep intrinsic fear he couldn't dare share with anyone. The troubling premonition that his luck was running out. That he'd beaten the odds for too long and his number would soon be up.

Mitch knew he wouldn't fall back to sleep, so he lit the bedside lamp and glanced at the decorative onyx clock — 9:00 p.m. He had slept seven hours. It was now nearing bedtime and he was wide-awake. And would be wide-awake until the early hours of morning.

Mitch rose to his feet and walked into the shadowy sitting room. He retrieved his white linen underwear from the carpet and stepped into it. He crossed to the tall front windows, drew back one of the heavy curtains and looked down on the street, wondering how he could pass the time for the next four or five hours.

He could, he reasoned, get back into bed and finish the bottle of bourbon. Drink himself into a stupor. At the moment, that prospect didn't particularly appeal to him. He felt anxious, jumpy. He was tense, restless and lonely. He needed company. And not just the company of other sailors and soldiers filling the saloons down on the street.

It had been too long since he'd seen a fresh pretty face, had heard a soft female voice.

Mitch turned, went back into the bedroom and yanked on the bellpull to summon a hotel employee. When the dutiful young man came up without delay, Mitch requested that a hot bath be drawn for him immediately.

Half an hour later, Mitch Longley, freshly bathed, shaved and wearing a neatly pressed navy-blue uniform, stepped onto the street in front of the hotel and hailed a hansom cab.

"Where to, sir?" asked the coachman.

"Good question," Mitch said, rubbing his chin thoughtfully, realizing suddenly that he couldn't recall the address. "I'm not sure.

It's a big mansion on Massachusetts Avenue, but. Stay here while I go back upstairs and check the invitation."

"Mattie Kirkendal's place?" asked the driver.

"Yes. Mrs. Kirkendal's home. I don't know the address, offhand."

"I do," said the man with a smile. "You aren't the first officer I've carried to one of Mrs. Kirkendal's famous parties. Get in and I'll have you there in no time."

Ten-thirty.

Suzanna was spinning about the dance floor in the arms of a short, balding army major who was unquestionably mad about her. She pretended to listen while the major prattled on about how beautiful she looked tonight and that he wanted — if only she would agree — to escort her home at the end of this evening's gathering.

Suzanna inwardly sighed, glanced over her partner's shoulder and spotted a tall, dark, sinfully handsome naval officer stepping into the arched doorway of the ballroom.

He paused there for a moment.

He stood unmoving, perfectly framed in the portal.

A magnificent figure in a well-tailored blue naval uniform with shiny brass buttons and gold epaulets adorning his wide shoulders, he immediately attracted attention. He possessed the kind of good looks that had already attracted several pairs of female eyes.

Including Suzanna's.

She needed no one to tell her who the dark stranger was. There was little doubt in her mind that the striking officer who so effortlessly exuded confidence and masculinity was none other than Rear Admiral Mitchell B. Longley, the daring Union commander she'd heard so much about.

The admiral was, Suzanna realized with a mixture of excitement and alarm, looking squarely at her. She made a misstep and quickly apologized to her partner for her clumsiness. But she never took her eyes off the dark-haired, dark-complected officer.

Nor did he take his eyes off her.

Mitch stepped inside and started across the room. Suzanna could hardly get her breath. Her knees grew weak and her pulse quickened. He was coming directly toward her, and there was something frightening about his very presence.

When he tapped her partner on the shoulder and said in a deep, rich baritone, "May I cut in, Major Barrett?" Suzanna felt her face flush.

Frowning, the major said, “Well, I suppose so, sir, however . . .”

But neither Suzanna or Mitch heard what the major was saying. His attention focused fully on the flame-haired woman in the sky-blue ball gown, Mitch didn’t bother asking for her permission. He reached out, commandingly took her in his arms and smoothly danced her away. At once a disturbing heat flooded Suzanna’s entire body. She had a strong impulse to pull free of this man’s embrace, to quickly turn and run from this dark Yankee devil she instinctively recognized as dangerous.

But she didn’t.

Her hand was gently clasped in Mitch’s long, tapered fingers. His strong arm lightly encircled her waist. She didn’t try to free her hand from his, but she refused to lift her arm and place it around his neck. Instead, she let it fall to her side in silent protest. With his smoothly shaved jaw resting against her soft cheek, he spun her gracefully around the dance floor, not saying a word, not even introducing himself.

When Suzanna had regained a measure of equilibrium, she pulled away slightly and tipped her head back. She looked up at him. He looked down at her. They stared at each other for a few breathless seconds, and Suzanna felt a deepening tremor of apprehension skip up her spine.

His eyes took on a glow in which interest and admiration were unmasked. Snared by that frank expression in his heavily lidded, emerald-green eyes, Suzanna knew that Mattie was right.

Rear Admiral Mitchell B. Longley was not like all the rest.

Sixteen

He was a man born to lead, not only because of his splendid physique and the strength of his character, but because of his personality. He possessed an easy, yet authoritative manner that made his subordinates eager to please him. Moreover, there was about him an undefined air of command that clung to him like the well-tailored uniforms he wore.

Suzanna had heard all the accolades attributed to this darkly handsome officer, and already she, too, was becoming aware of his power over people. Over her. She felt this power enveloping her well before their first dance ended. Before he had properly introduced himself.

She sensed that this man, whose dark face was strong but brooding, would not be as easily bewitched as the others. Her task would not be simple where this complex man was concerned. She couldn't imagine him sharing vital information concerning the war with any woman, much less one who was not his wife or his lover.

Still, it was her duty to try and gain his trust. Therefore she would, just as always, carefully play her part, a role she had practiced and knew well. She would make every effort to charm and befriend this enemy officer, to get as close to him as possible. So close he might share useful secrets. Her goal in life, the only thing that mattered, was to serve the Confederacy until victory was theirs.

The waltz ended.

Pretending to be indignant, Suzanna quickly stepped back out of his embrace. "Are you always so rude?" she asked, making a face.

"Have I been rude?" he replied, with a hint of a grin tugging at his full lips.

"Indeed you have, sir. You impolitely cut in on my partner, who is a devoted friend. You didn't ask if I cared to dance and you've not even bothered to introduce yourself. If you do not consider that kind of behavior rude, then I can only assume that your upbringing was woefully lacking in instruction and discipline. Now if you'll kindly excuse me, I —"

Calmly he reached out, took hold of her

fragile wrist and said, "No, I will *not* excuse you." He lifted his hands and clasped them lightly around her upper arms. He drew her closer, looked into her eyes and said, "I'm Mitchell Longley and, although I don't know your name, this I do know. You are the one and only young lady with whom I want to spend every possible moment of my brief liberty here in Washington. Since twelve hours of that precious seven-day leave is already up, let's not waste any more time. Tell me your name quickly and then come with me to some quiet place where we can get acquainted."

"I'll go nowhere with you, Admiral Longley, so kindly unhand me."

Mitch immediately released her, but when she turned and haughtily flounced away, he followed. Just as she'd hoped he would.

"I'm sorry," he said, catching up to her, falling into step beside her. "You're absolutely right, I was rude and I humbly apologize. I'm asking for a second chance. Forgive me?"

She glanced up at him. "I shouldn't," she said, starting to smile.

"But you will?"

"I suppose."

"You won't regret it . . . ah . . . ?"

"Suzanna. Suzanna LeGrande."

"Please tell me it's *Miss* Suzanna LeGrande."

"It is," she assured him, then said sweetly, already plotting how best to hold his interest, "I'm quite thirsty, Admiral Longley. Could I persuade you to go fetch me a glass of champagne?"

Mitch shook his dark head decisively. "Not a chance." When her brow wrinkled in surprise, he laughed and stated, "Now that I've found you, I'm not letting you out of my sight. Come with me." He offered his bent arm.

She slipped her hand around it and they walked across the crowded floor, dodging dancers, oblivious to the turning heads and inquisitive stares. At the edge of the dance floor they stopped before a long, linen-draped table where sparkling glasses of chilled champagne waited. Mitch handed her one and took one for himself. But when she would have turned back toward the floor, he slipped his hand under her elbow and smoothly maneuvered her out the open French doors onto the side veranda.

"Isn't this better?" he asked, inhaling deeply the humid night air.

"It is," she agreed. "Yes."

And it was.

The wide stone veranda was deserted

except for the two of them. A slight breeze blew from the east, lifting tendrils of Suzanna's hair and swirling the chiffon skirts of her blue ball gown around her ankles. A mild mist rolled in from the river as it did each night, pleasantly kissing their faces and cooling their overwarm bodies. Crickets croaked in a nighttime chorus and a few fireflies still darted among the well-trimmed hedges in the gardens below, where the cherry blossoms were in full bloom.

For a long minute, neither spoke. It was one of those rare moments in time when words were unnecessary. For the battle-weary Mitch Longley, the war and all unpleasantries were momentarily forgotten. All was as it should be. Everything was right with his world.

The pair stood on the veranda in the moonlight and drank their champagne in companionable silence. Mitch, calm and content as he hadn't been in ages, had no idea that the beautiful young woman at his side was interested in anything other than parties and clothes and travel and the pursuit of pleasure.

"Tell me about yourself, Suzanna." He finally spoke as they leaned on the wide stone railing that overlooked the manicured gardens.

Suzanna took another sip of the champagne, shrugged slender shoulders and said, "What would you like to know, Admiral?"

Feeling wonderfully lighthearted, he said, "All the vitally important things, like what you prefer for breakfast. Which side of the bed you sleep on. Which foot is the smallest. What's your favorite time of year. How long do I have to wait before you'll allow me to kiss you."

Suzanna tilted her head to one side and smiled saucily at him. "Well, let's see. That would be hot cakes and sausage. The center, of course. My left. Summer." She laughed softly and warned, "And not for at least six months."

Mitch threw back his head and laughed. He spent the next enjoyable hour getting to know the playful Suzanna, and he liked her immensely. She was totally feminine and yet had a masculine directness. Quickly he learned that she could be wickedly funny, making him laugh as he hadn't laughed in a long time. He greatly admired her rapier wit and sassy charm. She was incredibly bright, and it was all he could do to keep his hands off her.

Mitch Longley was totally dazzled by Suzanna LeGrande.

And Suzanna, much to her dismay, found

herself drawn to this tall, handsome Yankee officer. No denying it, Mitchell Longley possessed a languid, seductive charm that was irresistible. His elegant style and witty sophistication made him an enjoyable companion. So informative, so entertaining.

Then, of course, there was his good looks, which could not be ignored. With his chiseled features, midnight hair, provocative smile and seductive, heavy-lidded gaze, he could easily turn any woman's head.

Including hers.

There was an instant attraction between the two.

Suzanna was mildly unnerved by it, but determined she would not let it get out of hand or limit her effectiveness in any way. She reasoned that, actually, she should be glad she found the Union admiral appealing. It would make her work that much easier. And it was work, she must never forget that. When the time came — and she fully intended to put him off as long as possible — for her to kiss and embrace this handsome Yankee, she would not let herself forget for a moment that he was the enemy.

Suzanna was cautiously fascinated.

Mitch was thoroughly enchanted.

He wanted Suzanna. Desired her. And he meant to have her. But he knew better than to tip his hand immediately. A man who knew how to handle the fair sex, Mitch was keenly aware that a woman as beautiful and as intelligent as Suzanna LeGrande had more than her share of smitten suitors fawning over her. Making fools of themselves. He had no intention of joining their number.

"We'd better go back inside, Admiral," Suzanna said.

"Call me Mitch, Suzanna."

She smiled. "Mitch, let's go back inside."

"On one condition."

"Which is?"

"You won't dance with anyone else. Just me."

"Agreed," she said, and took his arm.

The handsome pair went back into the crowded ballroom. But for the remainder of the gala, Rear Admiral Mitchell B. Longley and Miss Suzanna LeGrande danced only with each other, to the disappointment of the other officers and the dismay of all the jealous ladies. Senator Davis Baxter, watching the golden couple with a scowl on his weathered face, was nonplussed that the upstart admiral would dare to ignore him. Didn't the Union officer know who he was and how much power he wielded?

As they gracefully circled the floor, Mitch

was silently making plans for a whirlwind courtship of this lovely flame-haired charmer. He would, at evening's end, offer to escort Suzanna safely home. And perhaps en route he might steal a kiss or two in the back of the carriage.

Suzanna, feeling the pressure of his strong arm around her, was also planning. Keenly aware that this handsome naval officer contrived and carried out assaults on her beloved Confederacy, she was firmly resolved to do whatever it took to learn of his battle tactics and strategy. While she sensed that she would not be able to handle this self-assured officer as easily as she had the others, she knew that he was already strongly attracted.

It was up to her to cleverly play on that attraction. Since his stay in Washington was limited, she couldn't wait too long. By the time his leave was up, she had to have him where she wanted him.

Suzanna decided then and there that she was willing to do whatever was necessary to gain this Yankee's trust.

If her decidedly dangerous flirtation could save but one precious Rebel life, she would count her endeavor a success.

Seventeen

"I appreciate the kind offer, but no, thank you," Suzanna murmured at midnight when Mitch offered to see her home. He didn't press, but she could see in his expressive green eyes that he was disappointed.

He nodded, then ushered her out of the mansion and down the front steps to where her carriage waited. There she paused, smiled at him and said, "I truly enjoyed the evening, Mitch."

"Spend the day with me tomorrow," he quickly replied.

"Well, I don't know that I should," she reasoned. "We've only just met and I —"

"It'll be quite proper. I'm committed to having lunch with my great-aunt tomorrow. She'll be delighted to have you join us. Afterward, I'll drive you directly home." He paused, then added, "If, at that time, that's what you want me to do."

"In that case, I accept your invitation."

"I'll hire a one-horse gig and come to collect you. Where do you live?"

She gave him her address and said, "I'll expect you at straight-up noon."

"I'll be there," he said, raising a hand and brushing a wayward lock of bright hair off her cheek.

"Good night, Mitch," she said, then purposely let her gaze move slowly down to his mouth. And up again. She noticed the minute tightening of his smoothly shaved jaw as he helped her into the carriage. She had made him want to kiss her, she was sure of it.

"Until tomorrow," he said, then stood and watched as the carriage rolled away.

Inside that closed coach, Suzanna released a sigh of relief. She was pleased. The evening had been a success. It had gone even better than she had hoped. The minute he arrived, she had caught and held the Yankee admiral's undivided attention. He was attracted and wanted to see her tomorrow.

Suzanna frowned suddenly.

She dreaded meeting Mitch's great-aunt.

Mattie had told her that Rear Admiral Mitchell B. Longley was from an old, monied family, an only child. His glamorous parents had perished in a yachting accident off the coast of Monte Carlo when Mitch was twenty-one and in his last year at Annapolis. He had inherited the family's stately Washington mansion, a sprawling villa in the south of France and a comfortable beach house off the South Carolinian coast. Not to mention the vast Longley real estate and banking fortune.

His only living relative was a wealthy spinster aunt. The younger sister of Mitch's paternal grandfather, Edna Earl Longley was a tall, horse-faced woman with snow-white hair, permanently arched eyebrows and a purposeful stare, who tolerated no nonsense from anyone. The never-married Edna was considered one of Washington's most influential women. With advancing age, she had finally relinquished her crown as the city's premier hostess, but she remained a force to be reckoned with.

The eighty-six-year-old spinster continued to receive visitors in her Connecticut Avenue mansion every Sunday afternoon from two to six. Military officers, ambitious senators, foreign ambassadors, Italian counts, international lawyers and diplomats — all streamed in and out of the mansion on those afternoons. The powerful gentlemen brought with them handsomely dressed wives and treasured sweethearts, among their number some of Washington's most beautiful women. All came to pay their respects and to drink champagne and share the latest gossip with the woman who was — in her day — the reigning empress of Washington society.

"Should you by chance ever meet the admiral's great-aunt," Mattie had warned Suzanna, "expect to be mercilessly questioned. Answer as though you have nothing to hide, but never divulge anything more than is necessary. And don't worry that she'll suspect anything. She will not. I've known Edna Earl Longley for forty years and she has no idea that I'm a Southern sympathizer. Nor will she ever guess that you are."

Suzanna was not so certain. The prospect of meeting Mitch's great-aunt troubled her. It was never as easy to fool a woman as it was to fool a man.

Suzanna's unease escalated the next day when the one-horse gig rolled to a stop before a big redbrick mansion with iron filigree balconies.

"We're here," Mitch told her. Then he gently warned, "Suzanna, my aunt can be one formidable old woman. Put her in her place. Don't let her bully you."

Suzanna's dread increased.

A uniformed butler answered the bell, but before he could usher them into the drawing room, Edna Earl Longley stepped forward, elbowed the butler aside, looked directly at her uniformed nephew and said, "Well, it's high time you came to visit your lonely old auntie. You think I don't know that you got into the city at noon yesterday? I waited all afternoon and evening for you to show up, but you never came. I decided you had forgotten me!"

Mitch merely smiled, reached out and swept the old woman up into his arms. "Have you been a good girl?" he asked, brushing a kiss to her wrinkled cheek.

"You put me down, young man!" she snapped, but her eyes sparkled with pleasure.

Mitch gingerly lowered her to her feet, then took Suzanna's arm and drew her forward. "Aunt Edna, I want you to meet my friend, Miss Suzanna LeGrande." He turned to Suzanna. "Suzanna, allow me to present my aunt, Miss Edna Earl Longley."

"Miss Longley," Suzanna said, extending her hand. "How nice to meet you."

Eyes narrowing in a deliberate stare, the tall, white-haired woman said, "LeGrande. LeGrande? I'm familiar with that name. Are you one of the Virginia LeGrandes? You live in that big white mansion on the banks of the Potomac, do you not? Have you been here to my home before? What about your family, are they — ?"

"That's enough, Aunt Edna," Mitch interrupted. "We're here to enjoy your company, not to be questioned as if we were suspects in a crime."

"It's quite all right," Suzanna said with an easy smile. She had expected no less, rightly assuming that this woman Mattie had warned her about would ask questions Mitch would never have posed. Wise beyond her years, Suzanna made no effort to be evasive. She said calmly, "Yes, ma'am, I'm proud to say that I amone of the Virginia LeGrandes." She shrugged and added, "Actually, I'm the last of the Virginia Le-Grandes."

Frowning, the older woman said, "But you're so young. Both your parents . . . ?"

Suzanna stated without hesitation, "My dear father, Lawrence LeGrande, passed away years ago, and I lost my frail mother, Emile, only recently."

"I knew the name was familiar!" exclaimed Edna, snapping her fingers. "Your father was the son of Timothy Douglas Le-Grande!" When Suzanna nodded, her hostess added, "I have an old acquaintance,

General Edgar Clements, who was a very good friend of your paternal grandfather. Edgar Clements and Timothy LeGrande attended Virginia Military Institute together many years ago."

Again Suzanna nodded. "Yes, I remember hearing about General Clements, but I can't recall if I ever met him."

"A dear, dear man," said Edna. "The old general still joins me for dinner occasionally when he's in the city."

"How nice," said Suzanna, then hurried on. "My only sibling, an older brother, was killed in the early days of the war at the first Battle of Manassas."

"No! Oh, child, I'm so sorry," offered a sympathetic Edna.

Mitch interjected, "We lost a lot of good men at Manassas. I'm saddened to hear that one was your brother, Suzanna."

Suzanna shook her head and breathed a bit easier. Just as she had supposed, both Mitch and his great-aunt took for granted that her brother had fought with the Union.

"Yes, we did," she said. "Too many." Then she hurried on. "I no longer live in the riverside mansion, Miss Longley. Since I'm now all alone, I sold the estate and moved to Georgetown to be nearer my friends." Suzanna quickly named a half-dozen acquaintances who were loyal to the Union. She concluded by saying, "My dearest friend is Cynthia Ann Grayson, but she and her family fled Washington when the war began. You probably know Cynthia's mother, Jennie Grayson."

At the mention of Jennie Grayson's name, Edna Earl Longley smiled. "I've always been fond of Jennie. Such a gracious hostess."

Suzanna smiled back. "Yes, she is. I've attended many glittering receptions Mrs. Grayson hosted at Stratford House." Suzanna paused, then added, "Mattie Kirkendal is about the only prominent hostess left in the city."

Edna snorted. "I taught Mattie everything she knows." She looked from Suzanna to Mitch. "That where you two met? At Mattie's? Did you meet just last night?"

Mitch shook his head at his aunt. "No more questions. Keep it up and we'll leave."

"Ah, relax, Mitchell, my boy," Edna said, and took Suzanna's arm. "Come on inside, Suzanna. Let's have a glass of port before the meal."

The old woman was cagey. She made pleasant small talk, but skillfully slipped in probing questions throughout the conversation. By the time Mitch and Suzanna bade Edna Earl Longley good-day at shortly after three o'clock that afternoon, Suzanna felt completely wrung out. And she had a nagging headache brought on by nerves.

Outside, the sun was high and hot. Not a hint of a breeze stirred the heavy, humid air. Feeling wilted and weary, Suzanna dreaded returning to her broiling rented rooms. In the west-facing structure, there would be no relief from the muggy heat until the summer sun finally went down.

Mitch lifted her up into the gig, circled around and swung up onto the seat beside her. He took up the reins, then turned and looked at her. He noted her flushed cheeks and the sheen of moisture covering her bare throat. She frowned and shaded her eyes with her hand.

"Look at me, Suzanna." She turned and gazed up at him. He said, in that low rich baritone, "It's uncomfortably hot and muggy today. But I know a place that's shady and cool and quiet."

His vivid green eyes held an unsettling power, and Suzanna's first impulse was to look away. She started to speak. He stopped her.

He said softly, but firmly, "I'm going to take you there. Now, this afternoon."

Eighteen

Suzanna was unconcerned.

She assumed Mitch intended to take her to his Washington residence. At lunch his aunt had asked if he was staying at home or in a hotel during his leave. Mitch hadn't replied, had just shrugged broad shoulders. Miss Longley had made a mean face at him, then turned to Suzanna and explained that Mitch's primary residence was a palatial house off Dupont Circle.

"Part of the estate my nephew inherited from his parents." She had added, "Keeps a full staff of retainers there with very little to do, since he is never in residence." She had again looked at Mitch, adding accusingly, "He refuses to get rid of any of them." She then pursed her lips in disapproval.

Suzanna concluded that while it might not be exactly proper, she would nonetheless be totally safe going to his home, since there was a full staff in residence. The two of them would not be alone. And even if they were, so what? She was a spy and had to take risks.

Now, as Mitch turned the gig down a boulevard to the south of Dupont Circle and headed in the other direction, she became curious and slightly uneasy. She started to ask where they were going, but her attention was quickly directed to a park just ahead, where those despised blue uniformed men were everywhere. It was like that all over the city. Parks had become campgrounds. Churches were hospitals. Forts ringed the town.

The capital had been an armed camp since the war began. It was a principal supply depot for the Union Army and an important medical center. She had heard that three thousand soldiers slept in the Capitol Building and that a bakery had been set up in the basement. The streets were constantly filled with the wounded.

Suzanna gritted her teeth and closed her eyes against the unsettling sight. She kept them closed until the shouts and calls of the soldiers had died away behind them. When finally she ventured a look, she was surprised to see that they were on a narrow lane leading into a dense grove of trees ahead. The Capitol and the city had seemed to disappear.

"Where are we?" she asked, feeling the cool of the forest quickly envelop her as the gig rolled under the canopy of trees.

"Almost there," he told her, skillfully guiding the horse around a sharp bend and down a gentle incline.

After they'd traveled another mile, a rustic cottage appeared before them, nestled in the trees, almost completely hidden at the end of the narrow lane. When Mitch stopped the gig in front of the cottage, he turned, smiled at Suzanna and said, "Welcome to my personal piece of paradise."

Eyes wide, she asked, "Exactly where are we?"

"A little island of tranquility in the heart of the city." He laid the reins aside, swung down out of the gig and came around for her.

"You're teasing me," she said.

"I wouldn't do that," he answered, taking her hand and leading her to the cottage. "My family has owned this forty acres of forested land for as long as I can remember. They never did anything with it, but never sold it, either. I used to come out here as a boy when I wanted to be alone. A dozen years ago I had this cottage built for a retreat. It's a convenient place to get away from everything and everyone, to read and rest and enjoy the solitude."

Mitch unlocked the front door and handed Suzanna into a small foyer. Once inside, she turned and entered a large parlor where an abundance of floor-to-ceiling windows brought the outside in. She stood for a long moment looking around. Across the spacious room was a stone fireplace with a huge fur rug spread out before it. Overstuffed chairs and sofas looked big and masculine and comfortable. Shelves reaching to the ceiling were filled with leather-bound books. A writing desk sat in the corner beneath a window. A polished mahogany bar stretched along half the back wall, near a door opening to the outside.

Mitch took Suzanna's hand and led her across the room and out that door, onto a shaded porch that afforded an unobstructed view of a brook spilling down a rocky streambed. The tinkling sound of cold, clean water splashing over the smooth boulders was soothing to the spirit, just as the deep shade was cooling to the body.

"No matter how hot the summer day, it's always cool here," he said.

"And beautiful," she replied as she looked around.

A hammock hung at one end of the porch.

Mitch looked pointedly at that hammock,

then at Suzanna. She was tempted. But if she stretched out in the hammock, he might try and lie down beside her. She thought better of it. Instead she sank into one of the matching rockers at the far end of the porch. Mitch followed suit. He dropped down into the rocker beside her, stretched his long legs out before him, laced his fingers atop his stomach and sighed with pleasure.

He said, "Would you believe me if I told you I've never brought anyone else here?"

"No." She was quick to reply. He chuckled softly and said no more. "Why did you bring me here?" Suzanna finally asked.

He reminded her, "You were warm and uncomfortable when we left Aunt Edna's. You're not now, are you?"

"No," she had to admit. "I'm quite cool and very comfortable." She leaned back, breathed deeply of the fresh air and couldn't keep from smiling as she watched a robin redbreast sail down to land on a slippery rock in the middle of the tinkling brook and wet its beak. She released a deep sigh and felt herself starting to unwind after a tense afternoon spent with the inquisitive Miss Edna Earl Longley.

For the next hour, the pair sat on the shaded porch, talking and laughing and being companionably lazy. Suzanna knew — had always known — how to entertain her audience, and she was intent on amusing Mitch. She regaled him with tales of her ancestors. She purposely embellished the stories she had learned at her grandparents' knees, making them more colorful, more interesting.

Suzanna had a happy faculty for forgetting things she didn't want to recall and remembering things as she would have liked them to happen. Therefore, when she related an event, it was exactly as she would have wanted it to be. She called on her storytelling talents to spin humorous yarns of her forebears' brave exploits.

Laughing at her anecdotes and the changing expressions on her face, Mitch was charmed and delighted. He felt a wonderful exhilaration just being around this high-spirited young beauty. She was capable, as no one else was, of making him forget everything. And everyone.

Which was exactly Suzanna's intent. She broached every subject under the sun, except the war. She was far too clever to so much as mention it. She wanted this naval commander to assume that she was just what she seemed to be, a frivolous, pleasure-loving young woman who knew little or nothing about the conflict. And was not the least bit interested in hearing about such disagreeable things as troop maneuvers and battles and casualties.

As she talked and Mitch listened, Suzanna made no effort to draw him out, to learn more about him. She judged that this handsome officer was reflective, poetic and innately private. A gallant man who possessed a quiet, mature authority. Not the kind to let anyone ever get too close to him.

Suzanna was undeterred by this knowledge. She fully intended to get close to him. Very close. So close he would share vital secrets.

Now, as she sat here on this shaded porch, cunningly drawing Mitch into her web, Suzanna found that she was rather enjoying herself, despite the fact that he was the enemy. This place, this remote cottage in the woods, was very conducive to rest and relaxation, to letting down your guard. She could understand why he liked coming here. It was so pretty and peaceful and . . . and . . .

All at once it struck Suzanna that this secluded cottage was more than likely where this handsome Union officer would conduct his clandestine romantic trysts.

Jaw tightening at this disturbing thought, Suzanna turned her head and looked at

Mitch. His eyes were closed, dark lashes resting on high cheekbones. Her own eyes narrowing, she stared at him while he was unaware of her scrutiny. She swallowed hard. He looked beautiful and sullen and dangerous all at the same time.

And despite her inherent hatred of him, her heart tripped in her chest when his beautiful emerald eyes opened and he turned and looked at her. Wordlessly he reached out, took her hand in his and placed it over his mouth, not just kissing it, but running her little finger back and forth, rubbing it sensuously over his warm, smooth lips.

"Have dinner with me tonight, Suzanna," he said in a low, persuasive voice.

"I've love to," she said without hesitation, her fingers tingling from the touch of his lips.

Mitch took her hand from his mouth and laid it on his chest. She felt his heavy, rhythmic heartbeat against her palm. "The cottage is well-stocked. Let's dine here, just the two of us."

"Absolutely not." Suzanna withdrew her hand and stood up.

Mitch quickly came to his feet. A mischievous half grin on his face, he said, "Afraid?"

"Of what?"

"Me."

"No." Suzanna flashed him a radiant smile and said honestly, "But you, Admiral Longley, should be afraid of me."

Mitch laughed, enchanted.

NINETEEN

It came as a surprise.

Suzanna hadn't meant for it to happen so soon. She had fully intended to wait until the very last minute of his seven-day leave before allowing this Yankee suitor to kiss her for the first time.

Mitch had other ideas.

Suzanna was turning to go back inside the cottage when he reached out, clasped her elbows and drew her to him. He looked at her for a long minute, then lowered his dark head and placed the gentlest of kisses in the shadowed valley between her breasts, where the bodice of her yellow organza dress dipped into a V.

Stunned, Suzanna felt her breath catch in her throat as his mouth moved alarmingly close to the lace-trimmed edge of the low-cut neckline. She held her breath when he caught the lace in his teeth. And she shuddered involuntarily when his smooth lips brushed a warm kiss to the bare swell of her left breast.

"Mitchell Longley!" she scolded, pushing him away, hoping she sounded properly offended.

Mitch raised his head and looked at her, unsmiling. He had a slightly sullen demeanor. He gave no sign of emotion, no hint of what he might do next. But there was an air of smoldering menace about him, and Suzanna was alarmed. She didn't really know this Union officer, and here she was alone with him in a remote cottage. If she screamed for help no one would hear her.

His hooded gaze fixed on her mouth, Mitch drew her up against him and kissed her squarely on the lips. At first Suzanna made a halfhearted attempt to pull away. But she didn't really struggle. Mitch clasped his wrists behind her waist and continued to kiss her, very carefully, very deliberately, molding her lips to his. A surprisingly soft, nonthreatening caress that was, to her dismay, pleasing and thrilling to Suzanna.

Just when she was starting to really respond, he took his lips from hers and set her back.

"We better get going," he said, and Suzanna could only nod, confused by his behavior. Had he not liked kissing her?

Would he cancel dinner? Never want to see her again? Move on to some more experienced woman?

Mitch was quiet on the way back to her place, and Suzanna grew increasingly troubled. She had the sinking feeling that her less-than-expert kissing had left him cold, and he would turn to someone else who could better excite him. While she was an adroit flirt, she knew little about actually making love. A man like Mitch wouldn't want to spend his brief leave with someone as obviously naive as her.

And she would have failed miserably in her assignment to captivate him and gain his trust. She would never be allowed to get close to him, would never learn those secrets that could aid the beleaguered Confederacy.

When the gig rolled to a stop before her set of rented rooms, Suzanna turned to him and asked, "Mitch, do you still want to have dinner with me this evening?"

His answer was to lean over, press a kiss to her cheek and say against her ear, "You know I do, sweetheart." He lowered his voice to a near whisper and added, "And perhaps breakfast with you in the morning?"

She wasn't sure how to take the remark, and gave him a reproachful look.

He laughed and winked at her.

When Mitch came to pick her up at dusk that evening, it was in a shiny black brougham with a uniformed driver atop the box. Mitch handed Suzanna into the backseat of the luxurious coach, then crawled across her and sat down close beside her.

Immediately, he reached for her hand, and she smiled at him. But when he placed her hand atop his trousered thigh and covered it with his own, her smile slipped and she felt her face flush hotly. She could feel the steely muscles bunch and pull beneath her fingers, and knew that she should quickly move her hand away. She meant to but was distracted when he put a long arm around her shoulders and said, "Kiss me, Suzanna. Kiss me just the way you kissed me at the cottage this afternoon."

Before she could reply, his mouth covered hers. Her hand remained on his trousered leg as he urged her head back against the lush leather seat. After her initial surprise, her lips eagerly clung to his. Mitch deepened the kiss, his tongue parting her lips and sliding between her teeth. At the first touch of his tongue on hers, Suzanna's fingers involuntarily tightened their grip on his thigh and her mouth opened a little wider. It was a passionate, prolonged kiss of the kind she had never before experienced.

She was breathless when their lips finally separated. She felt dazed and weak and hoped he wouldn't kiss her again. She anxiously moved her hand from his leg.

"It's quite warm this evening, isn't it?" she said nervously.

"We could always go back to the cottage," he suggested, a devilish gleam in his eye.

"No! Certainly not!" She shook her head for emphasis and her eyes flashed.

Mitch responded with an ever-so-slight play of a smile around his lips. He laid a hand lightly on her bare throat and said softly, "Relax, Suzanna. I'll never take you anywhere you don't want to go."

"Promise?"

"Promise."

"Then kiss me again."

He did. And he kept on kissing her all the way to the hotel where they were to dine. Responding, kissing him back, Suzanna laid a hand briefly on his chest before sliding it up around his neck. Her fingers entwined themselves in the silky raven hair at the back of his head.

His arms encircling her, Mitch pressed her close against him. Suzanna could feel her breasts flatten against the granite muscles of his chest, his heart beating heavily against her own. His lips smothered hers in kisses so hot and exciting she felt as if she might faint. It was a fever-inducing experience, and she was flushed and chilled at the same time.

Lost in his blazing hot kisses, caught up in the passion of the moment, Suzanna didn't realize that the carriage had rolled to a stop.

"Excuse me, sir," the embarrassed driver said, clearing his throat after opening the coach's door. Mitch and Suzanna broke apart, Mitch unfazed, Suzanna appalled. Respectfully looking in the other direction, the driver added, "We have arrived at your destination."

"Not quite," quipped the aroused Mitch Longley.

Twenty

"I've failed miserably!"

"No such thing, child."

"Yes, I have, Mattie. Admiral Longley has revealed nothing. Nothing at all," said a disillusioned Suzanna. "And tonight is my last chance. He returns to duty at dawn tomorrow and I may never see him again."

Suzanna and Mattie Kirkendal were drinking iced lemonade on the broad veranda of Mattie's stately mansion. It was a warm, muggy afternoon with storm clouds gathering and thunder showers threatening. Suzanna had shared a long leisurely luncheon with Mitch and would be with him again this evening for an elegant dinner at his residence.

For the past week — beginning the very night they'd met — she had spent almost every waking hour with the increasingly ardent Mitch. But they had attended none of the galas or wine suppers or garden parties to which they had been invited. Not even Mattie's. Mitch did not, he had told her honestly, want to share her with anyone. He had so little time; he wanted to spend it with her and nobody else.

So they had dined alone at his mansion. And taken long carriage rides around the heavily fortified city. At an intimate picnic for two on the grounds of his vast estate, Mitch had woven a garland of flowers for her hair and they had romped like happy children, falling on the grass, laughing and kissing. One warm evening they had even danced under the stars in the white lattice pavilion at the back edge of his property, a hired five-piece orchestra playing just for them.

And they had returned daily to the secluded cottage in the woods where they shared good food and mindless gossip and burning kisses. Suzanna had insisted on telling Mitch's fortune, and he had agreed. Carefully studying his palm, she assured him that he would live a long and happy life. He told her he had never doubted that he would. They had waded in the babbling brook and swung in the hammock on the back porch and stretched out on the fur rug before the cold fireplace.

Throughout, Suzanna had done everything in her power to get the closemouthed Union officer to confide in her. To talk about the war and his role in it. To reveal some small tidbit of useful information she could pass on to the Confederacy.

It hadn't worked.

Now, on the eve of his departure, she had come to Mattie to confess her inadequacy and to seek the older woman's advice.

"How can I break down his defenses, Mattie?" she asked as the two of them rocked back and forth and the first light drops of summer rain began to fall. "What must I do to convince him that I can be trusted? How can I possibly get him to talk?"

"You've done quite enough, Suzanna," Mattie said. "I warned you that Admiral Longley was not like the others. While I'm sure he's infatuated with you, he's obviously far too intelligent and wily to divulge anything. Doesn't matter, there are other sources. Give up on Admiral Longley and —"

"Give up? No! I will not give up! The Cause is too important, Mattie, you know that. Too many precious lives depend on our success."

"Yes, but you've done more than your part where the admiral is concerned. I'm hosting a dinner party this evening. Several pro-

Union contacts have promised to attend. Why don't you break your engagement with the admiral and come to my gathering?"

Suzanna wasn't listening. Her eyes narrowing with determination, she was thinking aloud when she snapped her fingers and said, "I know how to get Mitch to talk."

Comprehending instantly, Mattie turned beet-red. "No, Suzanna! That's too much to ask! The Confederacy does not require you to give up your innocence."

To the older woman Suzanna said, "Oh, Mattie, I didn't mean that. I would never . . ." She shook her head and waved a dismissive hand.

"Ahh. That's a relief," said her friend, placing a palm on her fluttering heart. "I could never forgive myself if I thought you'd even consider making such a sacrifice."

"I won't, so don't worry."

"I feel responsible for you, Suzanna, and I worry about you. And I'm so afraid that the handsome admiral is too worldly for you, too experienced at the art of seduction. He might try to take advantage of you and you wouldn't know how to handle him."

With a sly smile, Suzanna said, "Don't concern yourself, Mattie. I know how to handle Mitch Longley."

Then and there, on that sheltered veranda,

while the rain peppered the lawn below, Suzanna made up her mind to seduce Mitch Longley before he went back into battle.

The rain had begun in earnest when Suzanna returned to her rented rooms. The sky was pitch-black and thunder reverberated after bright flashes of lightning.

Inside, Suzanna lit a lamp in the dim parlor and walked into the bedroom. She glanced at the small clock on the night table — 6:00 p.m. Two hours until Mitch came to pick her up.

She began stripping off her rain-dampened clothes. When she was nude, she climbed up onto the high feather bed and stretched out on her back. She drew a shallow breath and wondered if she could actually go through with it. Could she allow this man who was her sworn enemy to make love to her? And if she did allow it, would she know how to respond? What to do? How to please him?

Suzanna recalled the times she and her best friend, Cynthia Ann Grayson, had eavesdropped on the young married women gossiping at parties. Some had professed to a strong distaste for making love with their husbands, while others had dreamily declared that they enjoyed every minute of the lovely intimacy.

Suzanna made a face. If a woman didn't enjoy the carnal act with a beloved husband, how awful might it be with this man she'd known for only a week and loved not at all? Would Mitch realize that she was repelled by his lovemaking? Would he know that this was her first time? If he did know, would he wonder why she had given herself to him?

Tormented by doubts, considering backing out, Suzanna laid a hand on her flat belly. She lightly stroked the bare flesh and shivered inwardly, envisioning Mitch's dark fingers stroking her stomach. She raised her hand to her left breast. With her forefinger she touched the sleeping nipple. She circled it slowly until it grew firm, the way it did when Mitch held her tight and kissed her passionately. She put her finger into her mouth, licked it, then returned it to her rigid nipple.

Wishing she knew more about making love to a man, Suzanna closed her eyes and let her free hand slip down over her ribs to her hip. She left it there for only a few seconds before slipping it across her belly and down to the triangle of fiery curls between her thighs. She couldn't do it, couldn't touch herself.

Suzanna opened her eyes and looked

around. She saw nothing she could use. She got up and hurried to the bureau, atop which the matching china pitcher and washbowl rested. She poured a splash of water into the bowl and dipped a washcloth into it. She wrung out the wet cloth, coiling it tightly.

She returned to the bed and stretched out on her back. She again closed her eyes. And she bit her lip when she passed the wet cloth down over her quivering stomach and into the crisp red coils. She moved her slender legs slightly apart and carefully lowered the wet washcloth between.

While the rain peppered the windows and the roof above, Suzanna lay there in the shadowy bedroom, shamelessly pressing the damp cloth to her sensitive feminine flesh. Intent on feeling sensuous, she tried hard to arouse herself. When it didn't work, she opened her eyes and scooted up in the bed so that her back was against the pillowed headboard. She raised her knees slightly and tried once more. Twisting the damp cloth into a rigid cylinder, she put it between her parted legs, rubbed it back and forth, then around and around until finally, after several tense minutes, she was panting with desire.

Pleased with her body's response, confident that she was an innately sensual woman who could be aroused by a handsome man even if he was the enemy, she stopped the shameful exercise. She quickly got up to draw herself a bath. Soaking in her tub, Suzanna hummed and thought of the way she felt when Mitch kissed her lips, her throat, the swell of her breasts. All tingly and warm and fluttery.

Her intent was to focus solely on the erotic aspect of her relationship with Mitch. To convince him that she was an experienced woman who tremendously enjoyed the act of lovemaking. To convince herself that she could hardly wait for him to make love to her.

To keep herself in a half-feverish state so he would sense it the minute he saw her.

And waste no time in taking her to bed.

Twenty-One

At exactly eight o'clock, Suzanna heard the bell. She gave herself one last look in the freestanding mirror. She nodded in approval. With her blazing hair dressed dramatically atop her head and the bodice of her turquoise chiffon ball gown cut daringly low, she appeared to be a sophisticated lady. Voluptuous and hedonistic. The kind of worldly woman who would think nothing of making love with her handsome escort of the evening.

Smoothing her frothy turquoise skirts, Suzanna opened the door. Mitch stood on the rainy stoop beneath a big black umbrella. He took one look at her and said, "Baby, what are you trying to do to me?"

It was exactly the kind of response Suzanna had hoped for. "Why, Admiral, what do you mean?" she said, eyes sparkling.

Mitch just shook his head. "Better grab a cape. It's raining cats and dogs."

"I won't need a cape," she replied. "Your umbrella is large enough for us both."

He smiled. "Then you take the umbrella and I'll carry you."

Before she could answer, he handed it to her, swept her up into his arms, locked her door, turned and raced down the front walk while she attempted to shield them from the pouring rain. But the wind had risen with nightfall and a strong gust swooped up under the umbrella and turned it inside out. Suzanna squealed and they both laughed. Their clothes were fairly damp by the time they reached the carriage. Suzanna didn't care. And she was delighted to see that he had come for her in the one-horse gig. No pesky coach driver to get in the way.

Just the two of them alone on a warm rainy night.

Once inside, Mitch turned and looked at her for a long moment. "What is it?" she asked.

He said, "Let's don't go to the house for dinner, Suzanna."

"No? Where then?"

"The cottage."

She smiled, catlike. "Yes. Let's go to the cottage."

By the time they reached it, both were soaked to the skin from rain blowing in under the gig's covering hood. Mitch again grabbed up Suzanna and carried her inside. In the darkened foyer they shook themselves like a couple of dogs.

Mitch handed Suzanna into the parlor, lighted a lamp and said, "I'll get you a robe so you can get out of those wet clothes."

She nodded, but felt a shiver of doubt skip up her spine. Now that the moment was at hand, she wasn't sure she could go through with her planned seduction. But she didn't have long to mull it over, for in seconds Mitch returned with a black silk robe over his arm and a stack of fluffy white towels. He kept one towel, gave the rest to her.

He inclined his head toward the bedroom. "You can change in there."

"Thank you," she said, taking the robe and towels.

Suzanna closed the bedroom door behind her, turned, leaned back against it and released a held breath. It was dark in the room, but she didn't light a lamp. Dripping water on the rug, she undressed down to the skin and blotted away the lingering moisture from her body with a couple of towels. A flash of brilliant lightning illuminated the big double bed, and Suzanna shivered. Naked, she stared at that bed, hugging herself.

She drew on the sleek black robe and tied the sash at her waist. It reached almost to her ankles and fell off her slender shoulders. She rolled up sleeves that were far too long. The robe's lapels kept parting over her bare breasts, despite her efforts to yank them together. Finally she gave up and left the lapels alone. They fell open almost down to her waist, yet her breasts were sufficiently covered as long as she didn't make any sudden moves.

Suzanna walked over to the floor-to-ceiling windows along the bedroom's back wall. She stood before them and watched the rain strike the glass. She turned and again looked at the bed. If she and Mitch were in that bed, they could watch the rain falling, could hear it pepper the glass, could see the lightning streak across the black sky.

Suzanna turned away, drew a spine-stiffening breath and rejoined Mitch in the parlor. Shirtless, he stood with his back to the cold fireplace, rubbing his dark hair dry with a towel. His naked torso gleamed in the lamplight and the sculpted muscles moved with the lifting of his long arms. The waistband of his tailored trousers fell away from his flat abdomen, revealing the small indentation of his navel. A dense line of dark hair led downward from there and disappeared inside damp dress blues.

He was the most beautiful man she had ever laid eyes on, a fact that could not be altered by the circumstances that had brought them together. Nor the reality that she would be his undoing if she had her way.

His sultry green eyes resting on her, Mitch dropped his towel to the floor. "Come here, sweetheart," he said, and Suzanna felt her knees grow weak.

She crossed to him and stood before him, her heart beating in her ears, hands balled into fists at her sides. He smiled at her, lifted both hands, put his thumbs and forefingers around the slippery lapels of the robe and modestly drew them together. Then he took her in his arms and kissed her.

Suzanna looped her arms around his neck and rose on bare tiptoes, leaning against him. He kissed her several times, each kiss lasting longer and growing hotter and more invasive. And as he kissed her, he cupped the twin cheeks of her bottom through the sleek black silk and pressed her to his stirring groin. Suzanna could feel the hard male flesh straining against his tight trousers, pressing insistently against her belly.

And then, never taking his heated lips from hers, Mitch found and tugged on the robe's sash, untying it. The robe was now held together only by their pressing bodies. Suzanna trembled when he moved back a little, swept the open robe apart, slipped both hands inside and placed them lightly on her narrow waist. Looking steadily into her eyes, he drew her back against his tall, lean frame. She winced and bit the inside of her bottom lip. She was now totally bare against him, her breasts crushed against his naked torso, her fluttering stomach and quivering thighs rubbing against the slightly abrasive fabric of his trousers.

His hands slid down to her hips and settled there. "I have dreamed of having you here like this," he told her. "In my cottage, in my bed, in my arms. Never have I wanted a woman more than I want you at this minute. Tell me that's what you want as well, sweetheart."

"It is," she said, hoping he couldn't tell that she was scared to death. "This is exactly what I want. Being here with you," she said, barely above a whisper.

"Baby," he said, his hands cupping her bare bottom. He kissed her as he'd never kissed her before, and Suzanna eagerly kissed him back, wanting to be as sexually aroused as possible for what was to come. Her lips moving beneath his, she grasped his bare shoulders in an attempt to hold him to her for just a little while longer.

She knew that once their lips separated and he set her back, she would be standing there naked and vulnerable before him. She dreaded that moment, so she frantically clung to him. As if he sensed her anxiety, Mitch took his lips from hers but continued to hold her close against him, sparing her the embarrassment of standing naked in the lamplight.

Warmly embracing her, Mitch gave her one last chance to back out. He said against her ear, "This much I promise you, sweetheart, I will never do anything that you don't want me to do. If you want me to take you home right now, just say the word."

"No. I don't want to go home. I want to stay here with you."

"You're very sure, Suzanna?" he said, and both knew exactly what he was asking her.

"I am." Her face against his bare shoulder, she said, "But the lamp. It's too bright, Mitch."

"There's no lamp lit in the bedroom," he said, and in one swift, fluid movement he swung her up into his arms, carried her into the other room and kicked the door shut behind them.

Twenty-Two

Mitch stood for a moment with his back against the door, holding Suzanna high in his arms, pressing kisses to her flushed face. As he pushed away and crossed to the bed, a jagged bolt of lightning streaked across the night sky and bathed the room in day-bright brilliance. The booming rumble of rolling thunder followed as, one-handed, Mitch reached out and turned down the bed's snowy-white sheets. He then kissed Suzanna and gently placed her in the very center of the mattress.

The black silk robe fell open, pooling at her sides, exposing her pale bare body. Thankful for the room's cloaking darkness, Suzanna fought the urge to hastily grab the robe and wrap it securely around herself. A firm resolve, born of her mission, made her refrain, but the palms of her hands were perspiring with nervous anticipation. She willed herself to appear composed and confident. She didn't want this handsome Yankee to think she was a starry-eyed innocent who might fall in love with him and quickly become a nuisance, tearfully demanding that he commit himself to her.

Suzanna reminded herself that she had but one purpose — to please Mitch Longley sexually. She had to convince him she was an experienced libertine, the kind of lover with whom he could enjoy a casual affair. An affair that was no more important to her than to him.

But her heart almost beat its way out of her chest when Mitch sat down on the bed facing her, placed a long arm across her and, bracing himself with a spread hand on the mattress, leaned down and kissed her hotly, hungrily. Suzanna quickly responded to his masterful lips, her mouth yielding to his, her nervous hands clasping his bare biceps.

As they kissed, Suzanna struggled valiantly to stay calm, but found that it was futile. She was anxious, yet eager. She was trembling, inside and out. She was chilled, yet burning hot. Patriotic duty was rapidly giving way to erotic desire. This tryst was to have been her grand sacrifice for the Cause. But here, in the arms of this formidable enemy, her generous offering was becoming eclipsed by selfish physical pleasure.

Suzanna sighed against Mitch's burning lips when he drew her up into a sitting position, wrapped strong arms around her and pressed her against his broad, muscled chest. Suzanna tingled at the ticklish brush of crisp hair against her bare breasts. She could feel her nipples tightening from the contact. Her skin burned from his touch and she was having trouble breathing.

Mitch urged the silk robe off her shoulders and down her arms. He freed her from the sleeves and the robe fell away. Suzanna felt Mitch's warm hands glide slowly up over her back and into her hair. He took his lips from hers and began removing the pins from her upswept tresses. As they spilled down around her shoulders, a flash of lightning struck nearby. Suzanna could see Mitch's handsome face; desire was clearly etched in his strong, masculine features. His eyes were smoldering with passion, and she felt a quick stab of fear.

Then the room went dark once more and Suzanna was back in his arms. The hairpins tossed onto the night table, Mitch's lean fingers tunneled into her hair, tightened their hold and urged her head back. He bent and pressed a kiss to the sensitive hollow of her throat, and Suzanna shuddered involuntarily. She winced when she felt his hand gently cupping her left breast, his thumb slowly rubbing back and forth across the stiffening nipple.

Mitch raised his head as another burst of lightning struck, clearly illuminating them and the entire room. Suzanna gazed into his hypnotic green eyes and heard him say, "If you want me to stop, sweetheart, I will."

The room again in darkness, she brazenly replied, "Don't you dare stop. Make love to me, Mitch. Make love to me."

Then she blinked in surprise and struggled to hold still when she felt his hot lips moving down over her breast. He kissed her nipple softly, tenderly. His smooth, warm lips felt like a flame singeing her flesh. Suzanna gave a strangled gasp of surprise when he opened his mouth and wetly enclosed the rigid nipple. She looked down, but in the darkness could not see the handsome head bent to her. She could only feel those beautifully sculpted lips tenderly tugging on her nipple, shocking her, thrilling her, setting her on fire.

Suzanna lifted a tentative hand, placed it on the back of Mitch's moving head. Her slender fingers toyed with the lustrous locks, and hardly realizing she was doing it, she pressed him steadily closer as she squared her bare shoulders and thrust her breasts forward.

Both dazzled and frightened by the new sensations she was experiencing, Suzanna felt herself beginning to sag weakly back onto the mattress. His lips never leaving her flesh, Mitch followed her down. Suzanna released a shuddering sigh as she stretched out on her back and continued to stroke his dark head while he teasingly licked, playfully bit and gently sucked at her diamond-hard nipple.

Guiltily, Suzanna longed for another flash of lightning so that she could see them, could witness this stunning act of intimacy. As if the heavens had read her mind, the strongest bolt yet streaked across the sky, and Suzanna was rewarded with a thrilling glimpse of Mitch's tanned face at her pale breast. His beautiful eyes closed, lashes fluttering restlessly on high cheekbones, his lips clasping her rigid nipple.

Again darkness fell and again Suzanna was glad the light was so quickly gone. Her face burning with a mixture of pleasure and shame, she lay there luxuriating in the stygian blackness, hoping there would be no more flashes of lightning, and wondering what he would do to her next. She bit the inside of her lip when Mitch's mouth abruptly left her breast and he rose from the bed. She strained to see where he was and what he was doing, but it was too dark. Seconds later he came down onto the bed and stretched out beside her. She was instantly aware that his trousers had been discarded.

He was naked.

Suzanna swallowed convulsively.

Mitch gathered her into his close embrace, tugged the silk robe out from under her and dropped it onto the floor beside the bed. Trembling uncontrollably now, choking with sexual excitement, Suzanna accepted his kiss, her mouth quickly opening beneath his, her tongue stroking his. She felt his tall lean body pressed against hers, his skin scalding hot to the touch and that hard, heavy, most male part of him throbbing insistently against her thigh. Her hand spread on his chest, she felt his thundering heartbeat and realized that he was as aroused as she.

Kissing her deeply several times, Mitch finally maneuvered her onto her back, then rolled up on his side and lay close against her. When their lips finally separated, he was resting his weight on a bent elbow. He whispered endearments as he toyed with her kiss-moistened nipple, his forefinger circling it. And as he unhurriedly set about readying her for the act of lovemaking, he told her in a low, husky voice how much he wanted her. He confessed that he had wanted her from the moment he'd walked into Mattie Kirkendal's ballroom and seen her in the arms of another officer.

"Yours are the only arms I've been in since that night," Suzanna shakily told him.

"I don't want you to be in anyone else's arms while I'm away, sweetheart."

Suzanna did not reply, didn't reassure him. She wanted him to worry and wonder, and therefore want her more than ever. Mitch didn't press her. He took his hand from her breast and moved it down over her ribs and laid it lightly on her flat belly. Suzanna tensed and waited, not sure what would come next, wondering what she was supposed to do, how she could possibly convince him she was experienced at this game of love when she knew next to nothing about it.

She felt Mitch's lips brush her temple and slide down to her face. His mouth moved slowly across her cheek to settle on her lips, while his lean fingers stroked her constricting belly.

Suzanna squirmed and her toes curled. When she felt his fingertips slip into the triangle of springy coils between her thighs, she stiffened and lost her breath entirely. She whimpered and he took his lips from hers. She anxiously gasped for breath, but Mitch didn't remove his hand. He brushed kisses to her feverish cheeks while his palm moved between her legs and he gently cupped her with all four fingers.

And he waited.

When Suzanna was breathing more easily, Mitch lifted his hand a little and deftly parted the flaming red curls. That slick button of female flesh now exposed, he whispered her name in the darkness as he touched her with just his long middle finger. Suzanna's hips involuntarily lifted from the mattress and she clamped her hand over her mouth to keep from gurgling in protest. She had not counted on him touching her with his hand. Nor had she supposed that he could so excite her with just his lean fingers. Her hot face reddened with embarrassment. He had said that he would stop anytime she asked, so that's exactly what she would do. She would order him to stop right this instant! But if she did, then he'd know that she was inexperienced. She couldn't let that happen.

Again Mitch waited while she calmed a little. Then he slid his finger down and dipped the tip into the wetness flowing from her. He spread that wetness upward and around the tiny button of throbbing flesh. He began to very slowly, very gently caress her, and Suzanna's young healthy body responded to his masterful touch. There was no further thought of making him stop. She didn't want him to stop. Ever.

Suzanna surrendered completely to the passion engulfing her, and from that moment forward, the heated lovemaking became a blinding blur of building ecstasy for her. A bolt of lightning exposed to her wonderment-widened eyes the sensual sight of Mitch's tanned hand between her pale legs, touching her, toying with her, pleasuring her so expertly that she totally forgot the purpose of this clandestine rendezvous.

When darkness returned, she was grateful. But she was profoundly awakened and highly aroused as well. What his fingers were doing to her was thrilling beyond belief. She had never dreamed she could feel like this, never considered that she might be suspended in such a state of delicious desire. She was growing hotter by the second and her feverish body was taut with yearning for more.

Suzanna's eyes opened when Mitch took his hand away, and she sighed deeply when she felt him move between her parted legs. Lightning flashed and his passion-hardened face and wide, muscular shoulders filled the entire scope of her vision. She was gazing into his flashing eyes as he entered her. Darkness returned just in time.

She was glad that Mitch couldn't see her grit her teeth and squeeze her eyes shut against the piercing pain as his hard, pounding flesh slid into her.

When he stopped abruptly, Suzanna was confused. Had she done something wrong? She waited, hardly daring to breathe, her heart pounding. Was she supposed to do something more? But what? Suzanna felt Mitch pressing gentle kisses to her lips, heard him say her name over and over as if offering an apology. She was confused by his sudden hesitancy and wondered again if she was doing something wrong, something that made him wish he had never started making love to her.

After what seemed an eternity, he began to move inside her, to thrust slowly, carefully. And to Suzanna's surprise, it didn't feel all that bad. She began to relax, to move with him, to recapture some of the joy she'd experienced earlier when his hand was touching her.

Then Mitch was kissing her again and she

was kissing him back. Her arms were around his neck and the two of them were moving together in a slow erotic dance of desire that made all prior pleasure pale in comparison. Suzanna hardly realized that she was saying Mitch's name over and over as she lifted her hips to meet each slow, driving thrust. And she had no idea that he was valiantly fighting to control his body's aching need for release.

A patient, caring lover, Mitch spent the next half hour delaying, with great difficulty, his threatening orgasm. Intent on pleasing his beautiful partner, he held back and took pride in smoothly tutoring Suzanna in the art of lovemaking. Skillfully, he began teaching her the secrets of her own lush body and how to derive the ultimate pleasure from making love to a man.

But finally the moment came when he could no longer stall the inevitable. He hated knowing that she hadn't attained orgasm yet, but he couldn't help himself. She was too beautiful, too sweet, too sensual.

Mitch tore his lips from Suzanna's as lightning illuminated their twined bodies.

"Baby, baby," he choked.

Then the echoing thunder drowned out his groan of ecstasy as his orgasm exploded, draining him until he collapsed, sated, atop the bewildered Suzanna.

Twenty-Three

Mitch, still breathing heavily, lay stretched out flat on his back, holding Suzanna close. Her head supported by his raised arm, she was curled on her side against him, her hand on his chest, nails absently raking through the dense crisp hair.

"Mitch," she said, finally breaking the easy silence.

"Hmm?"

"Where do you go when you leave in the morning?"

"I wish I could tell you, sweetheart."

"Why can't you? You do know where they're sending you, don't you?"

"I do, but I'm not at liberty to tell anyone."

Suzanna raised her head. "Surely after tonight, after we . . . ah . . . I'm not just 'anyone.' Am I?"

Mitch lifted a hand, cupped her chin. "No, of course not. You're the most special person in my life."

"Then tell me where —"

Interrupting, Mitch said, "I don't want you worrying, Suzanna."

"I'll worry a great deal more if I don't know where you are and what you are doing. In which battle you're engaged."

"Listen to me, sweetheart. I've come through almost four years of constant war without suffering so much as a scratch. I've been unbelievably lucky and I fully expect my luck to hold. And as I recall, you read my fortune and assured me that I'd live to be an old, old man. So you see, there's no need for you to be concerned."

Suzanna hid her frustration. She lay back down, brushed a kiss to his tanned throat and tried to sound casual when she ventured, "I'll bet I can guess where you're going. I've heard rumors that a major naval battle is brewing down at Mobile Bay in Alabama and . . ."

"I wouldn't put much store in rumors, Suzanna."

"Then give me some facts. What's the name of your ironclad? Which fleet do you command? What battles . . . ?"

"Darling, it's almost midnight. Only six short hours before I must report for duty. I have no intention of wasting that precious time talking about the war."

Bested, she graciously acquiesced. "You're absolutely right, Admiral Longley. If I'm not to see you again for weeks, perhaps months, then . . ." She shrugged bare shoulders.

Even then he was not forthcoming. He gave her no indication when he might be back, when she would see him again. He said, "Suzanna, if you're reluctant to stay out past a decent hour and risk being seen by those who might gossip about you, damage your sterling reputation, I'll take you home. Now."

"And if I'm not?"

"Then you can sleep here in my arms, which is what I'd like."

She snuggled closer. "If I stay I'm afraid you won't get much rest."

"I should hope not."

The pair didn't sleep a wink all night. They talked and kissed and touched while the blinding rain continued to pelt the windows and lightning intermittently illuminated the room and the bed where they lay.

The kissing and touching was but a lovely, lengthy prelude to the complete lovemaking Mitch was planning for his beautiful companion. It was sometime before 3:00 a.m.

that Mitch, promising Suzanna it would be better this time, at last made slow, sweet love to her again.

He was right.

Suzanna found the intimacy to be exquisitely pleasurable. Mitch skillfully drew out her escalating ecstasy, teasing and tormenting her until she was fairly panting with passion. A patient, tender and accomplished lover who knew how to give a woman extraordinary sexual elation, he purposely kept Suzanna at a heightened state of arousal for the better part of an hour before finally taking her over the top.

When she cried out and desperately clung to him as the last little tremors of her orgasm buffeted her, Mitch held her and soothed her as one might comfort a fretful child. When at last she had calmed, she confessed dreamily, "I've never felt like that before."

"I know," he said. "Why didn't you tell me, sweetheart?"

"Tell you what?"

"That this was your first time. When you agreed to come out to the cottage with me tonight, I assumed that . . ."

"And you assumed correctly. For heaven sake, I am twenty-three years old and have entertained more than my share of sophisticated suitors! My first time to make love? Certainly not!" she declared emphatically. "I've had any number of lovers."

"No, you haven't."

"I most certainly have. Why, I . . . I . . ." She shook her head. "You could tell?"

"Yes, darling, of course I could tell. I'm your first lover, and if I have my way, I'll be your last."

Suzanna liked his answer. It sounded as if he was already falling in love with her. Good! That's exactly what she wanted. Once he was madly in love with her and felt he could trust her completely, he would share all kinds of vital information, which she in turn could pass on to her Confederate operatives.

"Mitch, it was foolish of me to pretend I was an experienced woman, wasn't it?" she said.

"Why did you do it?"

"I was afraid you'd be bored with me, that you wouldn't want me if you knew the truth."

"My sweet, naive Suzanna, you have much to learn, I'm afraid. Knowing you were an innocent when you came into my arms tonight makes you all the more desirable." He paused and added, "But unfortunately, it makes a scoundrel of me."

"No, it doesn't. I wanted you to make love to me." She traced his beautifully sculpted lips with her forefinger and stated honestly, "You didn't seduce me, Admiral. I seduced you."

"My dear child, I'm so glad you came," said Mitch's aunt, the formidable Edna Earl Longley.

"Thank you for inviting me, Miss Longley," Suzanna said with a smile.

The invitation to join Edna Earl Longley for lunch had arrived at Suzanna's rented rooms not twenty-four hours after Mitch departed. When Suzanna opened her front door, a messenger had handed her a small vellum envelope. Inside was a brief note, scrawled in a large, shaky hand, stating that "the two of us should get better acquainted. Won't you join me for a light noon repast at one sharp on Friday, May 21." It was signed "Edna Earl Longley."

Suzanna was immediately apprehensive. Still, she had seen no way out. It would have been rude not to accept. But the prospect of being grilled by the indomitable old woman had filled her with dread.

Now, as she stepped into the front foyer of Miss Longley's mansion and smiled at the tall, rawboned woman who was giving her a thorough once-over as though she could see right through her, Suzanna's anxiety increased.

"So you dominated all my nephew's time while he was here on leave, did you not?"

"I . . . ah . . . yes, I suppose I'm guilty, Miss Longley," Suzanna said, smiling weakly.

Eyebrows lifted, the older woman motioned Suzanna into the spacious drawing room. Once Suzanna was seated on a long brocade sofa and her hostess was in a rocker nearby, a deadly silence filled the room for several seconds. It was Suzanna who broke it.

She said, "You have such a lovely home, Miss Longley."

"Yes, well, I didn't ask you here to listen to your comments on my domicile. Let's talk about the only thing we have in common, Miss LeGrande. My nephew, Admiral Longley."

Suzanna felt her face turn hot. But she smiled and replied, "I know how fond you are of Mitch and —"

"No, you don't. You have no idea. From the moment he was born, Mitchell has been like my own son. When he was twenty-one and lost both parents, he and I became even closer. I'm his only family and he's mine, and I couldn't love him more if he *were* my son. He's all I have in this world, and the only thing I really care about is whether or not he is happy."

"That's very sweet of you, Miss Longley."

"My dear child, there is nothing sweet about me. I am, admittedly, a selfish, overbearing old woman and I have no intention of changing my ways at this late date." She waved a bony hand and said, "All this, everything I own, will belong to Mitch when I die. Not that he needs it. He is quite wealthy in his own right, as you have probably ascertained."

"I hadn't really given it any thought," Suzanna said truthfully.

Edna Earl stared at Suzanna intently for a long minute, then slapped her knee and said, "By heavens, I do believe you mean that!"

"Let me assure you that I mean it." Suzanna leaned forward and added, "I don't give a fig how much money your nephew has, so if you're afraid I'm a callous gold digger, you've badly misjudged me!"

Edna Earl Longley chuckled merrily. "I like you, Suzanna LeGrande! You speak your mind and refuse to let me intimidate you. Now accept my apologies for being rude and let's be friends."

"I would like that, Miss Longley."

"So would I, child. And forgive me if I've been tactless, but as I said, Mitch is like my own son and I know him better than he knows himself. He's a handsome devil and he's had plenty of beautiful women, but he feels different about you."

Now it was Suzanna's turn to look surprised. "Really? How do you know?"

"Were you with Mitch last night?"

"Yes, I was," Suzanna said without hesitation.

Edna smiled knowingly and nodded. "I knew it! He came by here bright and early this morning to say goodbye. I've never seen Mitch like that before. He was beaming like a smitten schoolboy. Now, come, let's enjoy our lunch. Do you like champagne?"

The two women talked and talked, and when Suzanna finally left around three-thirty, she felt that she had been successful in gaining the elderly woman's confidence. The two of them had spoken at length about the war, and Suzanna had played her part well. When her hostess cursed the hated Confederates, Suzanna joined in, declaring she couldn't wait until "every Johnny Reb had been vanquished and the bloody rebellion was crushed."

"Do come again soon, Suzanna," Edna

said as she ushered her guest to the door.

"I'd love to," said Suzanna.

"Early next week then. My most trusted physician, Dr. Milton Ledet, is coming for dinner Monday evening."

"Ah, we do have something other than Mitch in common. Doc Ledet has been my physician since he delivered me twenty-three years ago."

"Then I'll have the good doctor come round to collect you and you'll join us for dinner."

Again Suzanna said, "I'd love to."

"Wonderful, wonderful," said Edna Longley, smiling warmly.

Suzanna went away greatly relieved. The afternoon had been a success. The older woman suspected nothing.

Twenty-Four

"I learned absolutely nothing from the Yankee admiral, Mattie," Suzanna declared disgustedly when she arrived early at the Kirkendal mansion for a soiree that same evening.

Suzanna didn't dare reveal to Mattie that she had allowed Mitch to make love to her, but she did tell her trusted accomplice that her kisses had not been enough to loosen the admiral's lips.

"He wouldn't tell me anything. Not a thing! He refuses to talk about the war, much less reveal anything that might be of help to the Cause."

"Ah, the impatience of youth," Mattie gently scolded. "Surely you didn't expect a seasoned, highly intelligent officer like Admiral Longley to disclose precious secrets so soon."

"So soon? But I was with him every waking minute for the entire week he was here on leave."

"And that, I would say, is a phenomenal success. In case you didn't notice, the admiral is a sinfully handsome man. And he's a very wealthy one, as well. This city's most beautiful women are drawn to him like moths to the flame. You should be very flattered that he picked you out of the crowd." Mattie smiled, took Suzanna's arm and guided her into the drawing room. "Since he spent all his time with you, my guess is the admiral is so captivated he will find a reason for being back in Washington sometime soon."

"You think so?"

Nodding, Mattie said, "Yes, I do. And the more he's with you, the more he will let down his guard. When he feels he can trust you completely, he will then, hopefully, be forthcoming."

"I suppose so, but it could be weeks or months before he comes back."

"It will be well worth the wait," said Mattie. "Now, this evening's guests will be arriving shortly. I've never seen you looking lovelier, so work your magic on the gentlemen, as usual. We never know when one of the dazzled officers might let something slip."

■ ■ ■ ■

Suzanna continued to regularly attend Mattie's galas, where she danced with Union officers and kept her ears and eyes open for any fragment of information she could pass on to the Confederate commanders in the field.

She continued to flatter and flirt and press the officers for news of the war. And she suffered each time she heard of yet another Union victory. Word of late May's Matadequin Creek battle in Hanover County had quickly spread across Washington. The elated officers, many drunk from too much liquor, bragged loudly about General Torbet's division attacking and defeating Butler's brigade near Old Church, a brilliant strike that had resulted in nine hundred Reb casualties.

Suzanna secretly took heart when she learned about the Battle of Cold Harbor. In early June Lieutenant General Ulysses Grant attacked Confederate forces at Cold Harbor and was soundly defeated by her old acquaintance, General Robert E. Lee.

Another June campaign that had appeared to be good news for the Confederacy turned out to be bad. Grant tried to take St.

Petersburg below Richmond and then approach the capital from the south. The attempt failed, but the defeat turned into a bloody siege with no end in sight and many lives being lost daily.

As the hot, hot summer progressed, Suzanna heard the men speak of so many battles it was impossible to keep track of them all. Trevilian Station. Wilson's Wharf. Yellow Tavern. And many many more, the majority of which were won by the mighty Union forces.

Suzanna paid special attention when she heard of a naval skirmish. And always she wondered, was Mitch in the thick of it? Had he been wounded? Killed even? She heard nothing from him, and when she called on his aunt Edna to ask if she had heard anything, the older woman told her Mitch was not the kind of man to be writing letters when on duty.

"Don't expect a letter and don't expect to see him anytime soon. It could be weeks, even months before he's back in Washington. He'll just show up one day when we least expect it."

Which was exactly what happened.

On the fifteenth of July, a hot, muggy morning if ever there was one, Suzanna was awakened from a deep slumber by someone knocking. Frowning, muttering to herself, she drew on a robe, pushed her hair out of her eyes and answered the door.

A young uniformed messenger stood on the stoop. He handed her a small white envelope.

"Thank you," she said, and started to close the door.

"No, miss, I'm supposed to wait for your reply."

"Very well." She tore open the envelope and read the brief missive:

> Suzanna,
> Just arrived in Washington. Have meetings with fellow commanders at Capitol Building this morning. Can you meet me at cottage at straight-up noon?
> Mitch

She looked up at the waiting youth. "Admiral Longley gave you this note?"

"Yes, miss," the boy said. "Half an hour ago Admiral Longley checked in to the hotel where I work. He gave me ten dollars to bring this note to you. He awaits your reply."

"Stay right here," Suzanna said, then turned and went inside. She plucked a pen from its inkwell and wrote across the note,

"Yes, Yes, Yes." She folded the note, stuck it into a fresh envelope, returned to the door and handed it to the young man.

"You'll see that the admiral gets this promptly?"

The boy grinned. "He'll have it in hand in fifteen minutes."

Twenty-Five

He was there when she arrived.

The cottage door stood wide-open. Suzanna raised her hand, but lowered it without knocking. She drew a deep breath and walked into the foyer. She turned into the parlor, looked around and saw that it was empty. She crossed the large room, walked out the back door onto the wide veranda and saw him.

He lay comfortably sprawled in the gently swaying canvas hammock at the far end of the porch, arms folded beneath his dark head, dozing peacefully. His shirt was open down his dark chest and he was in his stockinged feet.

On the porch's concrete floor, directly below the hammock, sat a round silver tray holding two stemmed crystal flutes, a bottle of champagne chilling in a silver bucket, and a small box wrapped in white paper with a blue bow on top.

Suzanna surveyed the scene and smugly told herself that this time she would get plenty of valuable information out of this unsuspecting Yankee. She would eagerly accept the little gift he'd obviously bought for her, and behave as though she were thrilled. She would also drink champagne with him until they were both quite giddy. And she would make love to him until at last he was putty in her hands and would tell her anything she wanted to know.

"Mitch." She softly spoke his name.

His eyes opened. He slowly turned and looked at her. He smiled, lowered his arms and extended a hand to her.

Suzanna crossed to him, leaned down and brushed a kiss to his lips. Then squealed in shocked surprise when he pulled her into the hammock with him. At once he was kissing her passionately and telling her how much he had missed her.

When she was quite breathless from his kisses, Mitch finally took his lips from hers and said, "I bought you a little present."

"I love presents," she said, smiling saucily at him.

He reached down, plucked the box from the tray and held it out to her. She grabbed it and tugged on the ribbon. She tore the paper away and opened the small blue velvet box. Resting on a bed of white satin was a dazzling sapphire surrounded by diamonds and suspended from a delicate gold chain. Suzanna's eyes widened and she was momentarily speechless. There was no need for pretense; she was genuinely thrilled to be receiving such an exquisite piece of jewelry.

When she could speak, she looked up at him and said, "Mitch, this is the most beautiful sapphire I have ever seen."

"The exact color of your lovely eyes," he said. "That's why I picked it."

"But it's too much . . . too expensive. I can't possibly accept it."

"Of course you can accept it," he said, lifting it out and tossing the box to the floor. "Now sit up and I'll put it on you."

Suzanna slowly complied. Mitch draped the chain around her neck, fastened it behind her head and drew her back down into his arms.

"Thank you so much," she said, knowing it was unforgivably wrong to take such a valuable gift from a man she meant to betray.

"Is that all the thanks I get?" he teased.

"No, it's not," she replied, then turned in his arms and kissed him soundly.

As they kissed, Mitch began working the tiny buttons running down the front of Suzanna's blue poplin dress. When it was open to her waist, he slipped his hand inside and slid long fingers down into her lace-trimmed camisole to gently caress a soft warm breast. Suzanna took her lips from his.

"We better go inside," she said.

"It's cooler out here," he reasoned. "Let's make love right here on the porch in this hammock."

"You can't mean that, Mitch Longley. What if someone should see us?"

"This is private property and we're surrounded by dense woods." He grinned then and added, "Besides, you won't be naked. You can leave the necklace on."

She thought that he was surely teasing. She found out he was not. While they drank champagne from the stemmed glasses and laughed and struggled to stay in the hammock as it swayed back and forth, they also managed to get undressed.

But, under the circumstances, it took quite a while.

A lovely, lively hour had passed by the time all their clothes lay discarded on the porch and they were totally naked. Then Mitch, telling Suzanna it would be safer if he were on the bottom to control the movement of the hammock, clasped her narrow waist and sat her astride his hips.

"Are you sure this is going to work?" asked the pleasantly tipsy Suzanna as she thirstily drained her glass. "I have no idea how to . . ."

"I'll show you, sweetheart," he said, enraptured by the knowledge that this lovely naked Venus had never sat astride any other man. "It's easy, you'll see." He reached down to grab the bottle and refill Suzanna's glass. "My task will be to keep us from falling out. Yours will be to make love to me."

Suzanna took another sip of the fizzing drink, wrinkled her nose at the tickling bubbles and nodded merrily. "You can count on me, darling," then she hesitated, awaiting his instruction, wondering what would happen next, eager to find out.

He said, "Dip your fingers in the champagne, Suzanna." She gave him a questioning look, but complied. He said, "Now, spread the wine up and down my . . ."

"Why?" she asked, giggling. "Is it thirsty?"

He grinned. "Just do it, baby."

"As you wish." She took her wet fingers from the glass and carefully spread champagne over the smooth tip of his throbbing erection. Then, with him urging her to take it slowly and not hurt herself, she balanced her half-full glass in one hand. With the other, she wrapped slender fingers around him and carefully guided him up inside her, as if she had done just such a maneuver a hundred times before.

"You learn quickly, sweetheart," Mitch praised as he set his own glass down on the floor and placed his hands on her shapely thighs.

While she carefully slid the rest of the way down upon him, Mitch flexed the cheeks of his lean buttocks and surged up into her, filling her, stretching her.

Suzanna sighed and took another drink of champagne as she began the slow, rhythmic rolls of her hips. The movement set the hammock to swaying, and Mitch had to use both hands to cling to the sides and keep it from throwing them out.

It was crazy. It was fun. It was hedonistic heaven.

On his back, holding on to the hammock for dear life, a highly aroused Mitch was looking up, watching his naked Venus erotically ride him. What a sight to behold!

Her flaming red hair was whipping around her head. Her full breasts were bouncing with her swaying movements. Her soft bottom was slapping up and down against his lifting pelvis. And the sparkling sapphire necklace, dancing at her throat, was catching the rays of the noonday sun and blinding him with its flawless blue brilliance.

"Mitch, I . . ." she murmured, rolling her pelvis forward to meet his deep surging thrust. "My glass. My champagne glass. I can't . . ."

"Toss it away," he instructed.

Suzanna immediately threw it off the porch onto the grass. Then she placed both hands on Mitch's shoulders, leaned down and kissed him, licking at his lips, thrusting her tongue into his mouth. When she raised her head, her wild red hair fell into his face. Mitch shifted her upward a little and captured a nipple with his mouth.

"Ooh," she murmured. Then, realizing that both his hands were now on her — one at her waist, the other clasping her bottom — Suzanna quickly gripped both sides of the swinging hammock to keep them from spilling out.

The blazing July sun had marched across the cloudless sky, its harsh rays now striking the covered porch and the joined pair making passionate love in the swinging hammock. Both were covered with a sheen of perspiration, and their dampened bodies slipped and slid sensuously together.

Searing summertime sex at its wicked best! Too splendid to end anytime soon. Too thrilling to last very long. Neither could stop the inevitable. They were coming and there was nothing they could do about it.

Their shared orgasm was intensely potent, exploding like Fourth of July fireworks and causing Suzanna to cry out while Mitch groaned aloud.

In their sexual frenzy, neither remembered to hold on. Miraculously, they didn't fall out onto the hard porch despite the wildly swinging hammock. When they regained their breath they found the situation to be hysterically funny, and began to laugh uncontrollably.

For a long time they lay there naked in the swaying hammock, laughing and teasing each other about their behavior. When they had calmed they continued to lazily lie there, reluctant to get up.

Mitch finally spoke. "I will never lie in a hammock again without thinking of this sunny afternoon here with you."

"Me, neither," Suzanna said. "Mitch, how long will you be in Washington?"

Tenderly caressing her bare bottom, he said, "I figure it's about one-thirty in the afternoon. Which means I have another hour."

"That's all?" Her head shot up.

"It is. We'd better get up and go inside."

They laughed again as they gathered their

strewn clothing and hurried in. In the parlor Mitch said apologetically, "There's no time to heat water for baths. I'll bathe and change at the hotel. Could you wait until you get home to . . ."

"Certainly," she said, stepping into her knee-length pantalets.

As they dressed, Suzanna attempted to question Mitch. It still didn't work. To her dismay he was no more forthcoming than he had been the last time she was with him. He stubbornly refused to talk about where he was going, where he had been or anything to do with the war.

When they were fully dressed, Mitch picked up a small black leather bag from beside the cold fireplace — a bag Suzanna hadn't noticed before.

"Ready?" he asked, gripping the bag's handle.

"What's that?" she said, inclining her head. "Did you bring your pajamas along, then decide you didn't want to spend the night with me?"

"You know better than that." He shrugged wide shoulders and said, "My musette bag. I take it everywhere I go."

"I see. And inside are . . . ?"

"Papers. Maps. Dispatches. Nothing that would interest you, sweetheart."

Suzanna wanted to kick herself. If only she had noticed the musette bag when she arrived! Mitch had been sound asleep then. She could have looked through all the documents the bag contained. She could have gone away from here with something valuable to pass on to her trusted couriers.

"Is anything wrong, Suzanna?" Mitch asked, noticing her frown.

"No, I . . . no, it's just I wish you could stay longer. Spend the night."

"So do I."

She stepped closer, laid a hand on his chest. "You'll come back as soon as possible?"

"You know I will," he said, and ran his fingers over the delicate gold chain lying on her throat.

"I love my beautiful necklace," she said. "How can I ever thank you?"

"You already have."

She smiled. "I'll count the minutes until you come back to me."

"Kiss me. Kiss me goodbye."

TWENTY-SIX

The passion Mitch Longley had awakened in Suzanna did not change her true feelings for him. While her body responded to his masterful caresses, her heart remained untouched. The physical relationship in which she so willingly engaged, had but one cold-blooded purpose — to aid in the defeat of the Union.

Her hatred of the Yankees was as strong as ever and she never forgot for a moment that Mitch Longley was the enemy. The enemy who had taken everything from her — her sweetheart, her brother, her mother, her home, her livelihood.

And now, finally, even her dignity.

She had nothing left to lose, a fact that imbued her with reckless courage. She had no fear of the future for the worst had already happened.

Suzanna genuinely liked spying. She considered herself to be an able espionage agent who proudly served the Confederacy. She would do so until the war ended. The parties at Mattie's and the trysts with Mitch were but a part of her duties. As bold and brave as any man, she galloped headlong through the night on more than one occasion, carrying cipher messages to commanders in the field. And when the rare opportunity arose, she even sneaked into rooms to eavesdrop on Union Army conferences.

Suzanna shocked friends and acquaintances — including Mattie Kirkendal and Dr. Milton Ledet — by visiting camps and calling on generals and colonels in their tents. She constantly courted danger, and on at least one occasion, Federal commanders heard that she had passed information to the Confederacy that might interfere with their well-laid battle plans. Called on the carpet and presented with the damning facts, Suzanna used her overwhelming femininity to save herself. She appeared frightened and young and apologetic, and assured them she'd meant no harm, her big blue eyes filled with remorse as she spoke in a soft, childlike voice.

It worked beautifully and she found that the Federal commanders were quite gallant, almost as chivalrous as any Southern cavalier. They let her go with a warning and reprimand.

As Suzanna carried out her assignments, she took care not to be away from her rented rooms too long at a time. She knew that any day or night Mitch might show up unexpectedly and want her to rendezvous with him. She was prepared to drop everything on a minute's notice.

To her surprise, Suzanna was afforded ample warning of his next visit. A note arrived on Friday, August 5, saying he would be in Washington late Sunday evening. Would she meet him at the cottage? Spend the night?

Suzanna read and reread the note. Her blue eyes turned wintry and her lips thinned as she said aloud, "Sure, Admiral. I'll spend the night with you, so long as you bring your musette bag."

Suzanna was waiting at the cottage on that warm August Sunday afternoon. She had considered bringing prepared food for their evening meal, but had quickly decided against it. She hatched a foolproof plan. Once Mitch arrived and they'd relaxed for a while, she would declare that she was absolutely famished. But, she would inform him, she didn't really feel like going out to dinner. Would he please go into the city and bring a picnic hamper back to the cottage?

Suzanna paced the parlor now, rubbing her hands together, planning her strategy for the night ahead. She was hopeful her plan A would work. If not, she would implement plan B. Plan A was that Mitch would leave her at the cottage and go out for food, giving her plenty of time to scan the dispatches in his musette bag. Plan B was if he refused to go without her. Then she would wait until he was sleeping soundly later tonight. She would get up, slip into the parlor and search through the dispatches.

One way or the other, she was intent on leaving here tomorrow morning with something worth passing on to the Southern generals.

Suzanna was abruptly pulled out of her reverie when she heard horses' hooves striking the ground close by.

Mitch.

She took a deep breath, swept her long hair back off her shoulders, pinched her cheeks and bit her lips. She flipped open three or four buttons of her white summer dress to ensure that he could see, resting in the hollow of her throat, the sapphire he'd given her the last time they were together. She smoothed the gathers of her full, bell-like skirts. Then, hands folded, a warm, welcoming smile on her face, she waited expectantly.

Mitch walked through the door and Suzanna felt her pulse quicken. In uniform, the eight gold stripes denoting his rank of rear admiral gleaming on the sleeves of his blue tunic, he looked handsome and weary and quintessentially masculine.

"Suzanna," he said in that rich baritone as he dropped his black leather musette bag and opened his arms wide.

"Mitch," she breathlessly replied, hurrying to him and feeling his strong arms immediately close around her.

For several seconds Mitch held Suzanna in his embrace, silent and unmoving, eyes closed, inhaling deeply of her clean, pleasing scent. Her face pressed against his tanned throat, arms around his waist, Suzanna realized, with no small degree of dismay, that she could hardly wait for him to kiss her. Stunned by the recognition, she quickly reminded herself that kissing him was all in the line of duty. She didn't actually enjoy it.

But deep down, she knew better.

Pressing her close against his tall, lean body, Mitch slid a hand up and gently clasped the back of her neck beneath her long tresses. He urged her head back, looked into her eyes for a heart-stopping instant, then bent his dark head and kissed her with a raw sexual hunger that instantly awakened her smoldering passions.

Suzanna felt her knees buckle.

When their lips separated, Mitch swept her up into his arms and carried her directly into the bedroom. Minutes later both were as bare as the day they were born, and making ardent love in the soft feather bed.

They were still there at twilight, luxuriating in the warm afterglow of lovemaking. Satiated, lazy and relaxed, Mitch groaned when Suzanna broke the comfortable silence.

"Mitch," she said, slowly running a toe up his hair-dusted leg, "I'm starving."

"Mmm. So am I."

"What are we going to do about it?"

"Get up and go out to dinner, I suppose."

"I've an even better idea." She raised her head, pushed her tumbled red hair back off her face, and smiled at him. "Let's dine here."

"Great idea save for one little problem. There's no food in the cottage."

"I know, but you could go to your estate or to the hotel and pick up something. Think what fun it would be to have a picnic right here in bed."

"You promise not to get dressed while I'm gone?"

"I promise," she said, and kissed him.

On that same hot Sunday afternoon, a strapping Scottish fellow, wearing a signature green fedora with a bright red feather in the sweatband, was in a secret meeting with a distinguished, white-haired vice admiral of the Union Navy.

The Scotsman was Allan Pinkerton, head of his own detective agency and a man who had gained instant notoriety a few years back when he'd discovered a counterfeiting camp headquarters. He had rounded up the gang in a coup that delivered the largest counterfeit ring ever caught in the United States.

Pinkerton was a lucky Scot. While he was performing a security measure for a railroad company client, he had come across a plot to have the newly elected President Lincoln assassinated before he reached Washington, D.C., to take the oath of office. The plot was uncovered while Lincoln was in Philadelphia. Pinkerton had requested and been granted an immediate meeting with Lincoln, thus saving the president elect's life.

When war broke out, Pinkerton was hired

to head up the newly formed secret service. His main duty was to spy on the South. Of late Pinkerton had begun hearing unsubstantiated rumors of an elusive, flame-haired female operative who was boldly passing cipher messages to the Southern commanders in the field.

"You have no idea who the young lady might be?" Vice Admiral Gregory C. Bond asked now as the two faced each other across the admiral's desk in the deserted Capitol building.

"I don't, sir. It's whispered she was caught once and managed to talk her way out of it." Pinkerton shook his head in disgust. "The Federal commanders let her go with a warning. Didn't even get her name."

"She must be one persuasive young woman."

"So it would seem. But she'll slip up sooner or later. They always do. When that happens, I'll be there to arrest her."

Admiral Bond nodded. "I know we can depend on you, Allan." He rose to his feet. "It'll soon be sunset. Can I buy you a drink?"

Pinkerton smiled. "Don't mind if you do."

He almost caught her.

Mitch returned to the cottage sooner than

Suzanna had expected. When she heard the drumming of hoofbeats, her heart pounded. She scrambled to gather up all the documents she had carefully spread out on the floor. Her hands shaking, she stacked the papers in the exact order in which she had found them. She shoved the bundle back inside the leather bag and placed the bag by the door where Mitch had dropped it earlier.

Suzanna raced into the bedroom, shedding his black silk robe as she went. She anxiously snatched up the nightgown she had brought with her, yanked it over her head and let it fall down her body.

When Mitch walked into the cottage, he called her name.

"In here, darling."

Mitch put down the heavy wicker basket, which was filled with delicacies and two bottles of fine wine. He walked into the bedroom and paused in the doorway. Suzanna, in a delicate, pale blue lace nightgown, was propped up in bed. Her flaming hair was fanned out on the stacked pillows and her legs were curled under her. One of the nightgown's lace straps had fallen down her arm. She was smiling seductively and toying with the sapphire suspended from the gold chain.

"I missed you," she said, and he believed her.

Mitch felt the muscles of his belly tighten. He couldn't take his eyes off her. She was a striking fair-skinned, blue-eyed beauty. But it was more, much more than that. She was a devastating mix of vulnerable innocence and underlying passion. An irresistible combination. He had never known a woman like her. Never wanted one the way he wanted her.

"I'm falling in love with you, Suzanna," he said honestly.

"Well, I should hope so, darling," she replied, getting out of bed and swaying provocatively toward him, the message in her heavily lashed blue eyes and lush, lace-covered body unmistakable.

But when Mitch took her in his arms and kissed her, all Suzanna thought of were the secret dispatches she had read in his absence.

She could hardly wait to pass on their contents.

Twenty-Seven

The information Suzanna gleaned from Mitch's dispatches proved to be invaluable to the Confederacy's navy. Intelligence she passed on to her couriers was promptly delivered to the Southern flagship, CSS *Virginia.*

The *Virginia*'s captain learned that a big Federal ironclad would be steaming into Chesapeake Bay to ambush his vessel. Forewarned, the Southern commander had the element of surprise on his side, and he was lying in wait for the enemy. The minute the frigate was spotted, the *Virginia*'s gunners concentrated their fire on the pilot-house.

A shell blinded the Union ship's commanding officer, forcing a withdrawal until he could be relieved. The advantage gained by the delay meant victory for the CSS *Virginia,* with not a single loss of life among the crewmen.

When Suzanna heard of the *Virginia*'s victory, she was proud of the small part she had played in it. She didn't spend a minute worrying that the tip she had passed on could be traced to her. Elated, she went at once to Mattie Kirkendal's to share the good news.

"Why, Suzanna, come in, come in," said Mattie. "Dr. Ledet is here and he'll be so glad to see you. You must have read our minds — we were just talking about you."

"Oh? And what were you saying?" Suzanna asked as she accompanied Mattie into the drawing room.

"My dear," said Dr. Ledet, rising to his feet. "How lovely to see you."

Suzanna smiled, came forward, gave the white-haired physician a hug and said, "Mattie tells me you two were talking about me. Should I be concerned?"

To her surprise, the doctor did not laugh or smile. Instead he looked her in the eye and said, "Yes. Perhaps you should be, child."

Suzanna blinked in confusion and glanced at Mattie.

"Sit down, Suzanna," said her friend. "May I get you something? Tea? Lemonade?"

"No, nothing. Thank you." Suzanna saw the identical expression on both their faces. Warily, she sat down on the brocade sofa, looked from one to the other and said, "Let's have it. What's bothering you two?"

Dr. Ledet looked at Mattie. Mattie waved a hand, indicating he should begin. The physician nodded, then cleared his throat. "Suzanna, while Mattie and I are proud of you and are, of course, eternally grateful for all you've done for the Cause, we're . . . Well, frankly, we're worried sick about you and we . . . that is . . ."

Mattie impatiently interrupted. "What you're doing is far too dangerous, Suzanna."

"Oh? And what exactly am I doing, Mattie?" Suzanna assumed that Mattie and the doctor had long since guessed the truth — that she was having an affair with Mitch Longley.

"You're taking too many risks," Mattie said. "You've been incredibly lucky, but you're courting disaster."

"Mattie's absolutely right, Suzanna," Dr. Ledet declared. "You've done more than your rightful share, have sacrificed enough. Why not quit before something dreadful occurs?"

Suzanna said, "I appreciate your concern, really I do, but you're both worrying needlessly. I'm a big girl. I know what I'm doing and I can take care of myself."

"We know you can," Mattie said, drawing Suzanna's attention back to her, "but . . . but . . ."

"But what?"

Mattie sighed loudly. "While Admiral Longley is obviously mad about you, he is not a stupid man, Suzanna. Sooner or later he's sure to find you out and —"

Interrupting, Suzanna said calmly, "As I recall, it was you who informed me that if I could captivate the Yankee admiral, we would 'have caught the biggest fish in the sea.' "

Mattie looked sheepish. "I did say that."

"Yes, you did. Well, I have captivated the Yankee admiral, and while Mitch wisely refuses to discuss anything having to do with the war, he trusts me enough to leave pertinent dispatches carelessly lying about." She paused, looked from one to the other and said, "I came here this afternoon to share some really good news with you. Have you heard about the CSS *Virginia* surprising a Federal ironclad at the mouth of Chesapeake Bay?"

Both nodded. The physician said, "I heard about it at my gentleman's club this afternoon and came right over to tell Mattie."

Mattie said, "I knew immediately that the intelligence you passed to our courier was responsible for the *Virginia* commander's victory." Brow wrinkled, she paused and added, "I'm so afraid Admiral Longley might suspect . . ."

"No, he doesn't. And he won't. There's no reason why he should," Suzanna said with quiet authority.

"How can you be sure?" asked Mattie, unconvinced.

Suzanna gave no reply. Shaking his head, Dr. Ledet said, "The poor unsuspecting fellow has fallen in love with you, hasn't he, Suzanna?"

"Perhaps." She shrugged her shoulders. "If so, that's his misfortune."

"Suzanna!" scolded Mattie, shocked by her indifference. "Have you no heart?"

"No," Suzanna said, her eyes as cold as ice. "I'm afraid not. And you can thank the slaughtering Yankees for its absence. So you'll both pardon me if I'm unconcerned about the state of Longley's tender heart."

For the remainder of the hot summer and on into the deepening chill of autumn, Mitch seized every opportunity to see Suzanna, if only for an hour or two at a time. And the cottage was no longer the only site of their feverish rendezvous. They spent long autumn nights at his opulent mansion, luxuriating in the comfort and privacy of his plush upstairs quarters. They seized stolen hours in a suite at his favorite hotel. They even snatched precious minutes in the back of the covered brougham when there was no time for anything more.

Mitch was so much in love with Suzanna he would have moved heaven and earth to hold her in his arms for a few breathless moments.

And she knew it.

Suzanna knew that he was in love with her, and believed that she loved him in return. She wished that it were not so, wished he didn't love her. She wished as well that he were not such a kind, caring, gentle man. Her heartless chore would be so much easier if he were less likable, less thoughtful and unfailingly considerate.

On that first evening, when he'd walked into the ballroom at Mattie's and paused in the doorway, she had sized him up and immediately supposed that he was the typical despised Yankee, arrogant and insensitive, Satan in dress blues. Handsome, cold and cruel. The epitome of everything she hated about the destructive Union military.

But it was awfully hard to hate Mitch.

Had he been on the other side, had he been a Confederate instead of a Yankee, it would have been so easy to fall in love with him. When he took her in his arms it was almost impossible to remember that he was the enemy, the man she intended to destroy. She had to constantly remind herself of that fact.

She remained determined, but twinges of guilt had begun to plague Suzanna. She was painfully aware that she was betraying not one, but two men. Her lost sweetheart, Ty, and her adversary, Mitch. The innocent Ty would have been sickened by the knowledge that she was giving herself to the enemy. And the deceived Mitch would hate her for what she was doing to him, would hate her as passionately as he now loved her.

Despite her growing regrets, Suzanna felt there was no turning back. She had come this far and would stay the course. She would continue the steamy affair with Mitch for as long as she could be useful to the Confederacy. She would not concern herself with how it all might end. If he found her out, she had no doubt he would have her thrown in prison. She had known from the start that such a dire fate might befall her.

So be it.

For now she would continue what she

considered to be a vitally important assignment — to break down Mitch's defenses and learn all she could about any upcoming Union naval operations. This was war, she frequently reminded herself, and she was on the front lines.

To Suzanna's chagrin, Mitch continued to staunchly keep his silence on anything having to do with the war or his role in it. She did everything possible to convince him that she would never disclose to another living soul anything they did together. Or anything they said to each other. Any secrets he shared were safe with her.

But Mitch was too conscientious an officer to reveal anything that might jeopardize Union troops, even to the woman he had come to love so dearly.

Still, Suzanna remained confident that in time she could break down his defenses. In an effort to have him hold nothing back from her, she held nothing back from him. She surrendered her body completely, willing and eager to please him. Certain the growing intimacy would breed total trust, she encouraged him to make love to her in any and every way he so desired. She was his for the taking, she often informed him. And she wanted, she added flirtatiously, to learn all he could teach her about the art of making love.

"You never fail to surprise and delight me, Suzanna," he would declare.

And despite the fact that he would share no pertinent information with her, Mitch was so dazzled, so blinded by passion, he never for a minute suspected Suzanna of spying. He thought nothing of dropping his musette bag on the desk or table in plain sight.

Or of leaving his beloved Suzanna in the room with the secret dispatches.

Twenty-Eight

"Darling."

"Hmm?"

"Do something to me you've never done before," Suzanna playfully challenged, knowing how Mitch loved it when she was saucy and daring and unpredictable. She laughed, then slipped her hand inside his open shirt and pressed a kiss to his throat.

It was a chill evening in late October. Moments earlier, Suzanna had hurried into the cottage on a rush of cold air. Inside, flames shot up the fireplace chimney and the large front parlor was as warm as toast.

Mitch was there waiting for her. He stood with his back to the fire, his uniform tunic tossed aside, his white shirt open down his chest and the sleeves rolled up over tanned forearms.

Suzanna had paused where she stood and, deliberately, slowly, had taken off her long cape and tossed it over the back of a chair.

They then stared at each other for a moment, neither saying a word. The only sound in the room had been that of the snapping, crackling fire in the grate.

Finally, Mitch came toward her, his movements catlike and sensual, the expression in his green eyes unmistakable. At once the warm room was suffused with subtle sexual promise, and Suzanna realized with no small degree of alarm that she wanted him as much as he wanted her. Enemy or no, he was the handsome lover of any woman's fondest fantasy, and she had experienced incredible ecstasy in his arms.

Mitch put out his hand. Suzanna took it. He slowly walked backward, drawing her with him toward the warmth of the fire. When he stopped directly in front of the fireplace, she eagerly looped her arms around his neck and lifted her lips for his kiss. It was a long, slow kiss of elemental need and intense yearning, his tongue delving deep into her mouth to taste and stroke and arouse.

When finally the drugging kiss ended, Suzanna tipped her head back and smiled dreamily at him. "Hello, admiral."

"Hi, yourself, angel. Thanks for meeting me on such short notice," Mitch replied, his hooded eyes dilated with passion.

Suzanna leaned her forehead against his firm chin. She whispered, "Let's get into bed."

"Let's don't," he said. She quickly raised her head and looked up at him in surprise. A muscle danced in his lean jaw when he added, "It's cold in the bedroom. Nice here." And he kissed her once more.

They kissed over and over again until finally, hearts thundering, breath coming fast, they sagged weakly to their knees, still continuing to eagerly and urgently embrace. Neither was fully aware of when it happened, but at some point during all the heated kisses, they fell over onto the soft fur rug and stretched out. Once their lips finally separated, they lay for a while saying nothing, the blood zinging through their veins, their bodies tense with thrumming passion.

It was Suzanna who broke the silence, by suggesting he do something to her he'd never done before. Love her in a manner he never had before. If there was such a manner.

"If there is still any way left that you haven't made love to me," she said. "Is there, darling?"

Mitch chuckled softly and drew her closer. "Yes, sweetheart. Numerous ways. Many things we've not yet done. Many physical joys await us."

"Show me," she quickly exclaimed. "Teach me, darling. I want to learn everything there is to know about making love with you. I'll do anything you want."

Mitch felt his pulse leap. "You mean it? You trust me?"

"You know I do," she assured him, her hand inside his white shirt, exploring the firm muscles of his chest, her mind already racing. What, she wondered, might he do to her that he hadn't done before? Would she like it? Would she hate it? Would it shock her? "I trust you totally," she purred.

"You have nothing to be afraid of with me, Suzanna," he said, his voice low, soothing. "Not ever. You know that, don't you?"

"I know," she managed to say, thinking that it was just the opposite. He had every reason to be afraid of her. "Yes, I know."

Mitch slowly rose up onto an elbow and looked down at her. Suzanna gazed into his luminous green eyes and knew, in that instant, that she actually was willing to love and be loved by him in any way he might desire.

"I want," he said, sliding a hand up from her waist to her breasts, "to make love to you here in front of the fire."

"Is that all?" she said with a teasing smile,

and made a move to sit up.

"No, not quite," he replied, pressing her back down. "You're to lie there and allow me to undress you. You're not to lift a hand to help."

"A capital idea," she said. "I can think of nothing I'd enjoy more."

And it was true.

Suzanna found the unique ritual of having him disrobe her as if she were a helpless child to be exquisitely exciting. He was quite adept at removing each and every article of her clothing, but he took his own sweet time. And he paused to kiss each new expanse of pale soft flesh he bared.

A good half hour had pleasantly passed before Suzanna was finally naked, save for the sapphire necklace she always wore when she was with him. She lay stretched out on the soft fur, totally at ease with her nudity, perfectly comfortable with allowing him to examine her unclothed body.

Mitch sat back and admired his handiwork.

The leaping flames tinted Suzanna's pale porcelain skin a honeyed peach hue, while her unbound hair and the matching triangle between her thighs blazed like the fire in the grate. His heated gaze moved slowly over her, appraising her, adoring her.

When finally he lifted his eyes to her face, he said, "God, you are exquisite. A rare work of art. Far too perfect to be real." He leaned down and kissed her parted lips.

"I'm real, Mitch," she said against his mouth. "Flesh and blood, just like you."

"Thank God."

Suzanna raised her hand and slipped it back inside his open shirt. "Why don't you get undressed now."

He gave no reply, but kissed her again. During the kiss she felt his thumb rub back and forth across her left nipple, and she squirmed with pleasure. Her shoulders sank more fully into the soft rug, while her hips lifted slightly. She finally tore her kiss-swollen lips from Mitch's and looked into his hooded eyes. She saw raw passion glowing in their depths and shivered.

"Your clothes," she again prompted.

"No, sweetheart," he said softly. "Not just yet. Let me cherish you for a while. Let me love you with my mouth. You're so sweet, so clean, I want to smell you and taste you and show you a new kind of loving."

Before she could reply, he pressed his lips into the curve of her neck and shoulder. Then he slowly, carefully, trailed butterfly kisses out over her shoulder and down her slender left arm. When he reached her hand, he turned it over, kissed her warm palm, then gently urged her arm up over her head. She swallowed with difficulty when his heated lips kissed a path from her elbow to her underarm.

Suzanna drew a quick breath of shocked surprise when she felt the lick of his tongue against the prickly flesh of her underarm. Her face afire, she closed her eyes tightly, then tingled and trembled as his mouth moved down her ribs to her waist.

Her eyes opened when he gently eased her onto her stomach.

"Relax now, my love," Mitch murmured, admiring her golden-skinned, long-limbed body stretched out on the dark sable fur like a glowing sacrifice to the gods of love. "Lie still while I adore you," he whispered, and Suzanna did everything but. She squirmed and sighed and clutched at the downy softness of the rug while Mitch's lips spread fire along the tops of her shoulders.

His strong brown hands leisurely caressed her bare bottom while he trailed the gentlest of kisses over her delicate shoulder blades and down her slender back. And as he brushed kiss after kiss to her sensitive skin, he spoke to her of love in a low, rich baritone that both soothed and disarmed and excited.

Supine, cheek pressed to the rug, taut nipples rubbing against the softness of the fur, Suzanna tried very hard to keep still, but it was impossible. It was one of those moments — which there were more and more of lately — when she forgot that her lover was also her enemy. How could she be expected to remember when his marvelous mouth was pleasuring her so completely? And when he was saying all those things every woman longs to hear?

"Suzanna, you're the only woman I have ever loved, will ever love," Mitch told her truthfully. His lean fingers stroked her pale buttocks and cupped the rounded cheeks. His mouth moved down to the twin dimples at the base of her spine and teased them with his tongue. Suzanna purred and arched her back, giving herself up to the elation of the moment.

She couldn't keep from whispering his name when his burning lips moved slowly down her trembling thighs. He nibbled playfully at the backs of her knees, kissed her shapely calves, her slender ankles and ticklish toes. It was all she could do to keep from swooning.

And then he turned her over.

The kisses he had sprinkled over her backside had been thrilling, but nothing compared with the heated caresses he now pressed to the tight-nippled, passion-heavy breasts that were rapidly rising and falling with Suzanna's shallow breaths.

His raven hair ruffling against her chin, his mouth captured an aching nipple as his hand stroked her flat belly. While she gazed down at his dark, handsome head, Mitch continued to pay slow, sensual homage to her bare, tingling body, sending shivers of sensation through her until she felt weak and dazed and unaware of her surroundings.

When his burning lips spread moist fire along the trembling flesh of her thighs, and his teeth gently sank into the warm skin inside, Suzanna gasped and thrust her hands into his lustrous hair.

"Mitch, no . . . no . . ." she breathlessly protested.

He didn't listen.

Didn't raise his head.

He continued to kiss and excite her, and by the time he was lying between her open legs, his hot face hovering just above the flaming red curls of her groin, Suzanna was too weak with wanting to offer any further protests. Her pelvis involuntarily lifting from the rug, she closed her eyes, flung her arm across her face and bit the back of her hand when she felt his tongue part the curls.

Mitch raised his head. "Open your eyes, Suzanna."

"I can't."

"Yes, you can. Open your eyes, sweetheart. Look at me."

Her face aflame with embarrassment, Suzanna reluctantly obeyed. And her face grew even hotter. His dark hands urging her legs wider apart, Mitch was gazing into her eyes as if she were the most precious thing in the world to him.

He said huskily, "I'd never hurt you, never. Let me, baby. Let me make you mine, all mine."

"I . . . yes, oh yes," she panted.

"Relax your body completely and I'll give you a kind of pleasure you'll never forget."

"But I . . ." Suzanna's words trailed away as Mitch bent back to her.

She gasped aloud when he kissed her in that most secret of spots where all her passion was now centered. His mouth was closed, but his lips were scalding hot, and she had never felt such a splendid sensation before. She involuntarily tensed, sure that she shouldn't like it.

"Mitch, Mitch." She whispered his name as his mouth opened on her and he touched his tongue to that throbbing button of sleek female flesh. "No, no . . ." She offered a halfhearted objection and frantically clutched at the fur beneath her.

Mitch never raised his head. With his eyes closed, his hands beneath her bare bottom lifting her, he set her on fire with his tongue, teasing, circling, licking until she was literally sobbing his name in a frenzy. On the verge of sexual hysteria, she rolled her shoulders off the rug and sat up, grabbing at the hair of his head, begging him to never, ever stop!

And then an unbelievable explosion of blazing ecstasy so overwhelmed her that she screamed and frantically pushed him away. Jerking uncontrollably, she sank back down onto the rug as though she were a rag doll.

Mitch quickly moved up beside her, gathered her into his arms and held her close, calming her, crooning to her, telling her how much he loved her. Trembling, she clung to him, burying her face against his chest and saying his name over and over.

"Tell me you love me, Suzanna. Just once, say it. Say you love me."

"I love you," she whispered, and wondered if it could possibly be true.

The next time Suzanna saw Mitch was the last time.

It was that snowy November afternoon she'd gone through his musette bag while he was taking a bath. She had learned of the upcoming strike, which was sure to catch the Rebels off guard and cost lives.

When Mitch had left her at the cottage, he'd had no idea that he would never see her again.

But she knew.

In his full dress blues, he had come to her and gently cupped the back of her head.

Looking at her with all his love in his eyes, he had said softly, "I'm not sure when I'll be able to get away again."

"Kiss me as if this were the last time," she replied.

He crouched down on his heels, kissed her and said, "I love you, darling."

"Please be careful," she'd murmured in reply.

Mitch had barely exited the cottage before Suzanna jumped up, took a sheet of vellum paper from the desk in the corner and wrote down everything she had read in the damning dispatch.

She then dressed and trudged through the deepening snow to reach the landmark — a carefully chosen leaning rock near her rented rooms — beneath which she consistently hid messages laying out information she had gleaned from her unsuspecting enemy lover.

But this particular message was different. Unlike the other dispatches she had memorized and passed on to her operatives, this one directly involved Mitch. He was to be in command of a Federal ram that would lead a surprise attack on the unsuspecting Confederates.

Once she passed on the contents of the dispatch, he would be steaming headlong into a death trap. He was sure to guess the truth about her, if he lived through the battle. She would be responsible for endangering his life. She might even be responsible for his death.

Her heart squeezed painfully in her chest. She felt suddenly dizzy and her cheeks were hot despite the cold of the snowy November afternoon.

She closed her eyes and strongly considered tearing up the note. She opened her eyes. She drew a labored breath, hardened her heart and dutifully placed the message beneath the cold stone.

Part Two

Twenty-Nine

The deed done, Suzanna turned away.

Heart aching now, she hurried through blinding snow, unmindful of the biting winds stinging her cheeks and slicing through her billowing cape. The chill of the storm could not compare to the coldness gripping her heart.

Early this morning she had awakened with a start, as one of those horrific psychic sensations had come over her. The strong premonition of impending danger. The kind of frightening feeling she'd not experienced since that terrible day she'd learned that Ty and Matthew had both died in the war.

Now it was happening again.

She had known this morning, well before he had summoned her to the cottage, that Mitch would arrive back in Washington and send for her. And that their rendezvous would be different from all the others. It would be their last.

It was almost like a prophecy. And so it had been with an added sense of foreboding that, summoned just as expected, Suzanna had hurried to meet him. She had carefully hidden her anxiety from him, but she knew when she found the dispatch that her eerie fears had been confirmed.

Their time together was all gone.

She was certain that after today, she would not see Rear Admiral Mitchell B. Longley again this side of paradise.

Suzanna felt tears stinging her eyes, but blinked them back and pressed on. She was sad and depressed and wanted nothing more than to go straight home and pull the covers up over her head. But she couldn't do that.

She had assured her increasingly unhappy landlady that she would pay the overdue rent she owed on her set of rooms before nightfall today. When she'd made the promise, she'd had no idea how she could keep it.

Now she knew.

Suzanna walked three long miles through the blinding snow until she reached the glass-fronted windows of one of Georgetown's finest jewelers. She hurried inside, setting the bell to ringing over the entrance.

From a curtained door at the back of the

store, a thin, bald man in a finely tailored frock coat appeared. "Yes, miss, may I help you?"

"I certainly hope so," said Suzanna as she unhooked the braided frogs holding her snow-dampened cape together.

She reached up behind her head and undid the clasp of the gold chain supporting the sapphire. For several weeks she had considered selling the necklace for much-needed cash, but hadn't dared. Mitch would surely have been suspicious had she shown up not wearing it. Since the day he had given the gem to her, she had always worn it in his presence. Now she no longer need worry that he might wonder what had happened to the necklace.

Suzanna took off the jewel, laid it atop the counter and asked, "How much will you give me for this?"

Ten minutes later she left the jeweler's without the necklace, but with several bills in the pocket of her cape. Suzanna hated that she'd had to sell the sapphire, but she'd had no choice. She had no money. None. There was nothing left of the small sum she had realized from the sale of Whitehall. Most of what the mansion had brought had gone to pay the back taxes. The purchaser had refused to close the deal until she agreed to clear that debt.

With the sale of the sapphire, Suzanna reasoned that she could survive for another month or two. After that, the future was uncertain. No matter. She didn't much care what happened to her. The good-hearted Mattie had repeatedly invited her to move into the roomy Kirkendal mansion, but Suzanna was too proud. She was a LeGrande, one of the blue-blooded LeGrandes of Virginia, and she did not accept charity.

Suzanna suddenly smiled ruefully and shook her head at her misplaced pride. She refused to be a beggar, but she'd had no qualms about becoming a whore.

On the day of the planned attack, Suzanna awakened before sunup and waited in her rented rooms until dawn, walking the floor and worrying. Had she done the right thing? Would Mitch be injured in the ambush? Even killed?

The thought made her physically ill. Nonetheless, she continued denying to herself that she had foolishly fallen in love with the enemy. It couldn't be true. She didn't love Mitch Longley. She just hated the thought of her actions being responsible for anyone's death.

Still, a great rush of emotion swept over

her and Suzanna wept bitterly. She wished more than anything in the world that she could take it back. Undo what she had done. Already she regretted her actions. She was sorry she had deceived Mitch, remorseful that she had put his life in jeopardy.

Maybe she did love him. Dear Lord, she had fallen in love with the handsome Yankee admiral she had coldly betrayed.

"Mitch," she sobbed, her heart breaking. "Forgive me."

It happened just as planned.

At straight-up noon on that cold December day a Federal ram steamed around a bend in the muddy Rapidan River. Rear Admiral Mitchell B. Longley, in command of the vessel, stood on the hurricane deck.

From a safe distance away in an abandoned building high up on the bluffs overlooking the winding waterway, a heartsick Suzanna watched through a field glass trained on her unsuspecting lover. Suzanna had hired a fleet-footed mount from a livery stable and had ridden the nine long miles to this well-concealed location to observe Mitch's date with destiny.

A destiny for which she alone was responsible.

Along the riverbanks, hidden in the tall

grass, Confederate soldiers waited to spring the trap. Her heart beating in her ears, her eyes clinging to Mitch as he stood with his back erect and feet braced apart, Suzanna waited what seemed an eternity for the battle to begin.

The ram moved closer and closer, unaware of what was about to happen.

At last a Confederate army captain raised a hand in the air. And brought it down.

Suzanna jumped as the firing began. A barrage of minié balls rained down on the slow-moving ram in a bloody firefight that ended almost as soon as it had begun. When it was over Union sailors lay dead on the deck of the ambushed ram.

Her eyes never leaving him, Suzanna winced when Rear Admiral Mitch Longley was struck by Rebel fire. She felt the pain slam through her chest as if she herself had been hit. As Mitch clutched his bleeding left side and began to go down, he clearly formed her name on his lips.

"Suzanna," he said, his eyes narrowing with hatred. "Damn you, you treasonous bitch!"

He knew! Mitch realized that she was responsible for the ambush. He knew that she had betrayed him. While she clutched the field glass, blinked away tears and attempted to swallow the lump in her throat, Suzanna watched as Mitch cursed her. And himself for leading his men into an ambush.

Now that it was too late, the truth became crystal clear to Mitch. The Rebels had had advance warning. And he knew there was only one way they could have gotten it. Suzanna. The beautiful, red-haired woman he loved more than life itself was a conniving Confederate spy who had played him for a fool. She had allowed him to make love to her in order to learn military secrets with which to bring him down.

God, how could he have been so blind?

It was she; it had to be. She had read the secret dispatches he had unwisely left unguarded, and had alerted the Confederates. Mitch gritted his teeth against the searing pain in his side. He was rapidly losing blood. The hand pressing the wound was wet and scarlet with it. He could feel the dense blackness beginning to envelop him.

His last conscious thought was he hoped that he lived long enough to admit he had been duped by a clever Confederate sympathizer. He could hardly wait to confess to his misplaced trust and tell of Suzanna's callous deception.

He should be court-martialed and hanged

for his unforgivable stupidity.

And she *would* be hanged for her crime against the Union!

Thirty

Mitch struggled to open his eyes. After several failed attempts, he finally managed it. Squinting, he looked straight up. And was surprised to see not a bleak gray winter sky overhead, but a high, white-painted ceiling.

Slowly, he turned his head and saw row upon row of beds. Beds that were filled with wounded, moaning men. He was in a hospital of sorts, though how and when he got here he could not recall.

Mitch tried to sit up, but faltered. The sudden movement caused him to wince in pain, and perspiration quickly dotted his upper lip and forehead. His head fell back to the pillow and he closed his eyes once more, his wounded side hurting so badly he could hardly breathe.

Still, physical suffering did not stop the flood of remembrance and regret that washed over him as it did each time he regained consciousness. He, a seasoned Union officer, had made an unforgivable blunder, and his lack of judgment had cost precious lives. He had led his trusting crew into a deadly Confederate trap, a trap that had been set for him by Suzanna LeGrande.

Looking back now, he found it easy to see that he had been marked from that first warm May night when he'd walked into Mattie Kirkendal's mansion and spotted a beautiful, flame-haired temptress across the crowded ballroom. The irresistible Suzanna had, no doubt, been the capable young lady designated to charm, captivate and seduce him. How she must have laughed and bragged to her Rebel friends about the ease with which she had led the Yankee swine to slaughter.

Gritting his teeth against the pain — both physical and mental — Mitch recalled with vivid clarity all those occasions when she had buttered him up and begged him to share news of fleet movements and upcoming battles and war room tactics.

He had never told her anything, but he had, on more than one occasion, carelessly left his musette bag — filled with dispatches and maps — within her reach. On their last afternoon at the cottage, that bag had contained the secret dispatch laying out the strategy wherein he would steam up the Rapidan, surprise a large number of unsuspecting Rebs amassing near a Confederate supply depot, and take out as many of the enemy as possible.

But the Rebs had been tipped off.

Leaving the supply depot deserted, they had dug carefully concealed ramparts along both sides of the river and had waited for the ram to steam into sight. As easy as shooting fish in a barrel.

"Yes, I believe he's awake." Mitch heard the soft voice of a woman.

He opened his eyes and saw a white-uniformed nurse coming toward the bed. Behind her were a couple of naval officers, a lieutenant commander and a vice admiral.

"Admiral Longley," the men said in unison, nodding to him. Mitch acknowledged them by attempting to sit up.

"No, no, Admiral Longley," the nurse gently scolded, placing a restraining hand on his shoulder. "You're to be very still or else I will not allow your visitors to stay."

The rotund, white-haired senior officer said to the nurse, "Give us a few minutes of privacy, miss."

She pursed her lips. "Five minutes, gentlemen. The patient is quite ill. He needs rest." And she hurried away.

Vice Admiral Gregory C. Bond looked down at the badly wounded man whose ashen face was etched with pain. While Lieutenant Commander James Brackett stood at ease with his hands clasped behind his back, Admiral Bond pulled up a straight-backed chair and sat down.

"Ready to tell me how this could have happened, Admiral Longley?" said Admiral Bond.

Mitch nodded. Oh, was he. He could hardly wait to reveal the identity of the conniving Southern bitch who had lain in his arms for the sole purpose of betraying him. Exposing her and knowing that she would get her just reward was what had kept him alive. It was the only reason he had wanted to live after the ambush. From the minute he'd felt the minié ball shatter his left side, he had been determined to live long enough to make Suzanna LeGrande pay.

Now, finally, the time had come.

His pain-dulled eyes cold, Mitch opened his mouth to speak. And found that he couldn't do it. He couldn't hand Suzanna over to the authorities, knowing she would go to prison, might even be hanged for spying against the Union. The chilling prospect of his beautiful flame-haired lover being executed made his heart squeeze painfully in his chest. No matter what she had done to him, he could not endanger her life.

Speaking slowly and distinctly, Mitch addressed his superior officer. "Admiral Bond, this tragedy is my fault and mine alone, and I accept full responsibility. I was foolish beyond pardon, and because I was, lives have been lost." Mitch drew a labored breath and stated, "I was in D.C. on a snowy afternoon in late November. After a war room meeting was completed I had two or three hours to kill before returning to my post. I spent that time with a woman. We shared a few drinks and had impersonal sex, after which I fell asleep. Apparently, the woman went through my musette bag and read the dispatches. Either she sympathizes with the Confederacy or else she sold the information for money."

For a time, the old admiral didn't speak. He simply stared at Mitch in disbelief, his anger rapidly rising. "The young lady, she was a prostitute?" the stern-faced officer finally asked.

"Yes," Mitch answered truthfully, bitterly. "The woman is most definitely a whore."

"And this . . . ah . . . woman? Does she have a name?"

"I'm sure she does," he said, adding the lie, "but I don't know what it is."

The vice admiral frowned and rubbed his chin. "Let me get this straight. You took pertinent military documents along with you to visit a common prostitute? Is that what you're saying, Longley?"

"Yes, sir," Mitch replied without hesitation, knowing but not caring that he could be severely punished for his lack of judgment. "That's exactly what I'm saying, Admiral."

"Why, you irresponsible son of a bitch!" Admiral Bond's face grew scarlet as he raged, "I ought to kill you with my bare hands! You put your entire crew in harm's way for a drunken roll in the hay with some cheap whore! By God, I'll have you court-martialed for this if it's the last thing I do!"

"I would expect nothing less, sir," Mitch said calmly.

The older officer exhaled heavily with anger and disgust. Fighting to regain control, he crossed his arms over his chest and drew several ragged breaths. "You're not fit to serve in the United States Navy, Longley!"

"I'm aware of that, sir," Mitch stated evenly.

After a pause, Bond said, "You love the navy, do you, Admiral Longley?"

"I do, sir. It's my chosen career, the only

thing I've ever wanted to do. I've been in the United States Navy since graduating from Annapolis when I was twenty-one years old."

The older officer, a basically softhearted man, couldn't help but be touched. He knew what it was like to love the military; he had spent his entire adult life in uniform. Markedly tempering his tone, he said, "Two things will save you from a court-martial, Longley. In the first place, you're badly wounded. I'm not sure you could hold up to a military trial. In the second place, and more importantly, your career up until this tragic mistake has been without blemish. I have gone over the records with a fine-tooth comb and have learned that you've been an able crewman, a model officer, a credit to your country. I'll save you from a court-martial, Longley." Hesmiled weakly, then added, "We all make mistakes. Unfortunately, yours was a costly one."

"Unforgivable," said Mitch, trying hard not to groan or squirm as the pain in his wounded side grew almost unbearable.

"I'm sorry, Admiral. You'll have to go now." It was the concerned nurse, hurriedly approaching the bed as if she had sensed Mitch's misery.

"Yes, yes, all right," said Admiral Bond,

getting to his feet. He looked at Mitch and told him, "You must be punished."

Mitch nodded in understanding.

The older man continued. "I'm having you cashiered out of the navy, effective immediately." He patted Mitch's shoulder and added, "Sorry, my boy."

Then he turned on his heel and left, with Lieutenant Commander James Brackett trailing after him.

Thirty-One

Allan Pinkerton was like a dog with a bone.

He would bury the scant information he had gathered on a suspected red-haired Southern female spy, then he'd dig it up again and sink his teeth into it. Anytime he had a few spare minutes, he took out the slim dossier on the mysterious agent and carefully studied it.

Pinkerton was frustrated. And intrigued. And determined. Though he had resigned as head of the government's secret service agency, he remained committed to catching the daring female operative, whom the Union commanders had once even apprehended, only to let go without so much as recording her name. Since then there had been only unsubstantiated sightings of the elusive spy Pinkerton had dubbed Blaze.

In an all-out effort to bring her in, Pinkerton had quietly begun sending out any agent he could spare to gather information on a handful of young red-haired woman in the D.C. area who might fit the bill. So adept were his deputies at trailing suspects, the women never knew they were being followed.

Including Suzanna LeGrande.

She never for a minute suspected that the noted detective had found out who she was and strongly suspected her. She had no idea that often when she left her rented rooms, someone was watching — and had been watching that fateful snowy November afternoon.

Allan Pinkerton had learned that the woman he'd been calling Blaze was Miss Suzanna LeGrande, a native Virginian and a striking young beauty who fit the description of the enchantress the Union commanders had caught and released. It was reported to Pinkerton that Miss LeGrande had secretly met with Rear Admiral Mitchell B. Longley at a secluded cottage in the city.

Pinkerton didn't know that the detective who had tracked Suzanna to the cottage had deserted his post while the lovers were ensconced inside. Had the detective remained staked out as he was supposed to, he would have seen Admiral Longley leave, and shortly thereafter, Suzanna trek through the woods to deposit a message under the leaning rock for her courier to collect. Had the detective followed orders issued by Pinkerton, he could have retrieved the missive, captured its author and thwarted the bloody Rapidan River ambush.

But it had been snowing heavily that afternoon and the man was freezing and coming down with a cold. Supposing it made little difference if he left, he had returned to his quarters, never knowing of the missive.

Now, less than thirty-six hours after the deadly ambush, Allan Pinkerton was again questioning the careless detective. And getting nowhere.

"You're absolutely positive that Miss LeGrande did not make a drop somewhere that afternoon, that she didn't rendezvous with a courier after leaving Admiral Longley?" Pinkerton plucked his green fedora off his head, slapped it down on his knee and toyed with its decorative red feather while he talked to his agent. "You saw her leave and followed her home?"

"Ah, yes, I . . . she . . . they . . ." The agent swallowed with difficulty. He knew that when Pinkerton took off his fedora and started twisting that red feather he was angry.

"Don't you lie to me, Detective Brodie!" Pinkerton said, his eyes narrowed.

Sam Brodie knew the jig was up. "I was sick that day, Allan. Really sick. I stayed for more than an hour and . . ."

"And left before either the admiral or Miss LeGrande did?"

"Yes," Brodie shamefully admitted.

"I knew it," said Pinkerton, and slammed his fedora back on his head. "Your one chance to do your job well, make a name for yourself, and you desert your post because of a runny nose."

"I deserve to be dismissed, sir," said Brodie, hanging his head.

"You most certainly do, but I'm too shorthanded to let you go." Pinkerton came to his feet and said, "Despite your bungling, I'll see to it that Miss LeGrande is locked up by sunset today."

Brodie looked up. "You will?"

"I will. I'll finesse the young lady into making a full confession."

"But how?"

"By making her believe that you actually were doing your job." Pinkerton stood up then and exhaled loudly. "Better let Lafe Baker in on this. He'll swear to Stanton he's responsible for catching her. He'll grab all the glory." Pinkerton made a face. "He'll want to take her in himself. You know what an egotistical ass Baker is."

Suzanna had waited. And waited.

Each time she heard horses' hooves nearing her rented rooms, she tensed, expecting a loud knock on the door.

She hadn't slept, had hardly eaten. She had walked the floor and intermittently wept, wondering miserably if Mitch was alive or dead. Had he died there on the deck of his vessel? Or was he in a field hospital somewhere in the city, suffering intolerable pain?

Arms crossed over her chest, eyes puffy from crying, Suzanna was pacing restlessly when the drumming of hooves snapped her out of the painful reveries.

This time the horses did not go on past. They stopped. And so did Suzanna's heart.

A resounding rap on the door set her pulse racing. Suzanna drew a breath and opened the door. She was not surprised to see two Union provost officers standing on the porch. As instructed, neither spoke, just looked at her accusingly, as if they knew of her guilt.

It worked beautifully.

Suzanna didn't doubt for a minute that the officers knew everything. Mitch had told them. He had turned her in to the authorities for spying.

Since there was no longer any need for pretense, she looked from one to the other and asked anxiously, just as Pinkerton had predicted, "Is he alive? Admiral Longley — did he make it?"

The two officers looked at each other knowingly. Then one spoke. "We know everything you've done, Miss LeGrande. You will stand trial for treason, and when convicted, you will be hanged."

Suzanna accepted the news with little emotion. She had but one question of her captors, which she repeated now. "Did Admiral Longley survive the battle?"

Neither officer replied and Suzanna suspected the worst. She was brokenhearted. Mitch was dead and she was responsible!

"You're under arrest," said the taller of the two officers.

"I understand," she said, "but won't you tell me if —"

"We'll do all the questioning, Miss LeGrande," said the officer. "Now step aside and let us in."

Suzanna did as she was told. She watched in silence as the pair ransacked her rooms, turning everything upside down in a search for maps and documents. They found nothing. But they were not deterred.

"Get a wrap, Miss LeGrande, it's time to go."

Suzanna looked up in surprise when she saw people gathering on the street, pointing and whispering. A carriage waited at the end of the front walk. As she neared it, a husky man in a finely tailored suit stepped down, took her arm and said to the two officers, "I'll take over now." He turned his full attention on Suzanna, and in a voice markedly gruff, introduced himself.

"Miss LeGrande, I'm Lafayette Baker, chief of the Intelligence Service for the United States government."

Suzanna gave no reply. For months she had been hearing of the infamous Union espionage leader, chief of the War Department detectives. It was said that Captain Lafayette Baker was the personal bullyboy of Secretary of War Edwin M. Stanton. He had shadowed, apprehended, interrogated and imprisoned a multitude of Washingtonians — many on the merest suspicion of disloyalty.

A sadistic, ruthless, cunning man, he seemed to take pleasure in roughly shoving her up into the carriage. And even greater pleasure in saying to the driver, "The Old

Capitol."

Suzanna felt her blood run cold. She had heard so much about that forbidding place, the aging prison that had housed Mrs. Greenhow and countless other Southern agents and sympathizers. She could well imagine what was in store for her.

The ride to the Old Capitol seemed endless. The cold, dreary weather matched Suzanna's sad mood. The sky was gray, the tree limbs bare. And everywhere, the city was filled with signs of war. Blue-clad soldiers slouched along the streets, rusting supplies sat outside warehouses and the unfinished Capitol dome rose against the pewter sky.

Her heart breaking, Suzanna found it almost impossible to recall the carefree days before the war. It seemed that the terrible conflict had been going on forever, would never end.

Beside her, Lafe Baker was speaking, bragging how he was responsible for exposing her, but Suzanna had no idea what he was saying. She wasn't listening.

Soon she looked up and saw the Old Capitol at First and A Streets. She'd seen the outside of the prison many times before. But now the tall red building, a series of connected structures rambling in several directions, looked more ominous. Staring at it, Suzanna wondered if she would end her days inside the historic old building that had housed Congress after the British burned Washington.

Suzanna gazed at the once-handsome arched entranceway and at a line of barred windows. She winced at seeing the hands of desperate inmates clenching those bars.

"Shall we, Miss LeGrande?" Lafe Baker asked sarcastically as the carriage rolled to a stop before the prison.

"Why, I'd love to, Captain Baker." She was equally caustic with her reply.

The captain's florid face flushed hotly and he said, "You'll be taken down to size after a few weeks in prison, Miss LeGrande." He then stepped down and directed her to a flight of stairs.

Inside, a heavyset man met them. "Superintendent Wood," he said, introducing himself, and Suzanna nodded. He grinned. "Welcome to our humble abode, Miss LeGrande. I trust you'll be comfortable here."

Suzanna gave no reply.

"Right this way," the superintendent said, and she followed him down a short passageway and up a staircase to a dark hall.

Suzanna recoiled at the stench of unwashed flesh. She heard the superintendent say, "It gets a bit fetid in here, I'm afraid. This building was not meant to be a prison, and there have never been so many people packed in at once. But you'll get used to it."

The place was gigantic, yet overflowing with prisoners crowded together in the crumbling brick rooms, with their cracked walls and splintered floors. There was squalor everywhere. Piles of filthy clothes and spoiled food lay strewn about. Trash and debris were scattered across the rotting wooden floors. Spiderwebs filled the corners and sagged from the ceilings.

The noise was as bad as the smell. From every direction came shouts, pounding and weeping, and loud raucous laughter from the guards. Following the superintendent, Suzanna walked into a second section of the prison, entering a dark, silent, narrow hallway. Finally he stopped and pointed to the right.

"This is number 4, your luxury accommodations, miss," he said with a smile. He turned and walked away.

Suzanna drew a ragged breath and stared into the tiny cell, with its one barred window, scarred iron bed and wooden table. An armed sentry motioned her inside. She went in, but whirled around when she heard the door clang shut.

The sentry passed her a sheet of paper through the bars. "Rules and Regulations," she read. And the first sentence: "No communication whatsoever with other prisoners." It became clear why there were no cries or shouts or laughter in this wing of the prison.

In deep despair, Suzanna sank down onto the thin mattress, wondering how long she could keep her sanity in the isolation of this dark, dirty cell.

Thirty-Two

News of Suzanna's arrest spread quickly across the fortified city of Washington. The Union officers with whom she had flirted and danced were outraged. Friends and acquaintances were shocked. None had suspected the lively young beauty of being a traitor.

Dr. Ledet heard about it the day it happened. Shortly after noon he called on a prominent, elderly patient who was under the weather. The eighty-year-old Alfred Thornbury was a man whose loyalties lay firmly with the Union. He supposed his trusted physician's did as well.

Dr. Ledet had hardly put his black bag down and taken off his heavy greatcoat before Thornbury, lying in his big feather bed, slapped the mattress, laughed heartily and said, "By the saints above us, they caught the snoop responsible for the Rapidan River ambush! Did you hear about it, Doc?"

Dr. Ledet felt as though one of his scalpels had been thrust into his chest. He struggled to keep his tone even when he said, "No. I wasn't aware that a snoop was responsible for the tragedy." He turned away, gritted his teeth, reached into his bag and took out his stethoscope.

"Well, of course it was the work of a spy, Doctor." The old man's eyes twinkled despite his illness. "You might know, it was a wily woman who did in the commanding officer of that Federal ram. The sneaky Rebs were lying in wait for the poor fellow."

Dr. Ledet felt faint and overly warm. Still, he displayed no emotion when he said, "A woman? Do they know who?"

"Damn right they know who she is! Suzanna LeGrande is the young lady's name. One of those haughty Virginia LeGrandes, I presume." The old man laughed again and confided, "She's already been arrested and thrown into Old Capitol prison."

"Have they any proof that this . . . ah . . . Miss LeGrande actually is a spy?"

"She confessed, is how I hear it! Admitted to the whole thing." Warming to his subject, the patient struggled to sit up. "Seems the saucy Southern miss easily seduced Rear

Admiral Mitchell Longley. I suppose the besotted officer — who should have known better — shared military secrets with her. The damned fool!"

Once the physician left his talkative patient, he went directly to Mattie Kirkendal's mansion. Mattie was smiling warmly when she came downstairs to join him in the drawing room.

"Ah, Doctor, to what do I owe this cold winter afternoon's unexpected visit?" Her smile immediately slipped when she saw the expression on Ledet's face. She lifted her voluminous woolen skirts and hurried to him. "Milton, what is it? What has happened?"

"Suzanna. They've found her out! She's been arrested and thrown into prison!"

"Oh, dear Lord," exclaimed a horrified Mattie. The doctor caught her when she tottered on her feet. He helped her to a sofa, where she dropped down onto the soft cushions. Ledet immediately took a seat beside her. Tears filling her eyes, Mattie sobbed, "It's all my fault. I should never have allowed her to . . ."

"My dear, no one could have stopped her. Suzanna is a headstrong young woman and . . . and . . ." He stopped speaking, exhaled heavily and admitted, "The blame belongs to me. It was I who sent Suzanna to you when she expressed a desire to aid the Confederacy. I should have known better. I should have foreseen the danger. My God, I should have supposed that something like this was bound to happen."

Mattie dabbed at her eyes with a lace-trimmed handkerchief, patted her old friend's hand and said, "We're equally responsible, Milton. What's done is done. Now we must right the wrong we've done poor little Suzanna. What can we do to get her out of prison? I've money. Perhaps we can bribe a guard to set her free. Once she's out of jail, we could get her out of the city. Out of the country if necessary."

Nodding, he said, "As soon as I leave here, I'll go straight to the Old Capitol and visit her."

"I'll go with you."

"No, Mattie. That hellhole is no place for a lady."

Mattie again teared up and said, "Suzanna is a lady and she's locked up in that hell-hole."

The doctor put a comforting arm around Mattie's stout shoulders. "We'll get her out. Somehow. Some way."

"How do they know she's a spy?"

"Alf Thornbury, one of my patients with war office connections, swears she confessed."

Mattie looked her old friend straight in the eye and asked, "What might they do to her, Milton? I mean besides keeping her imprisoned."

The doctor did not reply, just shook his head sadly.

Mattie understood, and declared, "You must waste no more time. Go to the Old Capitol and help that child. Then come straight back here and report to me."

Shortly after four o'clock that same afternoon a distraught Dr. Ledet returned to Mattie Kirkendal's with more bad news. He had not been allowed to see Suzanna, even when he informed the superintendent that he was a physician whose only interest was in the young lady's physical condition. No one, he was told, could visit the prisoner. Nor would the superintendent even agree to tell her she'd had a visitor.

"She'll wonder why we didn't come to her aid. She'll believe that we have deserted her," he worriedly told Mattie as she wrung her hands.

"We'll write to her, tell her in a letter that I'll summon my attorney to begin work on her behalf. We'll let her know that we're doing everything we can to get her freed." She hurried toward the inlaid writing desk in the corner.

"No, my dear. It would do no good. I was informed that the prisoner is in isolation and that she is not allowed to speak to anyone, not even the other prisoners. Nor is she allowed to receive mail or messages."

"But, Milton, we must . . ."

"Mattie, we must be very careful now. Your name cannot become linked to Suzanna's or you will become a suspect. And then we can do nothing to help her."

"What day is it?"

"Tuesday, Admiral Longley."

"What month is it?"

The nurse patted Mitch's thin shoulder through the covering sheet. "It's early February, sir." She smiled then and told him, "You have a visitor. Your aunt's here again."

Edna Earl Longley hadn't missed a single day of visiting her badly wounded nephew in the two months that he had been in the hospital. When she learned that Mitch had been wounded in the deadly Rapidan River ambush, Edna had immediately rushed to her nephew's bedside. The attending physician had gently informed her that Admiral Longley would not recover. His condition was critical, she was told, and death could come at any hour.

But the old woman who loved him like a son scoffed at such dire predictions. She informed the nay-saying physician that her nephew was not going to die for another fifty years! She quickly summoned one of the city's most respected physicians, Dr. Milton Ledet, and insisted that he examine her nephew.

She grew furious with Ledet when he confirmed what the other physicians had predicted.

"Miss Longley," Dr. Ledet had said softly, "the poor boy is mortally wounded. We know nothing of the spine, but I'm afraid his injuries are crippling. It will be a miracle if he survives."

"Get out of this room immediately," she had angrily ordered. "You don't know what you're talking about! You shouldn't be allowed to practice medicine! They ought to take your license away from you, you charlatan."

Edna Longley staunchly refused to believe her nephew might die. But she grew more and more worried as days and weeks went by and Mitch didn't rally. He continued to drift in and out of consciousness. His attending physician stated that, unfortunately, the patient did not seem to be fighting for his life.

"In my opinion, the admiral does not care if he lives or dies," the doctor said.

The statement broke Edna Longley's heart, but she knew that it was true. And she knew why. It was more than just physical pain and the fact that he was being cashiered out of the navy in shame. She had, in the long hours he lay unconscious, heard him murmur a single name over and over again.

"Suzanna. Suzanna."

And more than once he had repeated a sentence that had apparently been whispered to him by the red-haired seductress during one of their last trysts. "Kiss me as if this were the last time."

Edna knew that Mitch was in love with Suzanna LeGrande, the heartless enchantress who had destroyed him. The one and only woman her handsome nephew had ever loved in all of his life was a cunning Southern spy who was responsible for the Rapidan River ambush.

Edna had heard of Suzanna LeGrande's arrest and imprisonment at the Old Capitol prison. She'd heard that Suzanna was to be put on trial for spying on the Union, and if found guilty, would be put to death.

She felt no sympathy for the woman. None whatsoever. She was angry with herself for not seeing through Suzanna. The conniving little bitch had fooled her, just as she had fooled Mitch. Let her hang for the crime! And the sooner the better, for she deserved it.

Edna Earl Longley was filled with hatred for the duplicitous traitor who had come into her home.

And into Mitch's heart.

Thirty-Three

She had lost all track of time.

Suzanna wasn't sure if she had been in the Old Capitol for weeks or months. At times she wasn't even sure if it was day or night. The endless hours of solitary confinement all ran together, punctuated only by a plate of unappetizing food being shoved into her cell and by brief intervals of fitful slumber.

She had given up on trying to learn if Mitch was alive or dead. She assumed the latter. But she would never know for sure because no one was allowed to visit or write her. When blessed sleep finally came, she often dreamed about Mitch, and in those dreams they were lying in the hammock at the cottage, teasing each other, laughing and kissing. Then the lovely dream would turn into a nightmare and he'd be clutching his side as blood spilled through his fingers, and he cursed her name as he fell.

Suzanna realized it was daytime when the booming voice of the superintendent startled her. "You have a visitor, Miss Le-Grande."

The cell door clanged open and Suzanna blinked at the dapperly dressed man she recognized as none other than Lafayette Baker.

Looking smug, Baker stepped inside and without preamble said, "I understand you're still misbehaving."

"How could anyone misbehave in here?" she said with the best brave smile she could muster.

"By your continued refusal to sign a full confession."

Suzanna lifted her chin pugnaciously. "Confess to what, pray tell?"

"Don't play games with me, Miss Le-Grande," said Baker. "I haven't the time. When you were arrested you as much as confessed to spying on the Union, did you not?"

Suzanna rubbed her chin as if thinking it over. "No. No, I don't recall confessing to anything. You must have me confused with some other poor defenseless woman you snatched out of her home."

"You're testing my patience, Miss Le-Grande," said Baker. "I have plenty of proof, so let's waste no more time."

"I have plenty of time, so let's waste no more proof," she retorted, a biting rejoinder.

The veins in his forehead standing out in bold relief, Baker said, "Damn you, you arrogant Southern traitor. You *will* sign a full confession along with an oath of allegiance." He shoved a piece of paper at her.

Suzanna refused to take it. She crossed her arms over her chest and told him firmly, "I am signing nothing, do you hear me? Nothing. Not now, not ever."

"No? Well, let me assure you that Stanton is going to hear about this!"

"Good!" Suzanna reached out, grabbed the piece of paper from him, tore it into pieces, which she dropped to the cell floor, and wiped her feet on them. "There! Tell Secretary of War Stanton I said it will be a cold day in hell before I sign an oath of allegiance to the Union!"

"That was a big mistake, Miss LeGrande," said an angry Lafe Baker. "Had you cooperated, I might have been able to help you. As it is, may you waste away in this cell forever." He paused, looked her straight in the eye and added, "Or until you're hanged for your crime."

"Get out," Suzanna ordered. "I can't stand the sight of you!"

He smiled and said, as if it were an afterthought, "I've a bit of news to share with you, Miss LeGrande."

Suzanna didn't give him the satisfaction of asking what it was.

He continued. "The war of the rebellion has come to an end and the Union has been victorious. Yesterday, Robert E. Lee surrendered at Appomattox."

It was April 10, 1865.

General Edgar M. Clements, one of Washington's wealthiest and most powerful men, yanked on the bellpull by his bed to summon his manservant. The distinguished, white-haired, seventy-four-year-old general, revered as the Hero of Montezuma for his bravery in the Mexican War, had returned to Washington only yesterday from a lengthy sojourn in the sunny south of France. He had gone to the Côte d'Azur in the hope that his failing health might improve in a more temperate clime.

But it hadn't worked, and after almost a year of loneliness the homesick general had sailed for America, realizing that his days were numbered. He wanted to die peacefully in his comfortable Washington home.

Jules entered the bedchamber carrying a breakfast tray upon which lay a folded copy of the morning paper, the *Washington Ledger.*

Jules poured the general's coffee and reminded his elderly employer that his old friend Edna Earl Longley was expecting him for a welcome-home lunch at her residence at one o'clock sharp. Edgar Clements nodded and reached for his wire-rimmed spectacles. Jules quietly left the room as the general put on the glasses and unfolded the newspaper.

And blinked in astonishment.

There on the front page was an artist's rendering of a young woman identified as Suzanna LeGrande, juxtaposed with a tintype of Mary E. Surratt, the Confederate sympathizer who'd been strung up for her part in Lincoln's assassination.

The headline read: Second Woman in History to Hang for Spying!

General Clements devoured the entire article, which stated that the beautiful young Virginian, Miss Suzanna LeGrande, had been charged and convicted of spying on the Union. The punishment for her crime was to be death, just as it was in the case of Mary E. Surratt, who had been hanged on July 7. Suzanna LeGrande was to be hanged at straight-up noon on the eleventh day of August, 1865.

Today was the seventh of August.

His appetite gone, Edgar Clements lowered the paper and set the breakfast tray aside. He was shaken to the core by what he had read. Little Suzanna LeGrande a convicted Confederate spy? She was to be hanged?

God in heaven!

General Clements had not seen Suzanna LeGrande in years, not since she was a carrot-topped little girl. He didn't know the young lady she had become and had never met the convicted traitor to the Union — the Union that he had served loyally as a young, patriotic officer and still loved dearly as a sickly old man.

But Edgar Clements had known Suzanna's paternal grandfather well and had been beholden to the late Timothy D. LeGrande since the long-ago days when they were together at the Virginia Military Institute.

The general again rang for his manservant.

"Sir?" said Jules, appearing almost instantly.

"Get out my dress uniform."

"But, General, it's early and —"

"And lay on my ribbons and medals."

"General, you're not expected at Miss Longley's until one this afternoon."

"I'm not going to Miss Longley's. Send a

messenger to tell her I've had to cancel." Edgar Clements had already tossed back the covers and gotten out bed. "My uniform, Jules."

"Now, now, General Clements," Jules gently scolded, "you haven't even touched your breakfast."

"Get my clothes, man, before it's too late!"

Thirty-Four

Suzanna, thin and wan from the long months in prison, sat on the dirty mattress in her cell, resolutely awaiting the hour of her execution. She had endured a long trial, been convicted of spying on the Union and been sentenced to death by hanging.

But she had not been told when the execution was to take place. So each time the superintendent approached her cell, she tensed, supposing the hour had come.

Head bowed now, eyes closed, she jumped, startled, when the superintendent abruptly unlocked the cell door.

"You have a visitor, Miss LeGrande," the man said gruffly.

Expecting to see the self-righteous Lafayette Baker, since no one else was allowed to visit her, Suzanna didn't immediately recognize the white-haired, well-dressed old gentleman who stepped in front of the scowling superintendent. She blinked in the changing light when the distinguished-looking patrician walked into the cell and extended his hand.

Puzzled, Suzanna automatically took the offered hand and rose to her feet. The elderly man looked vaguely familiar, but she couldn't place him.

He smiled kindly at her and explained. "My dear, I'm Edgar Clements. The name probably won't mean anything to you, since you were just a child when last I saw you. A pretty little girl with blazing copper curls, dimples and a bright smile." He saw the light beginning to dawn in Suzanna's blue eyes. "You sat upon my knee and called me Uncle Edgar."

"Oh, yes. Yes, I do remember you," she said, delighted to see a friendly face after all the lonely days and nights spent in solitary confinement. "You were a friend of my grandfather's and . . . and . . . Oh, Uncle Edgar, they are going to kill me."

"No, they're not," he stated emphatically. He took a seat on the thin mattress and patted a spot beside him. "Sit down, child and listen carefully. I am here to save you from the gallows."

Suzanna sat down beside the old man, folded her hands in her lap and shook her head. "Sir, I don't think it can be done."

"You're wrong. You'll see."

Wanting to believe him, she asked, "But . . . but why? And how?"

"Let's start with why. Your grandfather, Timothy LeGrande, was as fine a man as ever drew a breath, and I have owed him a debt of gratitude for more than fifty years. Now, finally, I have been presented with the opportunity to repay him for a sacrifice he made on my behalf."

Suzanna said, "What sacrifice? What did Grandfather do for you?"

"It happened a long time ago. Timothy and I were cadets at the Virginia Military Institute and the best of friends." Clements paused and shook his head, remembering. "As youths we were lively and reckless, real hell-raisers. One warm May evening we went to a tavern against military regulations. We were both drunk when we left the tavern, I more than he. I insisted, against Tim's wishes, on driving the carriage." Clements fell silent then.

"Yes, go on," Suzanna prompted.

"I should have listened to Tim, but I didn't. On the way back to the barracks, I ran over and killed a young woman. I panicked and fled the scene of the accident, leaving Tim to take full blame, which he did. He never betrayed me, never revealed what actually happened that night, despite his being cashiered out of the prestigious military academy." Clements exhaled heavily. "I have never forgotten Tim's sacrifice. He's long since dead, rest his soul, so I can't do anything for him. But I can and will help you."

"I'm grateful, but I'm afraid there's little you can do for me."

As if she hadn't spoken, General Clements said, "I have just come from a meeting with the secretary of war, Edwin Stanton. I requested that leniency be granted to the woman I plan to marry."

Taken aback, Suzanna was momentarily speechless. She stared at him, her lips parted, brow furrowed.

Edgar Clements continued. "I called in some favors, and Stanton has reluctantly agreed to set you free, but only if I take full responsibility for you."

"I can't ask that of you, sir."

"Yes, you can. This is my opportunity to repay the debt of honor I owe your late grandfather. I've already alerted a justice of the peace and told him to be standing by." Again Suzanna gave him a questioning look, but he pressed on. "Suzanna, you're alone, with no family and no money, am I right?"

"Yes, sir, you are."

He nodded. "I'm alone, too. As you may or may not know, I never married, never had children. I'm a very rich old man, Suzanna, and I haven't long to live. This bargain would benefit us both. Accept my proposal and we will be married before the sun sets today."

"What do you get out of this bargain?"

"Simply this. You agree to take care of me in my failing health, and I will restore your lost fortune. When I depart this earth — which will be quite soon — all that is mine will be yours. You will be a beautiful, wealthy young widow and can live a life of splendid ease. Go where you want to go, do just as you please."

A sensitive man, Edgar Clements caught the flicker of concern on Suzanna's gaunt face and hastily assured her, "Nothing will be expected of you other than looking after a sickly old man for a short time."

While the youthful bride luxuriated in the first hot bath she'd had in months, in an upstairs suite at the general's mansion, the aging bridegroom was closeted downstairs in his study with his attorney.

The summer sun had set by the time the newlyweds arrived at the mansion, after a short civil ceremony performed by the justice of the peace. A wedding supper was being prepared by the general's able staff, and the pair were to dine by candlelight later in the evening.

Now, as he sat across his heavy mahogany desk from his attorney, the seventy-four-year-old Edgar Clements, the hero of Montezuma, instructed the astonished lawyer to draw up a new will and testament leaving everything he had to his twenty-four-year-old bride, Suzanna LeGrande Clements.

"I hope you know what you're doing, Edgar," said the skeptical Will Bonner. "The girl's a traitor, responsible for the deaths of brave Federal sailors. Who knows what she might do to you once you've named her your sole beneficiary?"

The old general chuckled. "You suppose she might murder me in my bed?" he asked in mock alarm.

"I'm quite serious, sir. The young woman is obviously a coldhearted Jezebel who used her charms to —"

"That's enough, Will. You're talking about my wife, so you'll kindly watch your tongue. As I instructed, she is to fall heir to everything I own, do you understand?"

"Yes, but . . ."

"You heard me. Draw up the papers and I'll have Jules witness my signature."

"As you wish."

Grateful for the old man's kindness and relieved that she would not be hanged, Suzanna vowed to take good care of the sickly old gentleman for as long as he should live, be it five, ten or twenty years. She would do nothing to undermine or embarrass him. She would keep her end of the bargain and he would not be sorry that he had saved her life.

After a sumptuous meal served in the formal dining room shortly after nine o'clock that evening, Edgar Clements rose, came around the table and pulled out Suzanna's chair. She stood up, smiled at him and took his offered arm.

He escorted her out into the wide center hallway, paused at the base of the curving staircase and said, "There's a library filled with books in case you'd like to read. In the music room is a golden harp and a finely tuned piano, should you feel like enjoying a bit of music. There's a decanter of cognac and a big box of Belgian chocolates in the study." He patted her hand, and said, "Entertain yourself in any way you choose. You may stay up all night or go to bed immediately. This is your home now. It's up to you. Do anything you please, child." He paused, then told her, "As for me, I am quite tired. It's been an eventful day, so I'll say good-night now."

"Thank you so much for everything," she said.

He smiled. "You're very welcome, my dear. Is there anything else I can do for you before I retire?"

Suzanna started to speak, but hesitated.

"What is it?" he asked.

She couldn't help herself. She had to know. She was desperate to know, had spent agonizing months wondering. Now, at last, she could find out. She said, "Do you know whether or not Rear Admiral Mitchell B. Longley was killed in the —"

"No, Suzanna. Admiral Longley survived the Rapidan River ambush." Clements saw the look of relief that came into her expressive eyes. In a soft, soothing voice, he added, "As I understand it, he was badly wounded, spent months in a hospital He was finally released in April, around the time the war ended. Anything else?"

"No," she said, "that's all."

"Then good night, my dear."

"Good night, sir."

Suzanna stood and calmly watched Edgar Clements slowly climb the stairs. But her heart was hammering with happiness. Mitch was alive! He was alive and here in the city. This very minute the man she loved was probably sleeping peacefully at his mansion.

Thirty-Five

Mitch was awake, wide-awake.

It was the same every night. He couldn't sleep. He would lie there, tossing and turning restlessly, well into the wee hours of the morning. One reason for his insomnia was the fact that he was in constant pain from the slow-healing wounds that had nearly cost him his life.

But it was pain of another kind that often robbed Mitch of his sleep.

On this hot, muggy August night, as the tall cased clock in the foyer chimed eleven, Mitch was in the ground floor library. He had made his slow way downstairs on his own, with the aid of a cane, a torturous endeavor that had left him weak and clammy with perspiration.

Restless, edgy, he had come to the library to choose a book, hoping to be distracted, entertained. But when he sat down and tried to read, he found the text could not hold his interest.

He laid the book aside, struggled up out of his chair and headed for the bar. He took a crystal snifter from the shelf behind it and reached for a decanter of cognac. He poured himself a drink, swirled the brandy around the bottom of the glass, then turned it up and drank it in one swallow.

He poured himself another.

By the time he'd finished the third drink, he set the empty snifter on the polished bar, grabbed up his cane, turned and hobbled out of the library.

But he didn't go upstairs to bed. With difficulty, he walked the length of the center hall to the very back of the house. He let himself out, crossed the back veranda and went cautiously down the steps, steadying himself with the cane.

Mitch headed directly for the stables, which lay beyond the vast lawns and manicured gardens. He was exhausted and in a great deal of pain by the time he reached the hay-filled stall where he kept his favorite mount, a coal-black stallion with stockinged feet. The black nickered a greeting and Mitch laid a hand on his sleek neck.

A dozing stable hand was awakened by the stallion's whinnying and came to investigate. "It's you, Mistah Longley," said the boy. "You need anything?"

"Yes. Saddle my stallion, will you, Rupert?" Mitch replied.

"Now, Mistah Longley, you know you're not supposed to be ridin' 'fore you get better."

"That day might never come," Mitch stated flatly. "Saddle my horse, I'm taking a ride."

"Yes, sir," said the boy. "Whatever you say."

Once the big mount was bridled, Mitch struggled to climb up into the saddle. It took every ounce of his strength, as well as the aid of the wiry stable boy.

The feat finally accomplished, a winded Mitch thanked the lad and told him to go back to sleep. On horseback for the first time since being wounded more than nine months ago, Mitch rode out of the stables with his walking cane stuck in the saddle's rifle scabbard. He walked the responsive stallion slowly up the pebbled drive to the front property line of the estate. There he neck-reined the horse to the left, turning him onto the main road. Then Mitch put the mount into an easy canter. Soon he gave the stallion his head, and the blooded creature quickly stretched out into a graceful gallop. Pain jarred through his lean body each time the stallion's hooves struck the ground, but Mitch didn't turn back. He sucked his bottom lip behind his teeth and rode on.

When he pulled up on the reins to halt the stallion, he had reached the secluded cottage. For a moment Mitch stayed in the saddle, gazing at the darkened building where he had spent the happiest moments of his life. He debated whether he really wanted to go inside. He wasn't sure. He knew it would be wiser to turn and ride away.

With a groan, Mitch swung down out of the saddle, looped the stallion's reins over its head and took the bit from its mouth. The horse immediately lowered his head and began to graze on the summer grass surrounding the place. Mitch took his walking cane from the scabbard, then ground tethered the animal.

He drew a deep breath, slowly exhaled and went to the cottage's front door. He opened it and stepped inside. Moonlight spilled into the parlor through the tall windows at the back of the room. He glanced at a lamp that sat atop the writing desk. He walked over to the desk, lifted the lamp's globe, turned up the wick and struck a match to it. He replaced the globe, picked up the lamp and moved across the room, glancing at the familiar furnishings.

Cobwebs, dust and a faint musty smell — all were evidence that no one had been here in a long time. Mitch knew how long. Ten months had gone by since that snowy November afternoon when he and Suzanna had made love before the roaring fire. Mitch gazed at the cold fireplace and at the rug spread out in front of it. Once again Suzanna's prophetic words came back to haunt him.

Kiss me as if this were the last time.

When she'd whispered those words to him, she had known that it was to be the last time. Damn her!

Mitch gritted his teeth and, carrying the lamp high, limped into the bedroom. He had decided he would try sleeping here tonight. He set the lamp down on the night table. One-handed, he began unbuttoning his shirt. His weight resting on the cane, he reached down, took hold of the top sheet and flipped back the covers.

Immediately, he saw the small article of clothing lying on the white sheet. Frowning, Mitch leaned closer to see what it was, and made an almost inaudible moaning sound in the back of his throat.

There in the center of bed was a lace-trimmed, blue satin garter. How well he remembered when he'd last seen that saucy feminine piece — and where it had been when he'd seen it. Memories of that frosty morning came flooding back. In his mind's eye he saw the beautiful red-haired Suzanna wearing, just above her left knee, the blue satin garter.

And nothing else.

Mitch snagged the item with the tip of his little finger, walked out onto the back porch and went to the far end, where the canvas hammock hung. After leaning his cane against the back wall, he climbed into the hammock, carefully placed the garter in the middle of his bared chest and pressed it against his aching heart. He lay there unmoving in the silence, thinking about the woman, who was cunning beyond belief.

Just this evening, over dinner at his aunt's, he had learned that Suzanna narrowly escaped a date with the executioner. Edna announced that General Edgar Clements, once her old friend, had used his considerable wealth and political power to rescue Suzanna from the gallows and then had promptly married her!

"The old fool deserves what he gets, if you ask me!" Edna had said, eyes snapping.

Now as Mitch lay sleepless in the hammock, he gave secret, silent thanks that Suzanna's life had been spared. He also came to a decision. He would leave Washington immediately. He didn't know where he would go and it didn't much matter.

Just so long as it was far away from Mrs. Suzanna LeGrande Clements.

Suzanna turned and walked into the library, where lighted lamps illuminated the tall shelves filled with leather-bound books. She took one down, leafed through it, then returned it to the shelf.

She left the library and wandered down to the music room, where she moved toward the golden harp, but did not touch it. Then she crossed the room to the square, intricately carved piano that rested before tall floor-to-ceiling windows. She sat down on the bench and placed her fingers on the keys. It was the first time she had sat at a piano since those happy days long ago when she'd lived at Whitehall with her family.

Suzanna began to play Stephen Foster's haunting "Beautiful Dreamer." But by the time she was halfway through the ballad, her eyes were filled with tears.

She stopped abruptly, rose and left the room, determined she would weep no more. Not for Mitch, not for the South and not for herself. Chin raised, Suzanna went in search of the study. Once inside the cozy, masculine room, she headed straight for the carved decanters of liquor that rested atop a polished mahogany bar.

She unstoppered the brandy, poured herself a healthy portion of the amber liquid and raised the snifter in a toast to herself and to the kind old man asleep upstairs. She found a box of delicious-looking chocolates and popped one into her mouth. Then she sat down in an overstuffed leather chair and threw her legs over the arm, letting her feet dangle. And as she sipped the brandy and devoured the chocolates, she vowed that she would stop looking back. From now on, she would only look ahead.

After two snifters and four pieces of chocolate, a tipsy Suzanna climbed the stairs to her suite. Waving away the uniformed maid who waited there to help her undress, she closed the door behind the woman and began stripping as she went around the large room, turning out the lamps. By the time the last light had been extinguished, Suzanna was naked.

A lace-trimmed, long white nightgown lay across the foot of the turned-down bed. Suzanna didn't immediately reach for it. Instead she crossed the darkened bedchamber to the tall French doors that were thrown open to the wide stone balcony. She peeked out and looked both ways, but saw no lights coming from anywhere in or out of the mansion. Cautiously, she stepped outside.

She sighed when a light breeze from out of the east stroked her bare, overly warm body. She stood for a long moment in the August moonlight, gazing out at the lights of the city. On this first night of freedom, after all the months in prison, she was reluctant to have the day end. She had learned that all the things she had once taken for granted were precious privileges to be enjoyed and savored. Like being allowed to soak in a suds-filled tub. And having clean clothes to don once the bath ended. And sitting down to a delicious meal served on fine china and sparkling crystal. And being permitted to sleep in a big, soft four-poster in a very private bedchamber.

And best of all, keeping the double doors open to the outside because blessed freedom was now hers.

Suzanna finally began to yawn sleepily. Almost reluctantly, she turned and went back inside, but she left the French doors ajar. She picked up the long nightgown from the foot of the bed, raised it over her head and let it whisper down her body. Then she unpinned her upswept hair and shook her head.

She was just turning to get into bed when she heard a loud thud in the suite adjoining hers. Heart hammering, Suzanna rushed to the heavy door connecting the two suites. She pounded on it and shouted the old general's name. No response. She yanked the door open and hurried inside.

General Clements, in his nightshirt, lay on the floor beside his bed. Suzanna fell to her knees, calling his name, but he didn't answer.

"No!" Suzanna shouted. "No, no, no! Jules, come quick!"

The manservant appeared immediately and knelt beside Suzanna, feeling for a pulse in the general's throat. "I'm sorry, Mrs. Clements," he said, "the general's gone. It was likely heart failure."

Suzanna nodded and slowly rose to her feet.

A prisoner, a bride and a widow all in the same eventful day, Suzanna LeGrande Clements was now also a very wealthy woman.

Thirty-Six

"Suzanna, dear, I do wish you'd reconsider. Won't you change your mind about leaving?" pleaded the perplexed Mattie Kirkendal.

"Yes, child," Dr. Ledet agreed, "there's no need for you to leave Washington. Johnson's in office now and he's an old-fashioned Southern democrat just as we are. We're your friends. We want you to stay close so we can look after you. What will you do on the Continent?"

"Why, enjoy myself, what else?" said Suzanna, more flippantly than she felt.

She yearned so desperately for the handsome lover she had betrayed that it had become a physical pain for which there was no balm. She had learned that great wealth was no substitute for love. But she kept her own counsel, hid her heartache and pretended to be gay and carefree.

She never mentioned Mitch's name. And

Mattie and Dr. Ledet, acutely aware that she did not want to talk about him, didn't mention him, either. If Suzanna wanted to bury the past and look to the future, they would respect her wishes.

Suzanna took consolation from knowing that Mitch had survived, and she wished more than anything that she could go to him and beg his forgiveness.

But she knew she could not.

She was certain that he now hated her as much as he'd once loved her. And so Suzanna had decided — less than a month after becoming a widow — that she would set sail for Europe. She was determined to forget Mitch and all that had happened.

Once she'd made the decision to leave Washington, she had posted a letter to her cousins in Baltimore, to whom she had sent her servants, Durwood and Buelah, during the war. Suzanna thanked the Thetfords for their kindness and confided that she could now afford to bring her servants back to her own household. She was planning a journey to Europe and the servants would travel with her. Suzanna also sent money, a generous sum to repay their kindness, as well as cover the pair's train fare to New York City. She would, she stated, meet them in New York, where together they would board

Cunard's finest ocean liner, the SS *Starlight,* bound for Southampton, England.

Missy Thetford promptly replied to Suzanna's missive. She wrote that, regretfully, old Durwood had passed away last winter after a bad case of influenza, but that Buelah was healthy and eager to accompany her mistress overseas.

Now, on the 29th of September, her last day in Washington, Suzanna had come to say goodbye to Mattie and Dr. Ledet.

"I really must be going," Suzanna said. "I haven't finished packing. And I need to give final instructions to Edgar's servants." She confided, "I intend to keep the old general's full staff on duty and allow them to pretty much do as they please while I'm away. They are free to take time off to visit relatives and friends."

"That's most kind of you," said Dr. Ledet.

Suzanna shrugged her shoulders. "No, it's most kind of General Clements. They were like family to him. I'm sure he would want them to be well taken care of." She rose to her feet.

"When will you be back, Suzanna?" Dr. Ledet asked, standing and helping Mattie get up.

"I've no idea," she said truthfully. She

laughed then and added, "When I tire of the grand adventure, I suppose."

Mattie and Doc Ledet exchanged glances. "You'll write to us?" asked Mattie.

In the foyer, Suzanna turned to face them. They wore identical sad expressions. Suzanna said, "Oh, you two! It's not the end of the world. Be thrilled for me. I've always wanted to travel and now I can."

Mattie sighed and put her arms around the younger, taller woman. "You forgive us for —"

"There's nothing to forgive, Mattie. I've told you that over and over. Everything I did was of my own free will. Now let's never speak of it again."

The white-haired doctor put his arms around both women and said, "Suzanna, you're young, rich and beautiful. Perhaps some thrilling escapades in London and Paris are just what the doctor ordered." He paused, brushed a kiss to her cheek and added, "My dear, Mattie and I just want you to be happy."

"I've never been happier, Doctor. I have everything I've ever wanted," Suzanna replied breezily. Then she freed herself from their embrace, turned and walked out the door.

■ ■ ■ ■

"You keep burnin' the candle at both ends, you're gonna lose your youthful beauty," a concerned Buelah scolded as she helped Suzanna dress for yet another gala evening.

"Ah, well, I've a few good years left, don't you think?" Suzanna replied. "I'll try to make the most of them."

The two women were in the spacious boudoir of an opulent hotel suite in the heart of London. They had been in the city for six months, and during that time Suzanna had hardly missed an evening out on the town with the smart set.

The darling of the day, she was squired to London's most fashionable clubs — the Midnight, the Garrick, the Savage. She was invited to soirees for England's royalty, lavish parties that were attended by European royals, sheiks and maharajas, barons, dukes and wealthy old earls. And fellow Americans with esteemed names like Vanderbilt and Astor.

She radiated a kind of confident charm that endeared her to everyone she met. The gentlemen were awed by her beauty and virginal freshness. Everything in her being hinted of sexual delight, therefore she easily dazzled the world's most eligible bachelors. Many even fell madly in love with her.

On this chilly March night Suzanna was to join the handsome Charles W. Strickland, fourth Duke of Charlbury, for dinner and the theater afterward. At first Suzanna had found the duke to be witty and charming, and she enjoyed their evenings out, but she was quickly tiring of him, as she had of so many before him. Charles had, in the past few weeks, become a bit of a bore with his frequent proposals of marriage.

Marriage was the last thing Suzanna desired. Freedom was all she wanted or ever would want, and she had told the duke as much. The confession had seemed only to further pique his ardor, and she knew the time was at hand to break off the romance.

Now, as she stood before the freestanding mirror while Buelah fastened the tiny clasps at the back of her blue velvet ball gown, Suzanna said casually, "I'm tiring of London, Buelah."

The maid's nimble fingers paused and she smiled at Suzanna in the mirror, her dark eyes flashing with hope. "Me, too. Let's go home."

"Home? No, we're not going home." Suzanna quickly set her straight. "But perhaps we should go to Paris for a while."

"Oh," said a clearly disappointed Buelah.

Suzanna turned to face her. "Why, you're homesick, aren't you."

"Yes, aren't you?"

She was, but she didn't admit it. Not even to herself. "Heavens no! We've just begun our travels. Tomorrow morning you start packing and I'll make arrangements for our departure to France."

Buelah groaned.

Suzanna shook her head, picked up her long ermine cape, tossed it over her arm and walked into the suite's drawing room to join the duke.

Charles Strickland came to his feet, beaming. Suzanna greeted him, then handed him the ermine and turned about. Strickland draped the lush fur around her bare shoulders, bent his head, pressed a kiss to the side of her throat and said, "Darling, marry me."

"No, Charlie."

"Please, Suzanna. I must have you, make you my own. I long to make love to you. Marry me!"

Suzanna exhaled with annoyance. "I do not wish to marry again."

Suzanna LeGrande Clements became the toast of the Continent. The beautiful merry widow was pursued by princes and plutocrats and potentates. Wherever she went, she caused a stir. Instinctively, she knew all the places to see and be seen. Be it Paris, the City of Lights, or the Eternal City, Rome, romantic Madrid or the spas of Baden-Baden, she stayed in the finest hotels and resorts, dined in the best restaurants and wore expensive designer gowns. She spent money as if there were no tomorrow. She sipped champagne from crystal flutes, danced till dawn on polished floors and favored the handsomest of her suitors with kisses.

And nothing more.

She stayed out late each evening and slept in late each morning. She went from country to country, party to party and man to man. Suzanna did everything in her power to enjoy life to the fullest.

And to forget Mitch Longley.

Nothing worked.

No other love had ever — could ever — take his place.

Five years went by in a fog, a neverending pursuit of pleasure. But happiness continued to elude her. And so did peace.

And then one afternoon, as she sat alone beneath a giant umbrella on the sun-splashed terrace of her hotel on the Côte d'Azur, high above the blue Mediterranean, Suzanna realized that the memories had faded. At times she couldn't remember exactly what Mitch looked like or how he sounded when he spoke her name. She felt confident that she was finally over him.

Restless, lonely and homesick, Suzanna decided it was time to return to America.

Thirty-Seven

Suzanna was astonished. It was as if the war had never happened, as though she had never been convicted of treason and had barely escaped the executioner's noose.

Having expected to receive a chilly reception upon arriving in Washington, she had prepared herself for snubs, insults and perhaps even death threats in this city where the majority of citizens had strongly sided with the Union.

She was apprehensive when she arrived in the nation's capital on a crisp, cold winter afternoon under clear blue skies. She was pleased to see no footmen, no servants and no driver. Her telegram firmly requesting that there be no fanfare had been obeyed.

Suzanna stepped down from the train and cautiously made her way through the crowds, wondering how long it would be before someone recognized her and began calling her names. How long before she was warned to get back on the train and get out of D.C.

She released a sigh of relief when she and her maid, Buelah, reached the covered carriage unnoticed, and hastily climbed inside, successfully maintaining a low profile.

While Buelah, glad to be home, chattered excitedly beside her, Suzanna looked out at the city on the Potomac. On this cold winter afternoon in 1870, Washington was beautiful again, just as it had been before the war.

She thought back to Mattie and Dr. Ledet admitting that, when the war had finally ended in the spring of '65, they had joined the throngs that rushed into the heart of the city. They had witnessed both elation and tears as the Union armies paraded down the avenue filled with sunshine, flags and roaring crowds.

"My beloved city will never be the same again," Mattie had sadly predicted at that time. "It's ruined! It will be an armed camp forever."

But Mattie had been wrong.

Washington was beautiful. And peaceful. On this brisk February afternoon, Suzanna gazed out on the wide boulevards, the dogwood trees that would soon begin to bloom and the fine carriages rolling past, filled with laughing people. It was almost impossible to believe that the city had been badly war torn just five short years ago.

At the stately house she had inherited from Edgar Clements — and which she still referred to as "the general's manse" — Suzanna was amazed to find that every loyal servant, save a couple of older ones who had passed on, was still on duty. And there was strong evidence that the house had been run as efficiently as if she had been in residence the entire time.

The respected law firm of Bonner and Barker, the entity overseeing the estate in her absence, had done an excellent job. Just as expected.

The staff were well-groomed, neatly uniformed and smiling as they welcomed her home. One of the parlor maids, a lively young woman who had been born, raised and spent all her life in this fine Washington house, offered to show the aging Buelah to her quarters. The two women went away laughing and talking as if old friends.

"A message came this morning, Mrs. Clements," said Jules, holding out the silver bowl in which a small vellum envelope lay.

Suzanna thanked him, then took the envelope and opened it. A dinner initiation from Mattie Kirkendal. And it was for this very evening! How Mattie knew she was back in Washington was a mystery, but then Mattie always seemed to know everything. Shaking her head and smiling, Suzanna lowered the invitation.

Suddenly she felt very guilty. Although she had promised she'd stay in touch, Suzanna had not corresponded with Mattie — or anyone else in Washington — in the five years she was in Europe. Save for the dry annual reports she'd received from the law firm administering the estate, she'd had no contact with anyone back home.

There had been a reason for her neglect. She had not wanted to hear anything about Mitch Longley. She hadn't wanted to know where he was or what he was doing or if he had married or anything else about him. She had hoped that not hearing from anyone would help her forget Mitch once and for all.

Dear understanding Mattie. Instead of being angry with her for not corresponding as she had promised, Mattie was inviting her to dinner the minute she was back in Washington.

Suzanna realized she was eager to see the kind woman, who had apparently forgiven her. She could hardly wait to see Mattie, and she hoped that Dr. Ledet would be joining them for the evening meal.

He was. But he wasn't the only one.

At eight sharp Suzanna arrived at Mattie's.

She was surprised to see lights blazing from every room of the imposing two-story mansion. Music and laughter floated out on the chill night air. Inside was a large gathering of people.

The minute a tense Suzanna stepped into the marble-floored foyer, Mattie spotted her and rushed to her side.

"Suzanna, my dear! Thank heavens you're finally home! You naughty girl, you," she declared, shaking her finger. "Not so much as a note in five long years!"

"Oh, Mattie, I'm so sorry. It was inexcusable of me, I know, but I do hope you'll forgive me."

"Of course I forgive you, Suzanna," she said, knowing without being told the reason Suzanna had refrained from corresponding. "I'm just glad to know that you're all right and that you're home at last." Tears filled the older woman's eyes. "I'm so happy to see you. You'll never know how happy."

"Ah, don't cry," Suzanna said, allowing herself to be warmly hugged. "I'm happy to see you, too, but I must have gotten my dates mixed up. I was under the impression that you invited me to dinner this evening."

"I did indeed!" Mattie assured her, pulling back and dabbing at her eyes with a lacy handkerchief. "I hope you won't mind that I've also invited a few friends to help celebrate your return to Washington."

"Friends?" Suzanna looked warily around. "Mattie, have you forgotten that I was convicted of spying on the Union and that —"

"Water under the bridge, child." Mattie waved her hand in the air. "Besides, tales of your exploits and derring-do have only added to your mystique. Why, old acquaintances are eager to welcome you back, and those who don't know you are dying to meet you. Especially the gentlemen." Mattie turned to the approaching white-haired physician. "Tell her, Doctor."

Beaming, Dr. Ledet said, "Little Suzanna! My dear, how wonderful to see you again and how beautiful you are." He embraced her and said, "Mattie's absolutely right. As soon as everyone knows you're back in the city, you'll be inundated with invitations to social events."

Suzanna was skeptical. "I'm not so sure about that, Doctor."

"We are," Mattie assured her, then, glancing at the doctor, added, "There's one little thing we should get out of the way before we go inside to join the others."

"Oh?" Suzanna held her breath, half expecting Mattie to announce that she had invited Mitch to dinner.

"Simply this, if you're worried about bumping into Mitch Longley now that you're back in Washington, don't be. It is not going to happen."

At the mere mention of his name Suzanna felt her pulse quicken. "How can you be certain?" she asked, in what she hoped was a casual tone.

Mattie explained. "At the end of the terrible conflict, while you were on death's row in the Old Capital prison, the admiral spent months in Bethesda Hospital recovering from his wounds."

When Suzanna nodded, Dr. Ledet picked up the story. "Longley was cashiered out of the navy, and left Washington sometime around August or September of 1865."

Suzanna felt as if she were suffocating. August or September of 1865? That's when she'd left Washington. Mitch had still been right here in the city when she married the old general. Had he known about the marriage? Had he cared? Had he, too, gone to Europe? Had he been there when she was there? Had they passed each other on a street somewhere and never known?

Unable to stop herself, Suzanna asked, "When Mitch left Washington, where did he go?"

"We're not sure. Some say he went abroad, but no one really knows," said Dr. Ledet with a shrug. Anticipating her next question, he said, "You can rest assured, though, that he will not be returning to Washington. His great-aunt and only relative, Miss Edna Earl Longley, passed away a couple of winters ago. It's said he slipped into the city for her burial, but was gone by sunset. And he had his attorney sell the old lady's mansion, which she left to him."

"But he still owns a home here," Suzanna said.

"No, my dear," said the doctor. "It, too, has been sold."

Mattie interjected hopefully, "So you see, you can stay right here in Washington because Mitch Longley will not be coming back."

"No. No, of course not," Suzanna said. "I mean, yes, I can stay in the city."

"Now, enough about that," Mattie said brightly. "It's time for new beginnings. Come, let's go inside and mingle with the guests."

Thirty-Eight

Mitch Longley slowly straightened, grimaced and mopped the sweat from his brow with a handkerchief. He automatically laid a hand on his badly scarred left side and gritted his teeth against the nagging pain in his hip and leg, which never fully left him.

He turned and squinted at the western horizon, where the sun was finally setting on this warm spring day. He glanced around at the vast field of sugar cane that stretched out in every direction as far as the eye could see. The laborers had begun gathering their belongings and were making their way to the edge of the field, many calling out a friendly "good night" to Mitch.

He was their employer, but they never thought of him as the boss. He was one of them. He didn't ride out to survey his property on a big snorting steed, shout orders to the workers and crack a whip over their heads. Instead, he worked alongside them at least three or four days a week under a broiling sun, and went home each night as weary as they.

It was not necessary for Mitch to work. He was a very wealthy man. If he never turned his hand again, Mitch had enough money to last for ten lifetimes. But money alone was not enough for him. He needed a purpose in life, a hands-on project that forced him get out of bed in the morning. And allowed him — due to sheer physical exhaustion — to fall asleep at night.

For years he had slept fitfully at best, and there were many nights he had never even closed his eyes. After he was cashiered out of the navy and finally released from the hospital, Mitch had struggled to regain his mobility. Determined he would not spend the rest of his life in a chair or flat on his back in bed, he had spent long, torturous hours working to regain his strength. The simplest tasks had seemed insurmountable, and more than once he had considered giving up and accepting the fact that he was an invalid, as helpless as a newborn baby.

But the will to survive and to regain his self-reliance had won out. He kept trying, kept fighting the odds. And despite the agonizing pain, he had learned to pull himself up and to stand alone. Finally, after many months of torture, he could walk with the aid of a cane. He had single-mindedly focused on being totally independent. Toward that one and only goal, he had expended every ounce of his will and energy.

But once the goal had been attained, once he'd endured strenuous exercises and his broken body had mended and he was completely fit again, he had become increasingly restless and miserable. Without the ever constant physical pain to battle, another more debilitating kind of pain engulfed him.

The idle hours had given him too much time to dwell on the beautiful red-haired temptress who had callously seduced and betrayed him. That heartless Jezebel who had successfully brought him down and cost him his naval career.

In an effort to forget Suzanna LeGrande, Mitch had traveled extensively. He had gone to England, Scotland, France and Spain. But she — witch that she was — had followed him wherever he went, not in the flesh but in his aching heart.

She would not let him go. Each time he caught sight of a well-dressed, slender young woman with blazing red hair, his heart skipped a beat. Finally he realized that he was searching for her. A thousand or a million miles apart, it made no difference.

He could not get away from Suzanna LeGrande.

Bored, weary of traveling, Mitch had returned to America and sold his house, as well as the mansion his aunt had left him. That done, he promptly left Washington for good. Having no desire to live where memories mocked him, he went in search of a new home, a new life.

He had found that home and with it a degree of peace and contentment. He had bought up thousands of acres of rich marshy lowlands on the southern coast of South Carolina. In the little village bordering his property, he had enlisted strong-backed men and women to help him work the land. Freed slaves and whites alike had all been eager for work.

Together they had brought the fallow fields back to life. Tobacco, rice, cotton, sugar and hemp now flourished in this warm subtropical climate, where the growing season was six to nine months long.

The temperate weather and the slow pace of life agreed with Mitch. He spent long, sun-filled days working the fields, and warm, balmy nights at the comfortable house he'd had built on an isolated stretch of beach.

The jalousied villa, with its latticed arches

and tied-back curtains, afforded a breathtaking view of the azure sea rippling in the distance beneath an indigo sky filled with puffy white clouds. It was as if he were the only person on earth. In the two years he'd lived in the comfortable villa, he had never seen anyone on the beach.

He had it all to himself.

Mitch had walked ten miles in either direction, on more than one occasion, and had spotted only one residence other than his own. About two miles south of his place, set back off the beach on a small cove, was a whitewashed, two-story house with a wraparound veranda.

He had never seen any lights on inside nor anyone around the grounds. No signs of life whatsoever. Obviously, no one lived there. Good. He hoped the place stayed vacant forever. He liked his world just as it was.

The pristine beach was virtually his. *His,* with no intruders. The isolation suited him. After a long, tiring day in the fields, he was lulled to sleep by the sound of the waves crashing rhythmically on the shore.

And on those rare occasions when he couldn't fall asleep, he needed only to walk out the door, cross the sugary white sands, and swim far out into the ocean.

■ ■ ■ ■

Midnight. Not a breeze stirred the tied-back curtains. The still air was heavy and humid.

Mitch got out of bed, his bare, overheated body glistening with a sheen of perspiration from head to toe.

He pulled on a pair of white duck trousers, ran a hand through his disheveled hair and walked out onto the villa's veranda. He clasped the railing and gazed out over the endless ocean. A full harvest moon silvered the waves beyond the one-story beach house.

On a whim, Mitch agilely vaulted over the waist-high railing and walked barefoot across the warm sands toward the cool, inviting sea. At the water's edge he unbuttoned his pants and shed them where he stood. Naked, he waded into the foamy water until it was lapping at his hair-dusted thighs.

He dived headlong into an approaching wave and began to swim, his powerful arms moving with precision as he sliced through the salty water, feet kicking to propel him forward. Exhilarated, he swam until his arms grew weak with exertion and his lungs felt as if they might burst.

Mitch turned over onto his back and floated in to shore. At the water's edge he picked up his discarded trousers, but did not put them on. There was no need. The beach was his and his alone.

Pants draped over his shoulder, he returned to the villa, tired, yawning, feeling blessedly relaxed. Inside, he tossed the trousers over the back of a chair, then grabbed a towel and began drying the moisture from his flesh. From habit he slowly, carefully, blotted water from the network of slashing white scars that marred the smooth brown skin. Scars that started just under his left arm and went down past his hip bone.

His body still half-damp, Mitch tossed the towel aside and crawled back into bed. He raised his arms above his head, folded them on the pillow, exhaled heavily and felt his muscles slacken.

The only light was that of the moon, the only sound that of the tranquil ocean.

His eyes closing sleepily, Mitch said aloud, "Solitude. Sweet soothing solitude. May it last forever."

THIRTY-NINE

Suzanna sighed wearily when Buelah came into the bedroom with a frothy pastel ball gown tossed over her arm.

"I don't want to go out this evening," Suzanna told her maid. "I'm just not up to it. Have Jules send the Graysons my regrets."

"No such thing!" Buelah scolded, shaking her head. "You promised Miss Cynthia Ann you'd attend her engagement party tonight and you are going to keep that promise."

Suzanna sighed again, but turned away from the tall French doors that stood open onto the balcony. Buelah was right, as usual. She couldn't possibly decline such an important invitation at the last minute. It would be unforgivably rude, and Cynthia Ann would be terribly hurt and disappointed if she didn't attend.

Cynthia Ann Grayson had returned with her family to Washington in the autumn of 1865, after the war had ended. And despite all that had happened, she and Suzanna were still close. On Suzanna's very first week back from Europe, Cynthia Ann had hurried over to visit. For a long moment Suzanna had stared at the young, dark-haired woman she had not seen in almost a decade.

"Cyn? Cyn Grayson? Is that really you?" she had asked, eyes wide with surprise and pleasure.

"Oh, Suz, how I have missed you!" her old friend quickly replied.

Then the pair threw their arms around each other and laughed and cried and behaved much as they had when they were spirited sixteen-year-olds.

When finally they'd calmed a bit, Suzanna pulled back, looked at Cynthia Ann and said, "I can't believe it. You've actually come to see me? You're still my friend after all that I've done? After all that has happened?"

"Of course I'm still your friend," Cynthia Ann assured her. She knew, as did everyone in Washington, that Suzanna had been a spy for the Confederacy and had sent soldiers and sailors to their deaths. But Cynthia Ann had never held it against her, despite the fact that Davy Williams — the man she was to marry — had been killed at Gettysburg wearing Northern blue.

"I'm so sorry, Cyn," Suzanna had exclaimed when Cynthia Ann told her of Davy's death.

"He died a hero in battle," her friend stated calmly, "and I shall always be proud of him."

She went on to confide that at that time she had vowed she would never, ever marry. But she had changed her mind recently when she'd met Cliff Dansforth, a shy, handsome attorney who was ten years her senior and well established in a thriving Washington legal practice. "You think Davy would forgive me if he knew?" she'd asked Suzanna.

"I'm certain of it, Cyn," Suzanna had assured her.

"You'll be my matron of honor?"

"You know I will, but are you sure you want me? Everyone knows that I . . ."

"Doesn't matter. Mark my words, Suz, the fact that you were a daring female spy will only make you more appealing."

Cynthia Ann had been right.

Just as in Europe, Suzanna quickly set hearts aflutter in the nation's capital, and hopeful swains swarmed around her. In the two months since her return from Europe, Suzanna had attended — and even hosted

— many glamorous parties. The fact that she had been a spy only added to her allure.

Everyone was eager to hear about her thrilling escapades, but Suzanna demurred with a playful smile and a shake of her head, refusing to discuss her past adventures. And in so doing, she added to her own mystique.

She never apologized for what she had done in the war, never attempted to hide the fact that she was and always would be totally loyal to the fallen South. Her nature as fiery as ever, she didn't hesitate to speak her mind when, at a crowded gala, a gentleman who'd had too much champagne swaggered over to her and said, "Haven't you heard the news, missy? The Union was victorious, no thanks to you. We whipped the arrogant Johnny Rebs and —"

Interrupting, Suzanna said, "You're mistaken, sir. The South was not beaten, only worn down by superior numbers and supplies!"

On another occasion a bitter Yankee veteran who had lost an arm at Vicksburg walked up to her, showed her the stump in his empty sleeve and said, "Just so you'll know what loss is like."

"Sir, I know a great deal about loss." Suzanna quickly set him straight. "I lost everything during the war. Everything. I lost my brother, my sweetheart, my mother, my mansion and my livelihood to the crushing Union, so don't lecture me about loss!"

While a number of guests had looked on, stunned, many had smiled and applauded her spirit. It was evident that Suzanna's admirers greatly outnumbered her detractors. So she went to the parties, and she laughed and danced and drank champagne and easily charmed her many acquaintances. At the frequent social functions she attended, she was consistently charming, cheerful and carefree.

But it was all a facade.

Suzanna was as unhappy here as she had been in Europe. Even more so. Here the memories were too vivid, too painful. More than one night she had lain awake reliving the times she had spent with Mitch at the secluded cottage in the woods.

She remembered making love for the first time in his bedroom while rain pelted the windows, lightning flashed and thunder boomed. And shamelessly undressing in broad daylight out in the hammock on the back porch. And on the soft fur rug before a blazing fire.

As she dressed for the Graysons' reception on this early April evening, she began to seriously consider getting away again. She didn't know where she could go, but she knew that she would never be content here in this city where so many memories haunted her.

She wished she could leave right now, this very minute, but knew that she couldn't. She would attend the Graysons' reception tonight and would wait at least until after Cynthia Ann was married before fleeing Washington. Suzanna had promised to be matron of honor and she would keep that promise.

"What you mulling over in your mind?" asked Buelah as she lifted the chiffon ball gown over Suzanna's head.

When the dazzling garment encased her slender body, Suzanna said simply, "Leaving."

"Too early to leave yet, child," said Buelah. "Jules said he'll have the carriage brought around at eight."

Suzanna didn't clarify her statement. "Eight will be fine."

Suzanna laughed merrily and tossed rice at the beaming newlyweds as they hurried away from the lavish, late-afternoon reception to the waiting carriage. Mr. and Mrs. Cliff Dansforth were to spend their wedding night in the bridal suite of the Willard Hotel, then leave in the morning for a yearlong honeymoon in Europe.

Suzanna's bright smile slipped a little as she watched the carriage — with the happily embracing couple inside — roll down the avenue and turn the corner. Before the gleaming black brougham disappeared around the bend, a glowing Cynthia Ann stuck her veiled head out and waved madly to Suzanna.

Suzanna laughed and blew her kisses.

But when all the other guests went back inside to drink more champagne and continue with the lively celebration, she stayed there on the street alone.

She felt a lock of hair tickle her cheek, and when she lifted a hand to push it back in place she touched a dogwood blossom that had fallen from a tree overhead and caught in her hair. Sweeping the blossom away, she watched as it fluttered slowly to the ground.

Now in late spring, the weather in Washington was near perfect. But all too soon the humid, miserable summertime would descend on the city, with its stifling heat. Suzanna dreaded the prospect of spending long, hot nights lying awake in the darkness, yearning for a man she could not have.

Instead of going back to the party, Suzanna impulsively summoned a carriage-for-hire and had the driver take her to the law offices of her attorney, J. Franklin Barker, the young associate who'd taken over the practice when the aging Will Bonner had retired from the firm.

On this sunny Saturday afternoon she caught the tall, thin lawyer just as he was getting ready to leave for the day.

"Mrs. Clements," he greeted her, quizzically studying her apparel. "What a pleasant surprise."

"I've just come from the wedding of my best friend," she explained, indicating her attire. "I couldn't wait a minute longer to find out. Has the deal been finalized?"

"I'm happy to report that it has." He indicated the straight-backed chair across the desk. "Do sit down and we'll discuss it."

The attorney explained that, as instructed, he had found a suitable purchaser for the big Washington residence. By "suitable," he meant not only was the purchaser agreeable to the asking price, but was also perfectly willing to keep any and all servants who wished to stay on.

"Mrs. Clements, you may want to take some time and think this over," the attorney said. "If you sell the general's mansion, you will be without a home here and —"

Interrupting, Suzanna said, "If the papers have been drawn up, I will sign immediately."

"As you wish," he said, and began searching for the stack of documents he knew were somewhere atop his cluttered desk. As he shuffled papers and frowned, he asked, almost as an afterthought if she wished to dispose of the South Carolina estate.

"South Carolina?" she repeated. "I still own property there?"

"Why, yes, I . . ." J. Franklin Barker looked up and smiled. "So neither your deceased husband nor Mr. Bonner ever mentioned that the property survived the war?"

She shook her head.

"Please forgive me. I guess I took it for granted that you knew about the South Carolina place. So, shall I sell it as well?"

"You say property. Is it raw land or . . ."

"Yes, there's a small bit of land and a comfortable house on the —"

"Really?" Thinking aloud, she mused, "And it's somewhat cooler there in the summer than it is here."

J. Franklin Barker said, "Oh my, yes. It's beach property. The house sits right on the ocean and is cooled by all those nice sea breezes."

Suzanna quickly straightened with interest as he continued. "General Clements, in ill health the last decades of his life, often visited the spas of South Carolina. He fell in love with the gentle climate, so he bought the beach property and had a house constructed on it. The structure is well-built and has been properly maintained all this time by a couple from the little inland village nearby. The pair looked after the general when he spent time there." The attorney paused, studied her face and asked, "So? Shall I sell it?"

"No, Mr. Barker. Post a letter to the caretaking couple and advise them to make the beach house ready for immediate occupancy." Suzanna stood up and smiled at the puzzled attorney.

"Occupied by whom?" He came to his feet. "Surely you're not considering going there? Why, that just wouldn't do, Mrs. Clements. It wouldn't do at all! The place is too remote, too far from a city. You'd be alone there, totally on your own. No friends, no social activities, no fine restaurants or hotels."

"You've just sold me on it, Mr. Barker," Suzanna said decisively. "Do not sell the property. I will spend the summer at the beach."

Forty

In May, Suzanna left Washington. Alone. Even Buelah chose to stay behind with the big, gregarious family who had purchased the general's mansion. Suzanna understood perfectly and praised it as a wise decision. In fact, she was secretly relieved that Buelah would not be accompanying her to South Carolina.

Buelah was quite old and frail, and Suzanna worried that uprooting her again might damage her failing health. And, truth to tell, it was mostly she who now looked after Buelah, not the other way around. It was best for them both that Buelah stay on where she was comfortable and content. Dr. Ledet promised he would keep an eye on her.

"But how will you get along without me?" the old servant had asked, tears swimming in her eyes.

"It will not be easy," Suzanna had told

her, "but perhaps it's time I learned how to take care of myself."

Left unsaid was that Suzanna actually looked forward to being on her own. She was weary of people and parties and pretense. She longed for solitude and silence and serenity. She knew she would never find happiness, and was accepting of that fact, believing that she did not deserve to be happy. But she did hope for a least a small degree of peace and tranquility.

Suzanna arrived in Savannah, Georgia, on a balmy May afternoon. She was met at the dock by a coach and six, and accompanied on the last leg of her journey up the coast by a dignified gentleman who introduced himself as Timothy Youngblood, Savannah attorney and South Carolina contact of her Washington law firm. He had, he informed her, made the necessary arrangements, and the beach house was ready and waiting for her arrival.

When they reached the little village, the attorney worried aloud that she might find the beach house too lonely and remote. But when Suzanna got her first glimpse of the white, two-story house on an elevated rise above the sugary white sands of the beach, she knew she had made the right decision in coming here.

Suzanna was out of the carriage before it came to a complete stop, eager to go inside and explore. The house was a handsome, well-built structure, and the minute she crossed the broad veranda and walked through the heavy, carved front door, she felt she'd found a home.

A wide center hallway and large floor-to-ceiling windows gave the place a bright, open feel. A gentle breeze off the ocean stirred the sheer white curtains and kept the air pleasantly fresh. At the back of the house, the kitchen larder was filled with food in anticipation of her arrival.

Upstairs, a big four-poster with snowy-white bed hangings and fragile mosquito netting dominated the master bedroom. Tall, glass-paned doors opened onto a broad balcony, affording a bird's-eye view of the endless ocean to the bed's occupant.

"I engaged the caretaking couple to make the place ready," said the solicitous lawyer as he carried her many valises inside. "I trust they have done a satisfactory job."

"The place is spotless," Suzanna replied, eagerly inspecting the residence. "And beautiful."

"Indeed," he said, then added, "but isolated. As you know, the village is a good two miles inland, and a very small community with few year-round citizens. Most of those are laborers who work a wealthy planter's vast sugar, cotton and rice fields." Suzanna nodded, and he continued. "A line of credit has been established with the merchants and the livery, and the bills are being sent to my office."

"You've thought of everything," she said.

"But have you, Mrs. Clements? This stretch of beach is particularly desolate and uninhabited. You're likely to go for days, perhaps weeks, without meeting anyone."

"I see," Suzanna commented, unworried by the prospect.

"The truth is I'm afraid you'll be terribly lonely here, Mrs. Clements. You're much too young and beautiful to be buried way out here away from civilization. Should you decide the property is too remote, I'll be happy to find you a lovely home in the heart of Savannah or up in Charleston."

"I'll keep that in mind."

"There's a small cottage on your property — about a mile back from the beach — where the caretaking couple are now living. The Tillmans — John and his wife, Martha — are quiet, unobtrusive servants and are available to stay on and tend to your needs — doing the marketing, the cooking and cleaning, making any necessary repairs to the property. Or they will move if you want to replace them with your own servants."

"Ask them to stay," Suzanna said. "But tell them I will not be needing their services for at least a couple of days."

"I sure will. You may have noticed the flagpole at the back of the house. Anytime you need something done, send the flag up, and one or both of the Tillmans will be here within minutes."

Suzanna smiled. "A perfect arrangement."

The attorney said, "Now, if there's nothing further . . ."

"Thank you so much for everything, Mr. Youngblood."

"You have my card. Feel free to contact me anytime."

The silence and solitude of the beach house perfectly suited Suzanna's melancholy mood. She felt as if she had been drawn to this secluded place, and hoped that it would be a soothing balm to her restless spirit.

As soon as the attorney left her, she hurried back upstairs to the master suite. She removed her hat, gloves, suit jacket, shoes and stockings. She took the pins from her hair and let it spill down around her shoulders. Barefoot, she walked out onto the balcony and stood at the railing, staring at the deserted beach, endless ocean and cloudless sky.

The loneliness of the place suited her even more than she had hoped. She stayed on the balcony until sunset, allowing the wind to toss her unbound hair about her head, and inhaling deeply of the clean, moist air. When she turned to go inside, it struck her that she would be spending the night all alone. Not a single servant would be under the same roof.

The thought did not disturb her. It pleased her. She was not afraid of the dark, nor was she afraid of being alone. And there was something quite liberating in being able to go about half-dressed or not dressed at all. Better still, if she felt like screaming or crying or cursing the Fates, she could jolly well do so without upsetting anyone. Here in this secret seaside getaway, she could finally withdraw from the tiresome bustle of life, become a total recluse and embrace her precious privacy.

At ten that night Suzanna blew out the bedroom lamp, stripped off her clothes and crawled, comfortably naked, into bed. Expecting to lie awake far into the night as she always did, she began to feel pleasantly drowsy the minute her head touched the pillow.

She fell fast asleep before she could draw the covering sheet up over herself. And she slept the night through without waking. For the first time in years she slept well and awakened feeling rested and relaxed.

Suzanna yawned, stretched and sat up. She hugged her knees to her chest and sat there in bed, planning her day. First on the agenda was a good long look at the ocean. She scooted to the edge of the mattress, swung her legs to the floor and stood up. She picked up her white satin robe from the foot of the bed and slipped her arms inside.

Loosely tying the sash, she crossed to the open French doors. She cautiously stuck her head out, then remembered that the attorney had told her the nearest house was at least two miles up the beach. No danger of being seen.

Suzanna stepped out onto the balcony and crossed to the waist-high railing. She stood there in the warming May sunlight, listening to the seagulls calling to each other, and watching the waves splash onto the shore. This was the way to start a new day. Or perhaps she should toss caution to the wind and take an invigorating swim in the ocean.

Giggling like a naughty child, Suzanna turned, went inside, crossed the big bedroom and skipped down the stairs. She glided through the foyer and yanked the heavy front door open. She rushed outside and raced across the sugary sands of the beach with her uncombed hair and white satin robe streaming out behind her.

At the water's edge she again looked around — and saw no one. She untied her sash and dropped the robe to the sand. Then she squealed with delight as she splashed into the chilly waters and fell over onto her belly. She swam with the ease and majesty of a sleek mermaid, her slender arms pulling her effortlessly through the salty tide.

She swam far out before turning and swimming back to shore, physically exhausted but wonderfully rejuvenated. When she stood up, out of the water, her teeth began to chatter. She swept her sopping hair back off her face, yanked up her robe and put it on, her wet body quickly saturating the satin. She hugged her arms to her chest as she headed back to the house, marveling at how well she felt.

Suzanna had, she decided, found paradise. She laughed then, realizing that already she was behaving like a pagan. How long had it been since she'd felt so wild and free and alive? Why, she hadn't behaved like this since . . . since . . .

No! She would not think about Mitch Longley. She wouldn't let herself think about him. It was a beautiful sunny morning and she was starting a new life. She was going to leave the painful past behind her — beginning today.

Suzanna spent the rest of the day in easy relaxation. Lazy, listless, lonely. And she enjoyed every minute of it.

Forty-One

In no time at all Suzanna had comfortably settled into her new way of life. She didn't miss the parties and friends she had left back in Washington. She never regretted her decision to leave the city. Days went by when she saw no one — and she didn't care.

She read the leather-bound books that lined the shelves of the library. God bless the general and his mother, Cordelia, before him. All the old popular British novels were here, including her own dear mother's favorite, *Cecilia.* As a child Suzanna had laughed and smirked at her mother's dramatic reading of Fanny Burns's silly suicide attempts and implausible plot points. Now, she herself read, enraptured, burning the lamp until dawn.

She took frequent swims in the ocean and long walks on the beach, collecting shells that she artfully arranged on her night table. And if she felt like seeing a friendly face, she sent the flag up the pole and had the caretaker, old John Tillman, drive her into the village.

On her first trip to the little community, she had leisurely browsed in the marketplace, stopping at a fruit and vegetable stall manned by a smiling young woman and two adorable children. Immediately drawn to the tiny, sweet-faced little girls, Suzanna stopped to visit, and found the woman to be cheerful and the girls open and friendly.

"I'm Suzanna LeGrande Clements," she had introduced herself to the trio.

"Anna. Anna Griggs," said the woman, wiping her hand on her apron before extending it to Suzanna. Nodding to the laughing little girls, she said, "My children, Beth and Belinda."

Suzanna stayed at the stall the better part of an hour. And in that time she learned that Anna Griggs had been widowed by the war and was very proud of her husband, a Confederate hero. She stated, with no self-pity, that selling fruits and vegetables provided for the care of her and her daughters.

Beth and Belinda Griggs had immediately stolen Suzanna's heart. And their uncomplaining mother had quickly gained her respect and admiration.

Suzanna bought presents for the little girls and attempted to slip money to their hard-working mother, who staunchly refused the offer. Suzanna was rewarded with laughter and hugs from the happy children and silent gratitude from their mother.

On a warm, sunny afternoon a few days after meeting the Griggs, Suzanna was again in the village. She had stopped in at Meadows' Emporium — the only general store in the community — to buy peppermint sticks for Beth and Belinda. Her back to the street, she was lifting the lid on the tall glass candy jar when suddenly she felt a strange sense of excitement she couldn't account for. The fine hairs at the nape of neck rose. She inwardly shivered and her heart began to race.

Suzanna put the lid down, whirled around and hurried to the front of the store. She stepped outside, looked up the street, then down. And caught the fleeting glimpse of a tall, dark man with midnight hair and broad shoulders just as he stepped into an alleyway and disappeared. Suzanna lifted her long skirts and hurried down the wooden sidewalk.

At the alley she stopped, blinked to clear her vision and looked expectantly down the narrow passageway. She saw nothing. No one. Her throat dry, breath short, she leaned against the building, placed a hand over her wildly beating heart and closed her eyes.

She was being foolish, seeing things. It wasn't him. It couldn't have been him. He was nowhere near this tiny South Carolina village.

Suzanna opened her eyes and pushed away from the building. Soundly lecturing herself, she went back to the emporium to purchase the peppermint sticks for the children.

The incident was forgotten as Suzanna presented Beth and Belinda with the candy and watched their eyes light with pleasure. By the time she left for home, she had totally dismissed the dark stranger from her mind.

Twilight was her favorite time of day. And her favorite place to spend the soothing solace of twilight was out on the upstairs balcony.

It was on just such an evening, while she reclined comfortably on a padded chaise longue and watched the fading light paint the clouds a darkening lavender hue, that a man suddenly crossed her line of vision.

A tall, lean man with midnight hair and

broad shoulders.

Suzanna blinked and sat up to get a better look. Barefooted, his pant legs rolled up to his knees and his hands stuffed deep into his pockets, the intruder walked aimlessly along the sandy beach, looking out to sea. His dark hair blew in the gentle ocean breeze and his half-open shirt billowed out behind him.

Suzanna couldn't take her eyes off him.

She leaned up from her chaise and stared, lips parted, eyes narrowing in the quickly fading light, her pulse beginning to quicken just as it had that afternoon in the village when she'd seen a tall, dark man disappear into an alley.

The tilt of his head, the set of his shoulders, the way he moved with such easy, fluid grace, even barefoot in the deep sand . . . There was something all too familiar about the tall, lean stranger.

Mitch! It was Mitch! It had been Mitch she'd seen that afternoon in the village! Dear Lord, her darling Mitch was right here on the South Carolina coast, strolling along the beach in front of her house!

Suzanna's initial impulse was to rush down to him. She jumped up from the chaise and turned to go inside, but quickly stopped herself. Heart now hammering, she sank back down onto the chaise and watched him go on past, unaware of her presence. She wondered if he lived in the village. Or was his the house two miles up the beach that the attorney had mentioned?

She wondered if he was married. Of course he was married. Married and a father as well, in all likelihood. What was he doing here? Perhaps he had brought his family to the beach for a long holiday. Were the children girls? Boys? Both? Did they look like him? Was his wife beautiful?

Tears now stinging her eyes, Suzanna watched as he stopped and turned to face the ocean. He stayed there for several long minutes, as if contemplating something. Then he turned and went back the way he had come. Hardly daring to breathe, Suzanna watched until he was well out of sight.

Her hands gripping the sides of the chaise, her stomach tied in knots, she stayed there on the balcony fighting the strong desire to go running shamelessly after him. It took every ounce of her willpower to stay where she was. By the time she finally went inside, her entire body ached from the coiled tension.

Suzanna couldn't sleep that night. She was too upset. Too excited. Too hopeful.

She lay awake in the moonlight telling

herself, over and over, that it didn't matter that he still hated her and would never have anything to do with her. Just being allowed to see him stroll down the beach was enough. She would never ask for anything more. She'd never let him know she was there. She would keep the lamps dark at night so that he wouldn't know the house was occupied.

And she would keep herself well-hidden.

Dawn was not far off before Suzanna finally went to sleep. After only a few hours of slumber, she awakened. Her very first thought of the day was that Mitch was right here where she was. He had been on the sidewalk in front of Meadows' Emporium a few days ago. He had walked past her house last night. Would he come again tonight? She could hardly wait for sunset.

Well before the sun went down Suzanna eagerly took up her station out on the balcony. She settled in with a field glass she'd found in the library. She wanted — had — to get a closer look at that dear handsome face.

But Mitch never showed up. Not that night, nor the next.

Night after night went by and Suzanna didn't see him. She began to wonder if she ever actually had. Perhaps it wasn't him at all, just a man who looked something like him. Or maybe the whole thing had been a figment of her imagination. She had yearned so long to see him, maybe she had conjured him up.

Suzanna became convinced that she had been mistaken. She had never seen Mitch in the village or down on the beach. Just wishful thinking, that's all it had been. The beach was — and had been all along — totally deserted. No one was down there. No one had been.

As the month of May drew to a close, the weather became markedly warmer — not uncomfortably hot, like this time of year in Washington, but warm enough to make wading in the ocean part of her daily routine. That and reading for hours at a time, and taking long walks on the beach. And going into the village to shop and see the sweet little girls, Beth and Belinda.

And half hoping she'd find Mitch there — but she did not. And she gave up on seeing him again.

Then, weeks later, when spring had turned into summer, she strolled down to the beach at sunset on an unseasonably warm, late June evening. Seeing no one around, she lifted her skirts up around her thighs and waded out into the surf. She laughed and carelessly kicked at the water, the sound of her laughter carrying on the moist air. She whooped and danced enjoying herself. But her pleasure was short-lived.

A sudden riptide caught Suzanna off guard. She lost her footing, fell and went under. She came up choking and spitting water, trying desperately to regain her balance, but was again tugged under by the dangerous tide. In horror she realized that she was being pulled out to sea.

Arms and legs flailing, Suzanna panicked, knowing she was in real danger of drowning. She tried to fight the current that was rapidly dragging her farther from shore, but was unsuccessful. She was sinking again. The forceful tide was pulling her down to a watery grave. She was going to drown out here alone, and no one would ever know what had happened to her.

Just as she was being sucked farther under, a firm hand came around her waist and she was yanked up into a pair of strong arms. Coughing and gasping for breath, Suzanna clung to her savior's neck as he carried her to safety.

At the water's edge, the man sank to his knees, placed her gently on the sand, lowered her soaked skirts down over her thighs and carefully swept her hair back.

And in the last fading light of day, Suzanna LeGrande and Mitch Longley found themselves face-to-face after all those years.

Forty-Two

For a split second there was an unmistakable look of love and relief on Mitch's handsome face, but his expression swiftly changed. His jaw hardened and pure hatred flashed from the depths of his emerald-green eyes.

"You!" he stated bitterly. "Damn you! What in the name of God are you doing here? How did you find me? *Why* did you find me?"

Struggling to get her breath, Suzanna quickly sat up, shaking her head. "No! No, I didn't . . . Oh, Mitch, I didn't know you were here."

"You expect me to believe you?" he said, levering himself up and shooting to his feet. "Oh, that's right," he added sarcastically, "I almost forgot. I'm the blind trusting fool who believed every lie you ever told me."

"I'm not lying now, I'm not. I swear it!"

As if she hadn't spoken, he said, "Christ,

you weren't content with ruining my life and ending my career. You still want more, is that it?" His hands balled into fists at his sides, a vein throbbing in his forehead, as he said, "Too bad, baby, I have nothing left to give."

He turned and stalked away.

Suzanna jumped to her feet and rushed after him. "Mitch, Mitch, I only want your forgiveness. I'm genuinely sorry for —"

"Save it, Suzanna." He sharply cut her off. "You're wasting your breath."

Grabbing his arm, she said, "Mitch, stop! I beg you, wait just a minute. Please let me —"

"No! I *won't* let you!" he said, shaking off her hand and walking on. "Never again."

Frantic, she again hurried after him, pleading with him to stop, to give her a chance, to let her at least apologize. But Mitch refused to listen. When she again grabbed his arm, he stopped abruptly, whirled about to face her and yanked his soaking shirt open, baring his torso.

"See this?" He turned slightly so that the last dying rays of sun struck his naked chest. Suzanna stared at the network of scars marring the tanned perfection of his body, and her hand went up to cover her mouth. "Pretty, isn't it?" he said sharply. "And I have you to thank for it."

Tears now streaming down her cheeks, Suzanna automatically reached out to touch the scarred flesh, but he was too swift for her. "No, you don't," he warned, and clasped her wrist. His fingers cutting into her flesh, he said, "I don't want you touching me ever again, do you understand me? I want you to stay the hell away from me, do you understand?" He released her wrist and again turned away.

"I will, but —"

Once more he cut her off. "No! Damn it, no. Whatever you're about to ask me, I won't do it. Whatever you want to tell me, I'm not listening. Whatever you need, I haven't got it. I'm all used up. Burned out. Empty. Useless. Unable to give you anything more."

"I . . . I don't want anything from you, Mitch. I just want —"

"I don't give a damn what you want," he interrupted. "Whatever brought you here, I don't care." He turned and walked away, leaving her shaken and sobbing his name.

Suzanna sank to her knees, trembling with emotion. But her innate pride quickly surfaced and she got to her feet. She ran after Mitch and shouted at him, "You think you're the only one who has suffered? Is that it? You're feeling sorry for yourself, and think no one else on earth has been hurt? Answer me, damn you!"

Mitch just shook his head, dismissing her and walked on. She followed, screaming, "I lost everything in the war! That's why I agreed to spy for the Confederacy. The Yankees had taken everything and everybody I ever loved." She drew an anxious breath and said, "Please, please try to understand! What I did to you is unforgivable — I know that — but it was not without reason. Surely you can understand." Frantically, she stepped in front of him and threw her arms around his waist. "I had lost everything and then . . . then I fell in love with you, Mitch. I did, I swear it."

He removed her arms and flung her away so roughly she sprawled in the sand. "That, Mrs. Clements, is your misfortune."

He left her there and never looked back.

Beaten, heartsick, Suzanna stayed where she was until Mitch was completely out of sight. Finally she drew a spine-stiffening breath, got to her feet and made her way back up to the house. There she stripped off her wet clothes, toweled herself dry and climbed wearily into bed.

But she didn't sleep.

■ ■ ■ ■

Suzanna was not the only one who couldn't sleep that night. Angry and upset, Mitch returned to his villa and immediately poured himself a stiff bourbon.

Damn her to eternal hell! Why couldn't she leave him the hell alone? Of all the places in all the world, why did she have to turn up on his little stretch of beach in South Carolina? He'd thought this would be the last place on earth he'd run into her.

Swearing at the cruel Fates that had brought them back together, Mitch paced restlessly and drank. His mood black and getting blacker, he realized that his hatred of her still burned brightly. But so did his desire.

A man who had grown increasingly cynical over the years, Mitch walked the floor and cursed the sight of her. And his own weakness. Seeing her again after all this time, he'd found his first impulse was to take her in his arms. And he hated her for that. She was the last person on earth he had wanted to encounter. And he'd be damned if he'd see her again! He would stay away from the beach. She could have the whole ocean to herself.

Mitch didn't know what she was doing here, but he reasoned that she would soon get bored and move on. From what he'd heard, she had spent five years seeing how many lovers she could collect on the Continent. He grimaced at the unpleasant thought. There had been a time when he was her first and only lover.

He shook his head and downed another shot of bourbon.

A whore, that's what Suzanna LeGrande was. A soulless courtesan who used her beautiful body to get what she wanted. Mitch gritted his teeth. He had spent far too many nights trying to forget how it felt to have her luscious lips on his and her silken arms and legs wrapped around him.

Mitch poured yet another drink and fought the unbidden desire she so effortlessly evoked in him.

Down the beach, Suzanna stayed awake far into the night, equally upset. Her eyes were red and swollen from weeping, and her heart ached painfully. For years she had told herself that she was over Mitch, that she no longer loved him, no longer cared where he was or what he was doing or if he despised her. But it wasn't true.

She loved him still, would love him until

she drew her last breath. Sadly, he hated her and would always hate her. And she didn't blame him. She had ruined his life, and for that she would pay the rest of *her* life.

Suzanna tossed restlessly in bed, her body awakened from simply seeing him again, hearing his voice, having his arms around her briefly. She moaned and beat on the mattress with her fists. She had spent far too many nights attempting to forget how it felt to have his burning lips on hers and his powerful body against her, atop her, beneath her. Inside her.

Suzanna turned onto her side, drew her knees up against her chest in a fetal position and fought the sweet agony he had so easily aroused in her.

Mitch stayed away from the beach. And so did Suzanna.

Neither dared risk bumping into the other again. Mitch strongly considered moving out of the little thatched beach house where he'd spent the last couple of years. Suzanna contemplated taking up the attorney, Timothy Youngblood, on his offer to find her a house in Savannah or Charleston.

But neither left. And each wondered if the other was still there.

After a string of muggy, miserable nights wherein he paced in growing frustration, Mitch finally decided that he was being a fool. Again. A beautiful, flame-haired woman was right down the beach from him and all he had to do was walk down there and take her. Why not do so? Why not avail himself of Suzanna's ample charms as so many others had?

Why not use her just as she had once used him?

Forty-Three

The night was hot and the moon was full when Mitch set out to settle the score with the beautiful witch responsible for the scars that slashed his left side from collarbone to hip. And for the invisible scars on his soul that did not show, but were there just the same. Incurable scars that had changed him forever.

It was well past midnight when Mitch left his beach house. He walked the two miles in a matter of minutes, each step in the fine sand taking him closer to what he despised, yet had to have.

When he reached his destination, Mitch stopped and looked up at the white, two-story mansion on the jutting bluff above. His heart hammering in his bare chest, he argued with himself. He should turn back, leave her alone. She was far too desirable, too dangerous.

His blood up, Mitch proceeded across the

sand to the set of wooden steps leading up to the house. He knew she was awake. Knew she was waiting for him, knowing he would come to her. Knowing he couldn't resist her. She was up there in the hot darkness waiting to wrap him around her little finger, just like before.

But she was about to learn a lesson, the same lesson she had taught him all those years ago. That he, like she, was quite capable of intimacy without affection. All he wanted from her was torrid lovemaking that involved only his body, not his heart. Sex without love. The best kind.

Suzanna *was* waiting.

She had been waiting since that night he'd pulled her from the ocean. She told herself he still cared, just as she did. She reasoned that he couldn't stay away from her any more than she could stay away from him. He would come to her; she knew he would.

Every night she took a hot bath, brushed her hair out around her shoulders and slipped into a gossamer gown of fragile, transparent lace. Every night she waited expectantly out on the balcony, watching for him to come down the beach. Every night she hoped that this would be the night he came.

Now, like always, Suzanna was out on the balcony.

Waiting.

She saw him coming down the beach in the moonlight. She didn't call out to him, didn't turn and go back inside. Instead she waited, knowing what was about to happen, knowing that she shouldn't let it. But knowing that she would, just the same. That she could hardly wait for it to happen and had planned for it to happen just like this.

She saw him step onto the veranda directly below, heard his knock on the front door. She didn't call out to him. Silent, she stayed where she was. In seconds she heard him come into the house and climb the stairs. She held her breath as he walked through her darkened bedroom and stepped out onto the moonlit balcony.

Her hands tightly gripping the railing, she continued to look out to sea as though she were still alone. She did not turn as he approached. But she knew he was there, could feel the heat emanating from his body.

Mitch didn't say a word. He stepped up behind her. He knew that she knew he was there. He reached out, gathered her lace nightgown in his hands and slid it slowly up her tensed body. Suzanna trembled with anticipation and dutifully raised her arms to help. When he lifted the gown up over her head and dropped it, leaving her naked and vulnerable in the moonlight, he cruelly told her, "This changes nothing. I want only one thing from you, Mrs. Clements. Do you understand me?"

"Yes," she murmured, her heart aching, but at the same time longing to be in his arms. "I understand completely."

Mitch swept her heavy hair to one side, then leaned down and pressed his burning lips to the side of her throat. "And I want it right here, right now. If you have a staff on duty or neighbors that might see us, so be it. I don't really give a damn."

Tears sprang to Suzanna's eyes as she nodded. She started to turn and face him, ready to accept his kiss, but Mitch stopped her.

"Stay as you are, Mrs. Clements," he instructed. "I've no desire either to kiss you or to look into your deceitful eyes."

Her tears spilled over and splashed down her hot cheeks. Mitch knew she was crying, but was unmoved. He unbuttoned his pants and dropped them where he stood. He kicked them aside and stepped up closer behind Suzanna. She could feel his heated body brush against her own, setting her on fire.

His jaw taut, Mitch placed his hands on her hips, gripped them tightly and, with a bent knee, urged her bare feet apart.

Suzanna bit her lip and continued to cling to the wooden railing, desperately wishing that she could hate him. With his spread hand on the middle of her back, he pressed her slightly forward over the railing. And then with both hands — those beautiful, long-fingered hands that had once touched her with such tenderness — he roughly spread the cheeks of her bottom and entered her from behind.

Suzanna never released her grip on the railing and Mitch never released his grip on her hips. He thrust forward into her as he drew her back against him, controlling her movements, setting a rapid pace, flesh slapping against flesh under the high, full moon above.

Too long denied the ecstasy they'd once shared, both climaxed almost immediately. His breath labored, his heart hammering, Mitch pumped into Suzanna until he was totally drained. Then he slid his arms around her and clasped his wrists in front of her waist. Suzanna finally let go of the railing. She leaned back against his chest and fought for breath.

When finally his arms loosened and he

stepped away, she felt embarrassed and quickly bent to pick up her discarded nightgown.

"No," he said, and took the gown from her. "You'll have no need of this."

He tossed the nightgown over the railing. The wind caught it and blew it across the sands and out to sea. As she watched it sail away along with the last of her dignity, Suzanna decided that she could be just as cruel, just as crude as this man who obviously despised her.

Pushing her hair out of her eyes, she looked defiantly up at him, then shoved him aside and swayed seductively over to the chaise longue. There she turned about, stretched out on her back and raised her arms above her head.

"I want more," she told him. "And I want it now."

FORTY-FOUR

"Too bad, Mrs. Clements," Mitch said through clenched teeth as he stooped and picked up his white trousers. "I've had quite enough of you."

"No, you haven't," Suzanna challenged as she seductively drew a long, slender leg up, bent her knee and placed the bare sole of her foot on the padded cushion of the chaise. Mitch watched, transfixed, as she allowed that knee to slowly fall outward into a cocked position, brazenly exhibiting her most intimate feminine charms.

Suzanna heard his sharp intake of air, saw his erection quickly spring to life.

She smiled and whispered accusingly, "You haven't had nearly enough of me." He made no response. Suzanna laughed throatily and commanded, "Come here, Mitch."

Mitch willed himself not to obey. He should leave. At once. To stay here with this insatiable little satyr would be courting disaster. He had taken what he came here for. She had nothing more to offer. It was time to go. Past time. She was too beautiful, too seductive, too dangerous.

"Never," he said, tossing his trousers over his shoulder and taking a step toward the open French doors.

"Now," she ordered, and extended a hand to him. "You still want me. I know you do. And here I am, yours for the taking."

A muscle spasmed in Mitch's tanned jaw and his eyes flashed with a mixture of disgust and desire. Suzanna held her breath as he hesitated, then turned and bore steadily down on her. He reached the chaise and looked at her for a long, uncertain minute.

Suzanna was mesmerized. She couldn't take her eyes off of him. He was all she remembered and more. The glorious physique, the strong features, the rich baritone voice — he was the embodiment of all that was virile male. Darkly alluring, he effortlessly exuded a potent, almost primitive sexuality.

But the expression on his handsome face frightened her. He looked at her as if he couldn't stand the sight of her. At the same time, his body told her he desired her.

Mitch stood there gazing down at her and

futilely fought the control she still had over him. She was all he remembered and more. The flowing scarlet hair, the exquisite face, the voluptuous body — she was woman incarnate. Exotic and bewitching, she radiated a strong, almost primal sexuality.

How could he possibly resist when she lay stretched out, shamelessly naked, blatantly offering herself to him? She was far too tempting, with her curls falling appealingly around her delicate shoulders and her pale skin looking luminous in the moonlight. That stunning body seemed to be fashioned solely for carnal pleasure.

And she was looking at him as if she could hardly wait to be in his arms.

Mitch surrendered.

He tossed his trousers aside and sat down astride the chaise facing Suzanna, between her parted legs. His gaze holding hers, he slid a hand along the curve of her calf, then up to the back of her bent knee. Suzanna's heart raced violently when his warm hand drifted along the inside of her thigh, the fingertips barely grazing the pale flesh as they moved deliberately toward her groin. She tingled with building excitement when finally those long, lean fingers reached the crisp red coils between her open thighs.

But her heart squeezed painfully in her

chest when, after only a few seconds of touching her with the kind of tenderness she remembered so well, he lifted his hand, showed her his damp fingers and said sarcastically, "No need wasting any more time. You're hot and wet and ready, so let's get to it."

"Why not?" she replied flippantly as she sat up and laid a possessive hand on his thrusting erection. "You're as ready as I am, so what are we waiting for?" She put her arms around his neck and tipped her face up for his kiss.

To her disappointment, Mitch still did not kiss her. Not on the mouth, anyway. He lifted her astride his lap, draped her legs over his muscular thighs, put his hands around her back and drew her closer. He bent his head and kissed her breasts, quickly licking the nipples into rigid points of sensation. Then he greedily suckled the stinging nipples until Suzanna was squirming and sighing and clinging to his dark head, pressing him closer, ruffling his silky, raven hair against her chin. While his mouth was at her breasts, his hard flesh throbbed insistently against her contracting belly.

Mitch's lips finally released Suzanna's left nipple and he raised his head. His eyes flashing in the moonlight, he lifted her slightly and gripped himself, ready to take her.

"No, you don't." She stopped him, her hands atop his wide shoulders. "Not until you kiss me."

"I told you before, Mrs. Clements, no kissing."

"No kissing, no nothing," she stated firmly, then thrust her pelvis up and forward, rubbing herself provocatively against him. "Feel good? Hmm?" she taunted, sliding slowly up and down his hard, heavy length. "Kiss me and you can have it."

His heart hammering, blood zinging through his veins, Mitch said through thinned lips, "I'll have it whether I kiss you or not."

"No, you will not," she firmly warned, then cupped his tanned cheeks in her hands, pushed his head back and pressed her lips against his mouth. Mitch shuddered but did not immediately respond. Determined, Suzanna carefully molded her lips to his and kissed him over and over again. "Come," she whispered against his lips, "kiss me. Kiss me, Mitch." She kissed the corners of his mouth and ran the tip of her tongue along the seam of his lips. "Just once."

Suzanna sighed softly when finally Mitch's mouth opened on hers and he kissed her, taking full command. His smooth, warm lips played with hers, soft, teasing, then demanding. His tongue ran along her teeth before thrusting inside to explore and possess and excite.

When the long, breath-stealing kiss ended and his mouth lifted to hover above hers, Suzanna looked into his glittering green eyes and put a hand between their bodies. She wrapped soft fingers around his throbbing erection, and Mitch shuddered involuntarily. He helpfully lifted her and held very still while Suzanna carefully guided his hot, hard flesh into place.

With only the smooth tip inside, she released her hold on him. She placed her hands on his broad shoulders and slowly, seductively, slid down upon him, impaling herself while he cautiously surged up inside her.

Their gazes locked.

They stopped breathing.

Suzanna took every taut inch of his pulsating hardness until he had filled her with himself. Then it was she who began the slow, sensual rolling of her hips and forward thrusting of her pelvis. Mitch exhaled heavily and took up her languid rhythm, clenching his buttocks and driving slowly into her.

"Mitch," she whispered against his burning lips as his mouth found hers again.

"Baby," he groaned, filling his hands with the cheeks of her bottom.

Sighing, gasping, the naked pair made heated love there on the balcony in the moonlight, while the waves rolled rhythmically onto shore. The lovers automatically took up the tempo of the crashing waves. Slow. Languid. Lazy. But that lasted only a little while. Unable to control that raging sexual hunger, they soon changed their tempo to a wild, frantic pace.

In and out, driving and bucking, building in momentum. Every thrust penetrated more deeply, bringing added pleasure, hurtling them toward that inevitable wild release. Her receptive body gripping him, squeezing him, Suzanna could feel herself opening wider, taking all of him, glorying in the fervent intimacy.

Their skin now wet with perspiration, they slipped and slid their way toward fulfilling ecstasy in a savage kind of mating neither would ever forget. They went at each other like a pair of uncaged animals who'd finally been given their blessed freedom. And just when the breathless Suzanna felt as if she could endure it no more, the pleasure became too intense and that wonderful wrenching release began.

"Mitch, Mitch," she gasped in a frenzy of escalating ecstasy.

Mitch knew what she needed and gave it to her, thrusting faster, harder, deeper, until she reached the apex and cried out in elation. He then let himself go, groaning as he exploded inside her.

Afterward they stayed as they were for several long minutes, arms around each other, gasping for breath, hearts thundering, damp bodies trembling. Suzanna was still sighing with bliss and happily assuming that she had been forgiven when Mitch abruptly clasped her upper arms, set her back and broke her heart by saying coldly, "Accept my accolades, Mrs. Clements. It appears you learned well from all your European lovers."

Crushed by the unfounded accusation, longing to hurt him as much as he had hurt her, she laughed in his face, pushed him away and got to her feet, saying, "Yes, I found the Frenchmen in particular to be quite instructive and —"

"Spare me the details!" Mitch said angrily as he rose to his feet.

Pleased with his reaction, Suzanna then told him truthfully, "Oh, Mitch, I never made love to a Frenchman or to anyone else."

He laughed cynically and said, "Not important. I don't care one way or the other." His eyes cold, he added, "Because I don't care about you."

Suzanna's temper flared. "Then get out! Get out of my house at once and don't ever come back!"

He calmly reached down and snagged his discarded trousers. Straightening, he said, "I'll leave now, but I'll be back." He stepped into his trousers and stood buttoning them over his drum-tight belly. "And you, my dear Mrs. Clements, will welcome me back into your house." He smiled and added, "And into your body."

Fury flashing from the depths of her expressive blue eyes, Suzanna shook her finger in his face and said, "Never! Do you hear me? If you ever try to touch me again I'll kill you, so help me."

Mitch shrugged bare shoulders and said, "You can't kill a man who is already dead."

Forty-Five

Suzanna was and always had been a fighter. If she believed in something, she gave it her all. When she wanted something, she was not afraid to go after it, even knowing there was a very real possibility that she might fail.

She wanted Mitch Longley. Wanted him to love her again the way he once had. Wanted him so much she was willing to sacrifice her pride if there was the smallest chance of getting him back. She was certain that Mitch would not heed her angry threats warning him to stay away from her. He would be back. And when he returned, be it a day, a week or a month, she would make love to him as never before.

If it took a year or a decade or the rest of her life before he learned to love her again, she was determined to make it happen. Slowly, after many days of easy companionship and many nights of exquisite lovemaking, he would surely fall in love with her again.

Toward that one and only goal, Suzanna focused all her efforts. From here on out she would be sweet and accommodating and amiable, no matter how uncaring he was or how much he hurt her feelings. She would not rise to the bait when he said harsh things to make her suffer. She would control her temper and would eventually conquer him with kindness.

If, for the time being, he wanted nothing from her other than carnal pleasure, so be it. But that would change; she would make it change. Eventually she would make him understand her reason for betraying him. And she would convince him that she had spent every moment since that fateful day regretting her actions. Believing that she was truly sorry, he would forgive her.

Until then she would be willing and ready whenever he desired her. She would be his playful wanton, his innovative lover, his undemanding mistress. And she would look forward to the next inevitable physical encounter, whenever it might happen.

Suzanna didn't even have to wait twenty-four hours, for it happened the very next afternoon. She was out on the balcony reading. The hot summer sun was high in the sky, but massive white thunderheads were boiling up on the eastern horizon when she looked up from her book and spotted Mitch.

Bare chested and barefoot, white duck trousers rolled up to his knees, he was coming down the beach. Suzanna immediately experienced a tingling thrill of anticipation. She had expected him to return, but not this soon. It was a good sign, a very good sign. He couldn't stay away from her. He wanted to, but couldn't.

A catlike smile on her lips, Suzanna silently promised the handsome beachcomber coming toward her that he was about to engage in a long, lovely session of abandoned delight.

Suzanna dexterously flipped a couple of buttons open on her bodice, then swung her legs over the chaise and stood up. Suddenly, a bright streak of lighting zigzagged across the rapidly darkening sky, followed immediately by loud, reverberating thunder. The first raindrops came in a wave of windblown fury as the storm quickly moved onshore.

Mitch's dark head and bare shoulders were being viciously peppered by the big wet drops. Suzanna turned and hurried inside. She hummed as she crossed to the big four-poster, raised the mosquito netting up out of the way and turned down the snowy-white sheets. She fluffed up the half-dozen pillows resting against the tall headboard, and stepped back to admire her handiwork.

Satisfied that the bed was thoroughly inviting, she dashed into the white bathroom and took a big bath towel from a shelf. She tossed the towel over her right shoulder and hurried downstairs. She yanked the heavy front door open just as a fully soaked Mitch stepped onto the broad veranda.

A dangerous bolt of lightning struck a few short yards behind him as Suzanna soundlessly said his name. Without a word he came to her. She put her arms around his neck. Giving him no chance to protest, she stood on tiptoe and kissed him sweetly as the booming thunder rattled the windows of the house.

Mitch's arms went around her and quickly tightened. The two of them stood there on the rain-lashed veranda eagerly kissing, sighing, touching. When at last their lips parted, Suzanna said softly, breathlessly, "We better get you out of these wet clothes."

His reply was cutting. "You know what I'm here for. The only reason I'm here."

"Yes," she said evenly. And looking steadily into his flashing green eyes, she brazenly reached between them and began unbuttoning his soaked white trousers. Mitch didn't lift a hand to help. He stood there, sweeping his sopping, midnight hair back off his face, while Suzanna wrestled the soggy pants down his slim hips and long legs. When the trousers pooled around his bare feet, Mitch kicked them aside.

He stood there shamelessly naked while Suzanna made a teasing game out of blotting the moisture from his tall lean frame. She started with his chest, pressing the thirsty white towel into the crisp black hair beaded with diamond drops of water. Her gaze holding his, she slowly moved the towel downward, but stopped just short of his flat belly.

She toweled his long, leanly muscled arms and his hands. She ordered him to turn around. He did. She dried his beautiful, deeply cleft back and then the tight tanned cheeks of his firm buttocks. She slowly sank to her knees behind him and briskly rubbed his long powerful legs, both front and back, all the way down to his ankles and feet.

She stood up and said, "Turn around."

Mitch turned to face her.

She looked directly into his eyes as she gently pressed to the towel to his groin. She felt him stir. She smiled at him, put out the tip of her tongue and licked her bottom lip. She loosely cupped him with the towel and began to slowly, gently, caress him.

Mitch stood it for as long as he could, which wasn't very long. A vein throbbing in his forehead, his pulse racing, he put his hand atop hers.

"Can we finish this inside?"

"I can think nothing I'd like better," she said, removing the towel and dropping it where they stood.

Inside, she led him up the stairs and directly into her spacious bedroom. Indicating the big four-poster, she said, "Make yourself comfortable, Mitch."

He nodded, then padded over to the bed and sat down on the edge. She motioned for him to lie down. He turned, stretched out and propped himself up against the stacked pillows. "Better shut the balcony doors."

"Let's not," she said. "Very little rain will blow in and this way the room is nice and cool."

Mitch held out a hand to Suzanna. She shook her head. "Not just yet. Lie there and relax. I'll be right back."

"Don't take too long," he stated. "I can't stay."

"No, of course not," she said, all the while

thinking, *You are going to spend the entire afternoon in that bed with me.*

Suzanna waltzed out of the room and hurried downstairs to choose a bottle of fine red wine. She placed a couple of fragile, long-stemmed glasses on a round silver tray along with the bottle, then went back upstairs.

"Good idea," Mitch commented when she placed the tray on the night table.

"Will you do the honors?"

Mitch reached for the bottle. He uncorked the wine and poured both glasses nearly full. He offered her one, which she declined. He shrugged and took a long swallow. While he drank, Suzanna began to languidly strip for his enjoyment.

She cleverly chose to stand at the foot of the bed, framed by the white bed hangings and directly in front of Mitch. She took her own sweet time, teasing him unmercifully as she slowly shed garment after garment.

Mitch drank thirstily of the wine and watched, entranced, as she seductively undressed. The storm outside gathered in intensity. The wind howled loudly and the rain blew in through the open double doors. The sky was black as night and Mitch had to squint to watch Suzanna disrobe. He welcomed the frequent flashes of lightning that intermittently illuminated her as she sensually shrugged out of her clothes.

Just as she tossed aside the very last article — her lace-trimmed pantalets — a bright bolt of lightning flashed and Mitch was granted a fleeting glimpse of the angelic-looking red-haired beauty in all her naked splendor.

She literally took his breath away.

Suzanna LeGrande was without doubt the most exquisite creature God had ever created. Her pearly white shoulders were delicate, her arms slender, her hands small. Her firm, full breasts were softly rounded, the satiny, rose-hued nipples standing out in tempting peaks. Her waist was narrow, her hips gently flaring. Her slender legs were long and beautifully shaped. Her belly was so flat it was almost concave.

And between her pale thighs, the triangle of fiery scarlet curls made his fingers ache to touch her.

The darkness returned.

Suzanna started to move. He stopped her.

"Stay where you are for a minute."

Suzanna didn't question him. She silently obeyed. When the next flash of lightning struck, Mitch gazed at her once more, savoring the sight. Then he summoned her to him. She stepped around to the side of the bed and sat down on the edge of the mattress, facing him.

"I am," she huskily promised, "going to make love you as you've never been loved before."

Forty-Six

Suzanna laid a soft hand on the steely, sculpted muscles of his bare, broad chest. Her long nails raking through the dense growth of crisp hair, she flattened her palm directly over his heart and thrilled at the immediate quickening of its heavy beating.

Mitch reached for her, but she adroitly evaded him.

"No. Not just yet," she murmured. "Let's take our time, get reacquainted."

Before he could protest, she leaned closer and urged his dark head down against the stacked pillows. She slanted her mouth across his, skillfully allowing her erect nipples to brush against his naked chest. She put out the tip of her tongue and ran it teasingly along his full upper lip. She placed the gentlest of kisses in the left corner of his mouth and asked, "Can you think of a better way to spend a stormy afternoon?"

"I can't stay," Mitch mildly protested.

Lightning flashed. Thunder boomed. Wind driven rain peppered the balcony just beyond the open French doors. A fine mist blew inside and made the large room pleasantly cool.

"You can't go out in this deluge," Suzanna reasoned. "Relax and enjoy yourself."

A nimble nymph, she climbed up onto the bed, threw a slender leg over Mitch's supine body and sat down astride his trim waist. Mitch's dark hands swiftly settled on her hips.

He scowled slightly when she levered herself up, reached out to the night table and picked up her glass of wine. She took a drink and offered the glass to him. He shook his head. Suzanna just smiled, took another sip and then — making certain she had his rapt attention — dipped her fingers into the half-full glass. Mitch swallowed hard. Suzanna put her wet fingertips to her breasts and provocatively spread the wine over her pebble-hard nipples. Fluted glass still in hand, she leaned up and offered her gleaming nipples to him.

Mitch groaned, clasped her ribs, drew her to him and eagerly lifted his head from the pillows. His mouth captured a wine-wet nipple and he licked and sucked the wine away, then moved across her chest to the other breast. Suzanna, still grasping the glass, closed her eyes and sighed with pleasure.

And finally, when every last trace of wine was gone from her tingling nipples, she lifted a hand and gently pushed on his shoulder. Mitch reluctantly raised his head. Suzanna felt a quick jolt of excitement rush through her body when she saw the undisguised heat in his glittering green eyes.

Pushing him back against the pillows, she sat up straight and again raised the wineglass to her lips. She took a drink, slowly swallowed, then again dipped her fingers into the wine. Watching cautiously, expectantly, Mitch stopped breathing when she slowly scooted back on his tense, tingling body until she was seated on his thighs. He shuddered involuntarily when she carefully placed her wet fingertips on him and began to sensuously spread wine over the smooth, jerking tip of his thrusting erection.

"No," he groaned, his heart hammering, his chest painfully tight.

"Yes," she breathed, and continued to spread wine up and down the entire length of his heavy, pulsating masculinity.

When she handed him the glass, Mitch took it and anxiously drained its contents.

"Let me love you, Mitch," Suzanna whispered softly. "Let me love you in every way a woman can love a man."

"Don't," he managed to say as he set the empty wineglass aside.

Suzanna simply smiled at him and slowly lowered her head.

At the first flick of her tongue on his glistening flesh, Mitch's neck bowed on the pillows and his hands balled into fists at his sides. He squirmed and shuddered as she licked her slow, sure way from base to tip. And when, cupping him gently with both hands, she brazenly opened her mouth wide and took him inside, Mitch's eyes closed with blinding ecstasy. His lean hands lifted from the mattress and settled on Suzanna's moving head, his fingers anxiously tunneling into the flaming hair spilling over his bare thighs and ticklish belly.

Mitch allowed himself only a few sweet seconds of the incredible pleasure before making her stop. His hands tightening in the silky red locks, he anxiously urged her head up. He clasped her upper arms firmly, sat her up and agilely rolled up into a sitting position facing her.

"Baby," he said, and aggressively kissed her.

During the hot, prolonged kiss, Mitch deftly changed their positions. His mouth feasting greedily on hers, he clasped his hands to her narrow waist and effortlessly lifted her. He turned her about, laid her down on her back and quickly moved atop her.

Suzanna eagerly looped her arms around Mitch's neck and breathed in approval when he pressed her legs apart and she felt his hard, heavy flesh throbbing insistently against her open thighs.

Mitch took his mouth from hers, balanced his weight on a bent arm and reached between their pressing bodies. Suzanna looked directly into his hot, hooded eyes as he gripped himself and thrust into her. He withdrew his hand, continued to balance his weight on his stiffened arms and began making love to Suzanna.

The raging storm was the perfect counter-balance to their tempestuous coupling, and Suzanna was at once reminded that the very first time they had ever made love was during a violent thunderstorm. Did Mitch remember, too?

While a fine mist of rain cooled their overheated bodies, Suzanna luxuriated in the lovemaking. She had never known such supreme physical pleasure. She wanted it to last forever, to never, ever stop. To lie here in the arms of this man she loved more than life itself was nothing short of paradise. To look into his heavily lashed green eyes while he made love to her was thrilling beyond compare.

The loving became even more thrilling when Mitch slid a hand beneath her left leg, pressed it up against her chest and then hooked it over his shoulder. The thought skipped through Suzanna's passion-fogged mind that they should never make love in any other position. This was the ultimate. This opened her more fully to him and he could thrust more deeply into her. She could become more his and he more hers.

Just when she was certain this was the best of all possible positions, Mitch pushed her leg off his shoulder, stretched out on his back and sat her astride his pelvis. They never missed a stroke. While he raised his arms above his head and folded them on the pillow, Suzanna gripped his ribs and rode him furiously, flawlessly, as if there were no other way to make love.

It was heaven.

For her and for him.

Mitch lay back and watched appreciatively as Suzanna seductively rolled her hips and thrust her pelvis forward, deliciously squeezing him with her warm, pliant body. The storm outside only added to the rapture.

The fury of the worsening tempest was exciting and dangerous, and so was the rapidly escalating passion of the feverish female writhing provocatively atop him.

The contrast of the ever-changing light was potently seductive. First the darkness enveloped them so completely that Mitch could hardly see Suzanna, could only feel her lush body imprisoning him, squeezing him, sweeping him toward that oncoming explosion of lust.

Then flashes of lightning brightly illuminated the wild, naked creature of such incredible feminine beauty that his heart was endangered by simply gazing at her.

During one of the dark intervals Suzanna began to pant and grip his ribs so tightly her nails cut into his flesh. Mitch knew she was on the verge of release, and he was glad. He'd been holding back and he couldn't make it much longer.

His arms came out from behind his head and he firmly clasped Suzanna's hips. While she bucked frantically against him, he clenched his buttocks and drove up into her. The tempo of their lovemaking became extremely rapid as their shared orgasm began. And just when both were about to fully climax, the brightest lightning of all flashed in the storm-darkened sky.

The room was temporarily as bright as day, bathing the joined lovers in its splendorous heavenly light. The boom of the following thunder perfectly coincided with their powerful eruption of orgasmic ecstasy.

"Mitch," Suzanna cried out as wave after wave of sexual bliss buffeted her, "Mitch . . . don't . . . let . . . me . . . go!"

"Never," he groaned as he wrapped possessive arms firmly around her and drew her trembling body down against his shuddering frame.

Forty-Seven

By late that afternoon the rain had stopped and the sun was out. The sky had turned a deep cobalt-blue, and the humid air was clean and warm.

Suzanna lay on her side, watching the man she loved sleeping peacefully. Mitch's face looked young and innocent in repose. And beautiful. She yearned to trace the strong contours of his handsome face with her fingertips. And it was all she could do to keep from kissing the gleaming midnight hair that fringed his high forehead.

Her gaze moved slowly down from his face to admire his magnificent form. A lean, masculine body marred only by the satiny scars on his left side. As always, Suzanna felt a deep sadness swamp her as she stared at the telltale scars. How could he ever forgive her when he carried not only the emotional scars of what she'd done to him, but the physical reminder of her betrayal as well?

Silently vowing that she would somehow, some way, make everything up to him, Suzanna eased out of bed, taking care not to disturb him. It was getting late, no more than an hour from sunset. The thought occurred to her that Mitch would surely be ravenously hungry when he woke. And she would surprise him with a tasty home-cooked meal.

Warming to the idea, envisioning the two of them sharing a long, leisurely romantic dinner, Suzanna freshened up, hurriedly dressed and rushed downstairs. She went out onto the veranda and retrieved Mitch's discarded trousers. The rain-soaked pants were now totally dry, thanks to the hot Carolina sun.

Suzanna shook out the pants, folded them neatly and carried them upstairs. She found Mitch just as she'd left him, stretched out on his back, an arm folded beneath his dark head, sound asleep. She tiptoed over and laid the white trousers on the bed beside him, then turned and left.

Downstairs, Suzanna hummed happily as she went about preparing the evening meal. She didn't know how to cook, had never learned. Fortunately, Martha Tillman, the caretaker's sweet wife, was an excellent chef and had spent the morning here in the kitchen baking a succulent smoked ham and fixing potato salad. And a melt-in-your-mouth, fresh blackberry cobbler.

Suzanna took down the finest bone china and sparkling crystal. She carefully set the damask-draped table in the formal dining room. She placed tall white candles in heavy silver holders, ready to be lit when dusk descended.

Sure that the table was perfect, Suzanna rushed over to check her appearance in the huge, gilt-framed mirror that hung suspended above the long cherrywood sideboard.

She frowned at herself, swept her hair back off her face and pinched her cheeks. She was turning to go back into the kitchen when she looked up and saw Mitch coming down the stairs.

Her face flushing at the vivid recollection of their wild afternoon of lovemaking, she smiled at him and said, "You're just in time. Dinner's almost ready."

Mitch glanced at her coldly and shook his head. "I'm not hungry."

Suzanna's smile slipped. Her heart sank. He was not going to stay. He didn't want to sit across the dinner table from her. He had spent the afternoon in her bed, but refused to spend another minute in her company.

Mitch walked right past her, heading for the front door. He stepped outside and left without saying goodnight. Suzanna took a long, slow breath and told herself not to despair. He would come around in time.

He had to.

Their heated physical affair continued throughout the long hot summer. Suzanna made herself available to Mitch anytime he wanted her, hoping that in so doing she could eventually break down his defenses and make him fall in love with her again.

Mitch's desire for her never diminished. He wanted her often and she willingly gave herself to him. But when they were not making love, he would have nothing to do with her. He never once spent the entire night with her. He refused to share a meal with her. Or take a walk on the beach. Or go for a horseback ride. Or have any kind of human contact, save for the raw, uninhibited sex.

Suzanna made the best of it. She was never demanding, never begged or pleaded. Never scolded or nagged. Never threatened or sobbed. She was cheerful and accommodating at all times, and made it a point to never be away from the house if there was the slightest possibility he might show up.

When she was certain he would not be coming to see her — or if he had just left — Suzanna would hurry into the village to visit with the two little girls she had come to adore, Beth and Belinda Griggs. The young sisters were always delighted to see her, and were not ashamed to show it. They never failed to throw their short arms around her neck and squeeze with all their might. Suzanna loved it. She would laugh merrily and bask in the warmth of their open and honest affection.

When she was in Mitch's arms, Suzanna repeatedly professed her love for him, determined that she, too, would be as open and honest as a child in an all-out effort to melt his hardened heart. But her sincere declarations fell on deaf ears. Mitch would not listen. He didn't want to hear it. No matter how hard she tried, she could not seem to change the way he felt about her.

She had shared incredible ecstasy with his body, but his heart remained untouched.

September was just around the corner.

Empty trunks and valises sat in the center of the drawing room, ready to be filled with her possessions. Martha was to start the packing at the beginning of next week.

Mitch noticed the luggage when he stepped into the foyer on a sweltering, late August evening, but he didn't comment. His expression didn't change one whit. And Suzanna once again experienced that awful sinking feeling that had become so much a part of her this summer.

Mitch didn't care. It was that simple. He saw the trunks and he knew she was going to leave, but he didn't care. Which was exactly why she had to go.

Suzanna looked into his eyes, hoping to see some unguarded sign, some small signal that he did care a little. But she saw only lust, so she gave him what he had come here for. Holding his gaze, she untied the sash of the robe she was wearing and let it slide down off her arms.

When she was naked, Mitch immediately reached for her. He put a hand into her hair, gripped the thick locks, bent his head and aggressively kissed her. He swung her into his arms and carried her up the stairs. He laid her on the bed, quickly undressed and joined her there.

An hour later he left, having never spoken a word.

Forty-Eight

Suzanna was dressing to go into the village when it happened. She stopped brushing her hair in midstroke. She shivered, despite the heat of the August morning.

It hadn't happened in years, that strange, unsettling feeling that sometimes came over her. The strong premonition of danger. A sense of fear she couldn't account for. The kind of terrible awareness like what she had experienced on that fateful day she'd learned that Ty and Matthew had been killed.

Her hand shaking, Suzanna laid the hairbrush down and rose to her feet. Her pulse was pounding, her heart racing. Something was wrong. Something bad was going to happen. Or had already happened. She knew it. But she didn't know what. Or to whom.

There was no doubt in her mind that something terrible had occurred or was about to occur. And there was nothing she could do to stop it.

With effort, Suzanna collected herself. She grabbed up a straw bonnet and went downstairs and out of the house. Old John Tillman was waiting to drive her into the village.

"Mornin', John," she greeted the old caretaker. "How are you today?"

"Jes' fine, Miz Clements, and you?"

"Martha? Is Martha well?"

"Yes'm, she's fine, too."

Suzanna nodded and climbed into the carriage. She made pleasant small talk with the old servant despite her distress. As soon as they reached the village, she was out of the carriage. She went immediately to the Griggses' fruit stand to see Belinda and Beth.

To her dismay, the little stand was closed down. No one was there. Her anxiety swiftly increasing, Suzanna turned and went directly to Meadows' Emporium.

"The Griggses?" she said to Caleb Meadows, the proprietor. "Mrs. Griggs and the children, they aren't at their fruit stand."

Caleb nodded. "The little girls are sick, is how I heard it."

"No!" Suzanna said, cold fear gripping her heart. "Do you know where they live?"

He nodded and gave her directions. Minutes later Suzanna knocked on the frame of an open door to a wood shanty that sat on the edge of an orchard. Mrs. Griggs came to the door, looking haggard and worried.

"My little girls," she said without preamble. "They're both real sick, Mrs. Clements."

"I'm here to help," Suzanna stated and stepped inside the modest, but clean, dwelling.

The two little girls were indeed quite ill. Both were running a high fever. Kneeling on the floor beside their pallets, Suzanna said over her shoulder, "Has the doctor been here?"

"No," said the worried mother.

Suzanna shot to her feet. "I'll go get him." She patted the woman's thin shoulder. "Don't worry, everything is going to be all right."

Suzanna spent every waking hour of the next seventy-two helping care for the sick little girls. Holding them in her arms. Rocking them gently. Pressing damp cloths to their burning faces.

When both finally rallied on the third day, she accepted their mother's gratitude and went home, dead tired but greatly relieved.

Certain the sisters' illness had been the cause of her frightening premonition, Suzanna gave in to a nagging headache and went to bed early. But at midnight she was awakened by a knock on the door. She knew it was Mitch, so she went downstairs to let him in.

"I know it's late," he said, half apologizing. "But I was here earlier and . . ."

"And I wasn't," she finished.

He stepped inside, towering over her. "I was here yesterday and the day before."

"Were you?" she replied, but offered no explanation of her absence.

"Yes," he said. "I wanted to see you. I wanted you." He put his arms around her and reluctantly admitted, "I want you all the time. I want you right now."

"Here I am."

He kissed her and said against her mouth, "It's been three days since . . . I'm not sure I can make it upstairs."

"You don't have to," she said as she took his hand and led him into the drawing room.

A wide wedge of bright moonlight spilled into the room across the stacked trunks and valises, and completely enveloped the large overstuffed sofa. Suzanna took off her nightgown, tossed it aside and sat down on the sofa in the pool of moonlight.

Mitch fell to his knees before her, urged her legs apart, wrapped long arms around her waist, drew her to the edge of the sofa and pressed his lips to her throat.

Nibbling and nuzzling, he said, "You're hot, baby. Burning hot."

"Mmm," she murmured, "hot for you, Mitch. I'm always hot for you."

Suzanna sighed, then turned about on the long sofa and stretched out on her back.

Mitch shot to his feet and stood for an instant, staring down at Suzanna. Never had she looked lovelier than she did now, lying naked in the moonlight, his for the taking. Then he bent down and picked her up. He lifted her high in his arms, turned about and sat down on the sofa.

It was then that Mitch realized Suzanna was burning hot to the touch. She sagged weakly against him, her head on his shoulder, her body pressed to his. Beginning to frown with worry, Mitch swept his hands over her back and hips and buttocks. Her skin was scalding hot, but her teeth were chattering as though she was chilled.

He anxiously sat her up, clasped her upper arm with one hand and laid the other against her forehead.

"Suzanna, you're feverish!" he said.

"Perhaps a little," she managed to reply.

"Jesus!" he swore, and rose to his feet with her in his arms. "You need a doctor."

"I'll be all right," she said, trying to smile.

"No! Dear God, no!" he declared, and carried her up the stairs. In her bedroom he gently laid her on the bed. "Listen to me, sweetheart, I'm sending old John Tillman for the doctor. Where do you keep your nightgowns?"

"What?" She tried to focus, but couldn't.

"Nothing. Don't worry." He patted her bare shoulder, then went in search of a gown. In a drawer of the bureau he found several, neatly stacked. He snatched one up, tossed it over his arm and hurried back to the bed. Suzanna was barely conscious. As one might dress a sick child, Mitch sat her up, leaned her against his chest and put the nightgown on her. He laid her back down, kissed her feverish cheek and said, "I won't be gone but a minute."

Suzanna was suddenly too tired to reply. The last thought she had before losing consciousness was that the terrible feeling of danger she'd experienced three days ago had been the premonition of her own death.

FORTY-NINE

"It's scarlet fever," said the physician after carefully examining Suzanna. He turned to Mitch. "Mrs. Clements has been helping nurse a sick family I've been treating. Two little girls with scarlet fever."

Mitch was astonished. "I had no idea that she —"

Interrupting, the doctor shook his head. "I warned her, but . . ." He shrugged, then added, "You'd better leave now. Scarlet fever is highly contagious."

"I'm going nowhere," Mitch said. "I'm staying with Suzanna." He swallowed hard and asked, "Will she . . . ?"

"I honestly don't know," the doctor admitted. "Scarlet fever is a killer, no doubt about that. Only time will tell." He picked up his black bag and started to the door.

"You'll come back in the morning?" Mitch asked.

"I'll stop in around noon to check on her.

Meanwhile keep her as comfortable as possible and pray the fever soon breaks."

"I will," Mitch said. "Thank you, Doctor."

"Shall I send Martha Tillman up?" asked the doctor.

"No. Tell the Tillmans they can both go home," Mitch said. "I'll take care of Mrs. Clements."

And he did.

Mitch refused to leave Suzanna's bedside. He stayed with her hour upon hour, both day and night. And it broke his heart that, in her unconscious state, while she shivered with chills and tossed fretfully, she talked and talked, begging his forgiveness, as if anxious to ease her conscience.

". . . and my brother and sweetheart were both killed . . . then I lost my mother . . . and my home . . . everything . . ."

"Shh, darling. Don't. It was a long time ago," Mitch whispered.

". . . and the Yankees took everything. I was alone . . . I wanted to help the Confederacy. . . ."

"Of course you did. I understand."

"I meant to deceive you. You were just another Yankee officer and . . ."

"Don't, sweetheart. You must stop torturing yourself," he murmured.

". . . but I fell in love with you, Mitch. I did and I . . ."

"I know, sweetheart, I know," Mitch soothed, trying to calm her. "Please don't worry, I'm here. I'm right here."

". . . they . . . they were going to hang me and . . ."

"Yes, darling."

"General Clements . . . old family friend . . . saved me from the gallows. . . ."

"Shh. Don't talk anymore, sweetheart," Mitch pleaded. "Rest, my love. Just rest."

But Suzanna didn't rest. She continued to toss fretfully and talk fitfully.

As her fever raged, Mitch was terrified that she was going to die. The fear of losing her made him realize just how much he still loved her, despite all that had happened. He was sorry now that he had been such a callous bastard, and he prayed that she would live so that he could make it up to her.

"Don't leave me, darling," he pleaded over and over as he bathed her perspiring face and body with cool water. "I love you, Suzanna. I will always love you. I'm sorry I've behaved so badly. I've been cruel and uncaring, and I'm asking you to forgive me. Please, darling. Forgive me."

But Suzanna never heard him.

Until . . . three days after falling ill, and still so weak and sick she was unable to respond, Suzanna faintly heard Mitch saying that he loved her. That he was the one who needed forgiveness, not her. Somewhere in her subconscious, his words registered. At last she was at peace.

She could die in peace.

Then finally — only hours later — she emerged from the enveloping darkness. When she regained consciousness and managed to open her eyes, Mitch's handsome, haggard face was the first thing she saw. And in his eyes, she saw only relief and love.

"Mitch," she rasped hoarsely. "Am I dreaming or did you say you love me?"

Tears quickly filling his bloodshot eyes, he smiled at her. "Yes, baby, you sure did. I love you, Suzanna. I love you with all my heart and I can't live without you."

"Oh, Mitch, I love you, too, and I've so much to tell you," she whispered.

"And I you. But for now, my love, rest. Just rest."

Suzanna managed a weak smile. "You'll stay with me?"

"For the rest of my life. I will never leave you, I promise. I love you, Suzanna. And if you'll let me, I'll spend the rest of my days trying to make you happy."

"I could never be happier than I am at this moment." Then she lifted a hand, laid it on his unshaved jaw and said, "Mitch, I'm hungry."

"Thank God!" he replied with a broad smile.

With Mitch at her bedside day and night, Suzanna survived the serious illness that had threatened her life. And during her recovery, the two of them really talked, each eager to confess and understand and forgive — everything.

By the time Suzanna was well, all the bitterness, all the distrust, all the betrayal and all the wasted years were left behind. Mitch proposed. And Suzanna accepted.

With only the Tillmans, Anna Griggs and her two young daughters, Beth and Belinda, as witnesses, the barefoot lovers were married at sunset on the beach in front of Mitch's house.

And then, for the first time, they slept together in the same bed. All night long.

Well, actually, they didn't really sleep.

ABOUT THE AUTHOR

Nan Ryan is the author of twenty-eight sizzling historical romances. Readers love her trademark style — American historical novels brimming with fiery passion and fast-paced action.

A winner of three Career Achievement awards from *Romantic Times BOOKreviews,* including Historical Storyteller of the Year in 2001, Nan is presently working on a novel. Entitled *The First Last Dinner Dance,* it is to be her first contemporary mainstream novel since *Stardust* was published in hardcover in 1988.

After nearly a decade in Scottsdale, Arizona, Nan and her husband, Joe, have returned to their native Texas, where they have built a new house in a northern suburb of Dallas, aptly named Fairview.

We hope you have enjoyed this Large Print book. Other Thorndike, Wheeler, and Chivers Press Large Print books are available at your library or directly from the publishers.

For information about current and upcoming titles, please call or write, without obligation, to:

Publisher
Thorndike Press
295 Kennedy Memorial Drive
Waterville, ME 04901
Tel. (800) 223-1244

or visit our Web site at:

www.gale.com/thorndike
www.gale.com/wheeler

OR

Chivers Large Print
published by BBC Audiobooks Ltd
St James House, The Square
Lower Bristol Road
Bath BA2 3SB
England
Tel. +44(0) 800 136919
email: bbcaudiobooks@bbc.co.uk
www.bbcaudiobooks.co.uk

All our Large Print titles are designed for easy reading, and all our books are made to last.